The Great Art of Life is Sensation

The Great Art of Life is Sensation
Book one in the series, The Risk of Being Tamed
by Ashton Rhodes

Cover design created by using Shutterstock images #60192943 and
#68124085

Cover design by Jacob Howe

Editing by Abby Prichard

Layout design by Mr. Larson

Printed in the United States of America
First Printing, 2014
ISBN 978-0-9915527-1-9

Ashton Rhodes Publishing
Mt Juliet, Tn 37122
https://www.facebook.com/ashtonandhendrix?ref=hl

For the one who climbs my walls.

The Great Art of Life is Sensation

The Warning

We walked into Club Inhibitions to find Tracy standing with two beautiful women. He would instruct me on what to do with them and how to please them. As his submissive, I would do whatever he wanted of me.

When we approached them, he put his arms around Tracy. I should have been jealous but not here, not with our arrangement. We weren't lovers; we were players in a game he devised, and emotions were not part of the agreement. He wasn't going to ease me into this. He was going to throw me in and hope that I learned to swim. Extending his hand for me, he directed Tracy and me, along with one of her friends, to a large couch at the center of the room. As a voyeur and an exhibitionist, the center was the only place he would want to be. Here, it was certain that no one could miss us. We would be everyone's entertainment, and no one's second glance.

Even though the club had only opened an hour ago, it was crowded with people writhing all around us, drenched in glistening sweat, some crying out in passion. A man next to me feverishly drove his cock into the woman splayed out before him. Two women were fondling each other's breasts with one of them sliding her hand in between the other's thighs, while a man watched them and stroked himself.

This club was definitely not for the straight and narrow set, what we refer to as, "vanillas." If the thought of this sickens or disgusts you, then I suggest you don't read any further because this is my very detailed story of surrender, in the most complete sense of the word, and I will not omit a single thing in the name of censorship.

The Teacher

You couldn't ignore a man like Hendrix. He had a way about him that attracted a multitude of women with his dark hair, styled into a modern pompadour, dusky blue eyes, and a build that suggested a physical career. His large chest and shoulder muscles pressed tightly to his white t-shirt, and underneath, the bright outlines of tattoos that continued to his wrists, the kind that begged you to question their meaning. Even his walk commanded attention, moving with determination, and the jeans he wore were dark and tight in the right places, allowing you to see his thigh muscles flex with every step. He wore his signature black Converse with white trim and stylish retro sunglasses, straight out of *Risky Business*. His overall appearance was a blend of modern and vintage with a debonair edge. You would look his way, and he knew it.

I could see women follow him with their eyes, wondering how to approach him, how to draw his attention, but his determined walk brought him through the door of my favorite café in Atlanta, straight to the small table by the window where I sat every weekend to write.

As he approached, his face was framed by the bright sun, making it seem like an afterimage I couldn't blink away, one that dredged up painful yet blissful memories. Not knowing which was worse, the pain or the bliss it caused, was my own fault. When you mingle the two, it becomes hard to distinguish them as separate emotions.

His earthy, rugged cologne filled the small space around me, invoking the vision of a steamy scene in his old car. I had tried desperately to forget that scent, but now it immersed me in unwanted recollection.

What brought him here today? I didn't like being caught off guard, and I wasn't prepared to face him. The least I could have done was dress in something more than a tight t-shirt and jeans, but even at my most casual, you could describe me best as Avant-Garde with a strange individuality that warned good, normal people to pass on by. However, Hendrix was anything but good and normal, and he loomed over me with palpable desire.

"It's nice to see you, Ashton. I thought you might be here. Can I sit down?"

"That depends. Are we going to talk about the weather, or do you need answers I can't give you?"

"You know I don't start conversations off with some clichéd excuse to talk. I just wanted to see you. Look, what we had is obviously over, but after eight months of not speaking, I'm tired of hiding. We had something different. I can't ignore that."

"Different, Hendrix? No, what we had was an experiment that went wrong."

Prelude

"The meeting of two personalities is like the contact of two chemical substances: if there is any reaction, both are transformed."

— *C.G. Jung*

A year ago, I saw Hendrix searching through records in a vintage store, the kind of store that sells cat clocks and smells like mildewed attics. It was the kind I loved because it reminded me that once upon a time people did more than watch bad TV or play video games. They made things, interacted with each other, threw lavish parties, and talked instead of texted.

The record selection wasn't much, but it beat going to the giant media stores with their overwhelming stock based solely on sales projections. I saw him pick up a Frank Sinatra album, pull the record partially out of the sleeve to inspect it, and drop it gently back in. He placed it under his arm to carry like a book and caught me glancing at him from across the room. My intermittent shyness took over, so I walked towards the bookcases and commenced to search for a collector's edition of Charles Dickens' *A Tale of Two Cities*. The first line always intrigued me, "It was the best of times, it was the worst of times." Contradictions seemed to define my life. I enjoyed the state of balance they created from their imbalance, like the scales of justice, adding a little to either side until you got it right.

If anyone really knew me, they would see that I was particularly off balance at the moment. I had ended a relationship a couple of months ago with another man who couldn't wrap his head around my true desires. I had all but given up on ever finding what I was searching for, which was to feel that I had no control for once in my life, to let go and trust that the man who took the reins could handle them no matter how hard I tugged. But somehow this man, carrying a Frank Sinatra album through my favorite store, saw right through me.

I tried to pretend he wasn't coming towards me by

continuing to search the shelves, but he was not to be swayed. His approach was slow and seemed deliberately to make me more nervous.

In a low and sure voice he said to me, "Of all the vintage shops in all the cities in all the world, you had to walk into mine."

Did he really just say that? Although, it was a good line to use on me, being that I loved old movies, and lucky for him, understood the reference. I laughed nervously, "I'm sorry. I was under the impression that it was mine."

He smiled and leaned against the bookshelf. "Witty and beautiful. You can't possibly be single."

"Well, you're wrong about that. I am frequently single, it seems."

"Too much for most men, I assume. My name is Hendrix Larson, by the way." He reached his hand out to shake mine. "It's nice to meet you."

Reluctantly, I extended my hand, not that I didn't want to touch him, because I most certainly did, but I was concerned that this handshake could be the start of something incredible or dangerous, or best case scenario, a little of both. My small hand was engulfed by his large, strong one. "Ashton Rhodes, and whether or not I'm pleased to meet you is still to be determined."

He laughed. "Fair enough. What would you say to having a drink with me?"

"What kind of drink are we talking about? Because they sell bottled water at the counter."

"Oh, you are trouble, aren't you? You should know though that attitude only makes me more attracted to you, so you're not doing a good job of running me off."

His unwavering determination made me want to push harder. "If I wanted to run you off, I would tell you to get lost. Maybe I'm just testing you."

"And that is admirable, not deterring. To answer your question, I was speaking of an adult beverage, and you are welcome to test me a little more or prove me wrong, whichever you prefer."

If he was welcoming me to test him, he really had no idea what he was getting himself into. I thought I might as well take the bait. "So if I agree, when and where are we having this hypothetical drink?"

"It's absolutely literal, I can assure you. How about now and right down the street?"

A moment of courage and I could be having a fun and exciting evening with this disturbingly handsome stranger or I could be led to a back alley and beaten with a baseball bat. Murder be damned, my curiosity won out.

I shrugged. "Sure, I guess." I had mastered the kind of disposition that kept men wondering if they had won the war of interest, while simultaneously being able to hide the fact that my heart was racing with excitement. This time it backfired.

He looked me straight in the eyes. "Because we've just met, I'll give you the benefit of the doubt, but from now on, I would prefer it if you answered direct questions in a more respectful manner." He said it kindly, but with authority.

I was honestly too awestruck to object. Who the Hell did he think he was? And why would I ever agree to go out with him? Although, his dominant attitude was exactly what my last boyfriend and all those before were missing. I craved it; I needed it to fill the other side of my scale, my counterbalance.

I still wasn't going to let him know this, even if he could see through some of my walls, it didn't mean I was going to let him in easily. "Um, I'm sorry?"

He just looked at me, and I felt both a little frightened and very attracted to him at the same time.

"You can start by answering me with 'Yes, Sir.'"

My sarcasm dwindled and my throat started to feel very dry. He was serious and I liked it.

Why not give it a try? "Yes, Sir." I found it hard to meet his gaze while acquiescing to him. Responding to him like he was in an authoritative position over me, made me feel embarrassed or ashamed but most of all very turned on by his commands.

"That's better."

He smiled then and seemed to be the most upbeat person in the world. Such a shift from the trepidation he invoked in me only moments before. He must be schizophrenic, but that would be my luck.

"Are you ready?"

It wouldn't hurt to play along and at this point I was far too curious to back out. "Yes, Sir."

"See, you can be good."

"Not usually."

Laughing, he put his record down on the nearest shelf, placed his hand at the small of my back, and led me to the exit. He opened the door for me. I wasn't used to this kind of treatment, both the chivalry and the assertiveness. In fact, most men were so intimidated by me that I automatically assumed the dominant role, but this strange situation looked like it could become the kind of scenario I had always fantasized about.

One

I had no idea where we were going, but was more than happy have him lead me.

When we walked outside, the fall air had turned cold, making my anxious breath visible. I glanced at him shyly when the opportunity that he wouldn't see me presented itself. With strong arms and a broad chest, he was built like a man who used his body as a tool. Men who performed physical labor always attracted me. The way they could drive their body to the point of exhaustion but kept working until the job was done showed such depth of character, and Hendrix seemed to flaunt that endurance and strength fashionably. In fact, everything about him showed character. Tattoos that were tasteful and artistic, a square set jaw, confident eyes, and a genuine smile. His demeanor seemed to emit strength and power that was deeply rooted and unbreakable.

I, on the other hand, was anything but rooted. I liked to move and change frequently, feeling like I was always outgrowing myself, or maybe it was a form of self-preservation. Either way, the juxtaposition between us made me all the more drawn to him.

He turned to glance at me briefly when he spoke. "Have you ever been to the Blue Rhapsody?"

The Blue Rhapsody was a jazz club I had always wanted visit, but never found anyone interested in going, so I avoided going alone. Just another winning point to the side of this being a good decision. "No, I haven't, but I've always wanted to."

"Great. It's one of my favorite places. I think you'll enjoy it."

We rounded the corner and arrived at a gold trimmed door. When we stepped in, the air was heavy with the smoke of cigars, the smell of liquor, and the sounds of piano and brass. I recognized immediately that the band was playing an instrumental version of "Fever." Jazz was music for the erratic mind, no rules, no restrictions, and slow jazz was sexy, velvety, and erotic, some of my favorite music. I was completely enamored with the air of seduction the entire place exuded.

Small tables spaced closely together throughout the room gave a feeling of intimacy. We made our way to a table at the back near the bar. He pulled a chair out for me and waited until I sat down before seating himself, close enough to make me nervous but not so close that I couldn't see his face directly.

"I'm going to have an absinthe. Would you like the same?"

"I've never had it, but yes, I would love to try it. Thanks."

He beckoned with a few fingers in the air, and a beautiful woman from across the room came walking towards our table. She had long, flowing blonde hair and wore a deep cut, black fitted shirt that showcased her overflowing breasts paired with a black mini skirt, black stockings, and black patent high heels. The monochromatic uniform made her full red lips and bright blue eyes even more noticeable. To say the least, she was my complete and total opposite.

Wearing my usual odd style, which was whatever my artistic brain told me was fashionable that day, I felt a little out of place. Today just happened to be a mash of 80s glamor and indie vintage. Tight jeans, boots, and a tank top with an oversized half shirt over it that read LOVE. My short dark hair was in its natural state of controlled chaos. Hendrix, on the other hand, dressed casually and looked like he had walked off of an album cover with a tight black crew neck t-shirt, faded blue jeans, and black Converse shoes with white trim. His dark hair was swept into a pseudo-pompadour that wasn't stiffened with hair product, but rather had some pieces hanging slightly over his right eye. When he pushed it back with his fingertips, it fell perfectly into rhythm with the rest of his statuesque features.

The waitress stood beside us. "Hi, Hendrix. What will it be for you and your friend tonight?"

"Two absinthes, please Tracy. Thank you."

He came here enough for her to know him by name. I was honestly a bit jealous after seeing the waitress, and I generally was not the jealous type. In fact, none of this peculiar scenario was like me at all, but that's why I liked it.

He smiled at me, as if on cue to my unease, "You know, I find you very captivating and beautiful, and I can assure you that you would not be sitting here if I thought anything less of you. So please try not to be too nervous. Are you?"

"Very."

"Ashton, I assure you that you're in good hands, and I'm not going to do anything that you don't want me to."

I loved the way he said my name. "Thanks. That makes me feel a little better, I guess."

"Only a little? It seems I have more convincing to do." He smiled devilishly. "But that's perfectly alright with me, convincing you is half the fun."

I smiled because I really didn't know how to respond to someone that was so straight forward and sure of his words.

He broke the tension for the moment. "Now, absinthe is not for the faint of heart, which I don't think I need to worry about with you. You seem very adventurous. After all, you did agree to come here without knowing a single thing about me."

I laughed quietly. "Well, that's true, and yes, I suppose you're right. I like to think of myself as adventurous and try new things. It makes me feel like I'm not missing any rare opportunities."

"I greatly admire that attitude, and it makes me all the more compelled to ask you something. But I'm going to wait a bit on that. For now, I'm enjoying your company."

If he was trying to ease my nervousness, this was not helping. I wasn't sure that I could wait for him to ask, but I was determined not to bring it up on my own. I told myself to be patient, which was not by any means one of my virtues.

The blonde waitress that greeted us brought out the absinthe. It had an unusual appearance. An entrancing, slightly green liquid in a short wide-mouthed glass, topped with a beautifully ornate slotted spoon. She sat a small bowl of sugar cubes on the table and a silver pitcher of cool water next to it and then quietly walked away. Hendrix picked up two of the sugar cubes and placed one on each of our spoons. Then, taking the pitcher of water, he slowly poured it over them, so that it flowed through the slots and made the sugar fade to a few left over crystals. The once clear, green liquid now had a cloudy appearance.

"The cold water makes the herbs in the absinthe louche, which is the white color it's taking on. You know, Oscar Wilde once said about it, 'After the first glass, you see things as you wish they were. After the second, you see things as they are not. Finally, you see things as they really are, and that is the most horrible thing in the world.' But I don't agree. I think we're captains of our fate and seeing things the way they truly are is in our power to be great or terrible as we create it. What do you think?"

He knew how to win my interest. Taking a drink, I thought about his observation while I became accustomed to the licorice taste.

"Well, Oscar Wilde is one of my favorite authors, and he may have seen things the way they truly were as horrible because he was gay and eventually jailed for it. I do agree with you though. I think our lives are our perception of them, and our so called fate is up to the decisions we make, based on that perception."

He laughed. "I was right. You are an interesting person. Of course, I was pretty sure of that, or I wouldn't have approached you in the first place. Fate is a strange idea but also pretty romantic, if you're into that kind of thing. I've been down that road myself, but I grew out of it, which brings me to the question I hinted at earlier."

"Ask away, please."

"Do you find me attractive?"

Why did he have to wait to ask me that? But I answered him truthfully. "Very."

"Well thank you. And as you already know, I think you're beautiful. But I have another question for you. Do you find our waitress Tracy attractive?"

That's why he waited. I was a bit sidetracked and annoyed for a moment, but what did I really have to lose? If he turned out to be a jerk, I could just walk out the door.

"She is beautiful," I said dryly

"But are you attracted to her?"

"I really don't know. I've never looked at a woman that way before."

"Have you ever truly given yourself permission to?"

"I would imagine that I have, but then again, I haven't ever given it any serious thought."

"Would you give it serious thought if I asked you to?"

"Can I ask why it's of so much importance to you? I'm a little confused here. I thought maybe this was a date, but if you brought me here just to tell you if you should date the waitress, then you definitely picked up the wrong girl!" I was ready to stand up.

"No, no, Ashton, please. I'm sorry I gave you that impression. That's not why I'm asking at all. I'm very sorry. Let's change the subject for a bit. I'll go into more detail later. I'm enjoying talking to you. I shouldn't have brought it up so soon."

I was considering leaving, but just knowing that I had that option made me want to stick around and find out more. That's the joy of not being in a relationship with this guy. I didn't owe him the time to listen to or argue points I didn't care to discuss.

He tried to recover our casual conversation. "I love your style. You give off a vibe of pure creativity, and I really like that. You're definitely an individual. So many people aren't these days. Since you love Oscar Wilde, I'm sure you know what he said about that? 'Be yourself; everyone else is already taken.' As you can probably tell, I'm also a big fan of his, and that particular quote has always resonated with me. So many people today are void of depth. They fill their time with meaningless television and try to make themselves into the image of someone they believe to be ideal. It's very hard to find someone who is a true individual and completely unafraid of being contrary to the norm."

"Yes, I know that quote, and thanks." I smiled. Damn it, I was trying to be uninterested.

"I am curious about your shirt though. It says 'love' in big, bold, black letters. I'm wondering if you wore that because you're subconsciously advertising love, if that's what you're looking for, what you're in, or announcing it to scare the people off who are afraid of it?"

"Well, Dr. Freud, to answer your question, I would have to choose option D. Maybe I am using it subconsciously to scare potential ex-boyfriends away. Didn't seem to bother you though, so what am I to assume that means?"

He laughed. "You are quick-witted and unashamed, and that's very refreshing. To answer your question, I'm not looking for love nor am I afraid of falling in love. Truth be told, I'm looking for someone to share an experience with. Something that I've dabbled in but not to the extent I'm wanting to explore. If you're convinced I'm not a total jerk now, I would like to continue our previous line of questioning. What do you say?"

"Okay, I'm interested. Not totally sure about the jerk part though." I laughed and hoped he wouldn't take offense.

He smiled. "Okay, here it goes then. Do you believe that you can separate love from sex?"

"I believe that some people can, though I don't think I ever have."

"So, in your past relationships, you were always in love?"

"There were times that I wasn't."

"And did you have sex with them anyway?"

"Yes."

"In those times when you were, we'll say not intoxicated by feeling in love, were you better able to concentrate on the actual sensations during sex?"

"That's a tough question. I don't know. I was probably too busy being angry."

"I think angry is okay. It's raw and rough, a lot like sex can be, wouldn't you agree?"

"It's the way I would have liked for it to be many times, but unfortunately I've never found anyone to experience it like that with."

"That's a shame. Someone as adventurous as you definitely should. It's carnal and exhilarating."

I'm sure I blushed a bit. "I would very much like to."

By this time, the absinthe was taking effect on me, and I think I was seeing things the way I wished they were because this gorgeous man was talking to me about carnal pleasures, and I was sincerely hoping he was going to show me what I had been missing. The flash of anger earlier completely wore off.

I saw Tracy at the bar, stretching slightly to reach the drinks she was gathering for another table. I was sure it was the alcohol imbuing me with the ability to see her through a man's perspective, and the fact that he had asked me earlier if I had ever given myself permission to be attracted to a woman. She did have beautiful breasts, hair I could wrap my fingers around, and legs that led my eyes up to the hem of her skirt, but I didn't dare go further with my imagination, at least not now. I could almost feel myself becoming aroused at even the idea of thinking that way, and truthfully, it frightened me a little. Never in my life had I touched a woman in a sexual way. I felt Hendrix's eyes on me then.

"Can I ask you my question again, the one that irritated you before?"

He had caught me looking at Tracy, and I think that I wanted him to, so that he could get back to our previous conversation. "Yes, you can."

"Do you find her attractive?"

I hesitated. "Yes, I guess I do."

That devilish smile again. "Wonderful."

14

He beckoned Tracy over. I got a little nervous to see her walking towards us, as if my secret thoughts were suddenly very apparent. Hendrix rocked back in his chair slightly and gestured for her to lean down towards him. I was thinking he was going to kiss her right there in front of me, and I wasn't at all sure how I would handle that. As he was putting his lips close to her, I realized he was only going to whisper in her ear. As he did, I saw Tracy start to smile coyly and glance at me. If I had been apprehensive before, I was even more so now. She might actually be interested in me and that scared me even more than my earlier admission of attraction.

Tracy stood up, and Hendrix came back to his original position in the chair.

"Tracy, can you please bring us another round?"

She looked delighted. "Absolutely, Hendrix."

"Okay, what is going on?" I looked from him to the waitress and back again.

"I suppose you could call it an experiment that I'm interested in about social and personal boundaries and sexual inhibitions. Do you think it's wrong to have sex with more than one person at a time? I mean, having sex with someone one night and someone else the next or possibly even two people at the same time?"

Wow, he was straightforward. "I've never done it, but I don't think there's really anything wrong with it."

"And why do you feel that it's okay?"

"As I said before, I do think you can separate love and sex, and if you can do that, then seemingly, sex is just sex, but once again I'm not speaking from experience."

"Have you ever talked about your fantasies to anyone?"

Tracy was suddenly at our table with two more glasses of absinthe. I didn't even notice her approach because I was too wrapped up in what Hendrix was asking me. She sat them down without a word and walked away. Hendrix again prepared them as he had done before, and we both began to drink. It gave me a little more time to drum up some courage.

After a couple silent minutes, I continued, "I have told others to an extent, but let me elaborate on my past situations a little without sounding like a 'woe is me' ex-girlfriend."

"Please do, and I don't think you would play that role well." He laughed.

"My boyfriends have never really understood me, to say the least. Please don't think me naïve when I tell you that I haven't done certain things that you've been asking me because I have my own interesting desires as well. As you so accurately pointed out in the store, I do tend to end up being too much for most men to handle. I'm independent and in charge of my life, but I am nothing of the sort when it comes to sex, or more truthfully, my sexual fantasies. I'm actually very submissive, and I want someone that can dominate me."

Holy shit, I said it. I can't believe I said that to a man I don't even know. I decided that I either detested this drink or loved it for making me so bold.

He smiled. "Well then, Ashton, you are in luck."

I was floored. Anytime I had even so much as mentioned this to other men, they had no idea why I would want something so strange and abusive. I hated that assumption, wanting to be dominated had nothing to do with abuse. It was about permission and trust. It was about giving and receiving in an altered format. In fact, I felt that you had to intrinsically trust someone to allow yourself to be dominated by them. I also didn't understand why this was such a fantasy for me, but chalking it up to my inherent weirdness, I moved on. And by moving on, I meant leaving them. This night was truly turning out to be memorable; Hendrix had actually said I was in luck.

I was obviously looking a bit stupefied, which was pleasingly disguised as having drank too much absinthe.

"Ashton, I don't want you to worry about telling me your deepest, darkest desires. You will not offend me. I can promise you that. What were you thinking just then when you were in a moment of silent surprise?"

"I was wondering why you don't think I'm some sort of freak."

"Oh, I wouldn't go that far. I was actually hoping that you were."

I laughed. "Well, yes, I guess I am. I'm just used to someone telling me how stupid it is that I would want to be ordered around or possibly spanked."

He made a satisfied "Mmmm" sound and shook his head from side to side. "No Ma'am, you are exactly what I have been looking for."

My entire body flushed with heat. "Normally, I'm offended when someone calls me Ma'am, but if you say it like that, I don't think I could ever get tired of hearing it."

"I hope that you don't. Now, do you mind if I tell you my fantasy?"

Loosening up quite a bit now, I could tell that I truly wanted to get to know this man and what he was like in other positions than sitting beside me at a small table. I was excited to hear what he had to say, but hoped that it was something I could help him fulfill. "Please, I would love to hear it."

"My fantasy, one that I have dabbled in, but only to a small extent and never had it end well, is swinging. Like you, I've had many people think I had lost my mind when I mentioned the mere idea of it."

"Like in a playground?" I laughed.

"No Ma'am. Like fucking other people and sharing each other. I hope you're not offended by my language. I'm sorry. I got a little carried away in the thought."

"No, I'm not."

"You're against it? You can tell me if you are, and I won't say another word about it."

I laughed. "No, no, the language! I'm actually interested in your fantasy. Maybe I have thought about it from time to time, but I haven't dwelled on it because I assumed it would never actually happen."

"Would you be willing to try with me?"

"Wow! That's a lot to decide on the spot, but I'm not saying no."

"Look, this is just about sexual freedoms, about pleasure. It has nothing to do with us becoming a couple. You would be free to stop anytime you wanted. No contracts or hidden agendas, just fun."

"Can I ask why you need me for this?"

"Because, I think you're the perfect woman for it. I could find people to have threesomes with or join in orgies, but I want another element to this. I want a submissive to order to do the things I want her to do to me, to a woman, to other men, anyone I choose. I want to dominate you while we explore having sex with multiple partners. But don't worry, you would be receiving just as much, if not more, pleasure than you were giving. The way I see it, it's a win/win situation. You have always wanted to be dominated, and I want a submissive. There's just the extra element of sharing ourselves with other people."

"When you put it that way, it does sound like it could be fun. And you promise I can get out anytime I want?"

"Absolutely."

"Well, then I think I might be up for it."

"Wonderful. I knew you would be interested. I sensed it as soon as I saw you."

I shrugged and smiled. "What can I say? Do you mind if I ask one more question though about the abnormal tendencies?"

He laughed. "Sure, of course."

"Does Tracy have anything to do with this, you know, because of the whispering and her smiling at me?"

"Yes, she does."

"Can I ask how?"

"Let's just say she's a fan and leave it at that for now."

I shrugged. "Okay."

"What did I tell you about answering me properly?"

Crap. "Oh, sorry, I mean, Yes, Sir."

He smiled. "That's better."

The suspense was killing me. I was sure Tracy was either an ex-girlfriend or a lesbian, or maybe some girl that he had already shared with someone. And maybe that wasn't all bad. Because again, I wasn't dating this guy, so what did it really matter? I planned to keep that idea in my head, so that it could ward off feelings of jealousy later on, if they decided to creep up.

He broke my silence again, steering the conversation towards another topic.

"So, in my daily life, I own my own business. I like to work with my hands, and after working for several small construction companies, I finally decided to open my own. I also do private designs, like furniture and cabinetry. All in all, it's pretty great. What do you do when you're not dreaming of being tied down and thrashed within an inch of your life?"

I laughed and almost inhaled the absinthe I was trying to swallow.

"Actually, I'm a writer."

"Well, that must be a rewarding job. What got you into it?"

"It is, most of the time. Sometimes I can't think of anything to write or I have a deadline and then it feels like work, but usually it's a great outlet. I got into it because I felt like I was constantly inhabiting two different worlds. The characters in my head needed to tell their stories. They just wouldn't be silenced until I began writing about them. It's like being schizophrenic in a way, but without the crazy, just a compelling urge to write."

"I like the way you describe it, and if you're crazy, then you're my kind of crazy."

We gave each other a knowing smile, the kind that you display when you're sure of what's to come, and the anticipation is controlling your thoughts.

"Ashton, I have enjoyed talking with you so much. I am very excited about what I have in store for us. Would you be opposed to coming over this weekend and talking more in depth about our endeavors?"

"Not at all. I would like that."

We finished our drinks, and he handed me one of his business cards to write my phone number on and another for me to keep. He stood up quickly so that he could pull the chair out for me to stand. Once again, I was not used to the gentlemanly treatment, and it surprised me, especially now knowing that what went on in his mind was not gentlemanly at all.

Making our way towards the front, he stopped beside Tracy, telling her he would be calling later that night. I looked up at her shyly, and she gave a girly wave in return. Hendrix opened the door for me and we walked back out into the growing darkness.

The city I had known for so long felt somewhat changed. I tend to put so much of my emotions into my surroundings that I start to blame them for my unhappiness and frustration. In fact, I wanted to move every time I felt that way, but now that I saw things taking an unexpected turn. Atlanta felt like the best and brightest city on Earth.

"Can I walk you to your car?"

"Oh, I live in the city. I don't own one. Thank you though."

"Then I'll hail you a cab?"

"Thanks."

We stood waiting for a cab to pass, which at this hour of the evening with all of the traffic passing by could take a few minutes. I didn't really want to leave him anyway, so I was thankful for the extra time.

He continued talking to me while we waited. "Does living in the city ever get to be overwhelming to you?"

"Not at all. I feel like I'm part of a living, breathing entity. Cities have always held such a fascination for me, the way they grow and change with the people who inhabit them."

He nodded. "I couldn't agree more. I live in a condo on Spring Street in Midtown."

"I love that area! I live right off of Moreland, down in Little Five."

"Perfect area for you, very artsy." He smiled.

I laughed. "Artsy. Nice choice of words, but pretty accurate."

A cab was turning the corner, and he raised his hand for it to stop. The driver pulled up to the sidewalk, and Hendrix opened the door for me. The awkward moment made me want to touch him, a hug, a handshake, anything. I just didn't want to get in the cab without a promise of what was to come between us.

I could tell he sensed my apprehensiveness. "I'll call you tomorrow to set up plans for the weekend. Don't worry. I'll see you again in three days, if you're still interested."

"Are you kidding? I couldn't be more interested." I looked up at him as I sat down in the back seat. He closed the door and gave a quick wave goodbye. Looking out the back window in a way he couldn't see, I watched him stand at the curb until the cab was ready to turn down the next block. My mind was reeling with the possibilities of what he had only briefly described. I wondered what I was getting into, but I didn't exaggerate when I told him I couldn't be more excited. Actually, I didn't think I had been this excited since my first novel was picked up by a publisher.

The rest of the way to my condo was like a dream. I saw the city around me, the people walking down the sidewalk, but I saw them through a haze, the colors of their clothes blurring to resemble a watercolor painting.

The cab drove up to the curb in front of my building, and I paid the driver. I couldn't get to the lobby door fast enough. Thankfully, no one spoke to me, it would have broken through my dream state and forced me to do something mundane. I stepped into the elevator, pushed the button for the ninth floor, and watched the doors close. It lurched to life and I was rising.

Stepping off, I hurried to my door, fumbled with my keys, and finally walked inside. Even my living room looked altered to me. I was in love with the feeling I had, and it was changing everything I encountered. I couldn't believe that Hendrix was real and that he wanted me to experiment in a crazy sexual fantasy with him. That probably wasn't many girls' idea of an awesome evening, but it was obviously mine. I was Hendrix's kind of crazy after all.

Two

After the bath had filled, and my nerves had calmed enough to think straight, I stepped into the warm water and sank to my neck. I even lit candles around my black claw foot tub. I hadn't done that in years, but the jazz club had left an impression, and I wanted to take it home with me. Grabbing the remote to the stereo, I turned it up. Luckily, I still had Jamie Cullum, Joe Bonamassa, and some other great jazz and blues artists on my playlist.

While I sat in the water, I began to think of what Hendrix had in store for me, what Tracy had to do with all of it, and if I could truly be attracted to a woman. As he had mentioned, he would want me to do something sexual with her or with other women, and I honestly didn't know if I could go through with it. I wondered though, how hard it could really be, after all I knew how to please myself, so I was sure I could please another woman. If Hendrix was coaxing me on, I felt I could do anything he asked. Closing my eyes, I began going over in my mind what I would do, using Tracy as a visual aid for now.

I envisioned the first step to be just a kiss; getting over that first fear would probably ease things up. After all, if Katy Perry could sing about it and make it a number one hit, it couldn't possibly be that bad. As I thought of what a woman's kiss would feel like, how running my tongue over her lips would taste, I started to feel excited. My clit began to gently swell, exaggerated by the warm water. Still keeping my mind on kissing Tracy, I ran my hand down my stomach to my thigh while imagining myself doing this to her. I wanted to know what it would be like to run my hand underneath her shirt and feel her breasts while I was still kissing her. My hand would move to the hem of her skirt and lift it up higher on her thighs. I moved my own hand between my thighs now and felt the wetness accumulating on my outer lips, even in the water. I began teasing myself by lightly running my fingers around my stiffening clit. Imagining Tracy still wearing her stockings, my hand made its way up her skirt to the warmth emanating from between her legs, and feeling her wetness behind both her stockings and panties made me want to break through them badly and see how I excited her.

At the same time, I began slipping my finger into myself. I thought of sliding my hand over the top of her stockings and moving her panties aside. She was kissing me deeply now, breathing heavily, and her body was begging me to plunge my fingers into her just the way I was doing to myself. In my mind I did, I felt her wetness, her desire, and her need for release, as I was feeling my own. While running my fingers in and out of myself, I thought of doing the same to her, feeling her tighten around them, as her hips begged me to thrust harder and stimulate her clit even more. My fantasy and motions were one now, and as I brought myself to the edge, I brought Tracy to hers. She threw her head back, cried out, and started grinding her hips and arching her back, forcing herself deeper onto my fingers. Her juices were running down my hand, pooling in my palm. She was grasping me around my shoulders and pulling me against her. I imagined Hendrix standing in a dark corner merely observing us, not even touching himself, simply enjoying the show. This thought drove me over the edge. I came so hard that I actually cried out and woke myself from my fantasy.

I sat there, lying my head back on the tub in pure shock. What had he done to me, making me think of things like that, a fantasy I had never explored? Truthfully, the most probable reason that I enjoyed it wasn't the idea of being with Tracy, but the thought of Hendrix watching us, like he orchestrated it and was making sure I followed it through to completion.

Coming back to reality, I lathered my sponge and ran it slowly over my body, paying close attention to the heightened sensation I felt on my skin. I never had a problem giving myself pleasure, but I had always wished that a man could do the same for me. Not that I had never climaxed with a man, but that he could truly make me come without any help from myself. I wasn't sure if it was a defect in me or in the men I chose, or that they could never convince me to surrender my control. But, I could never find a man that could truly overpower my stubbornness or that I had ever allowed myself to feel dominated by. The thought of being forced to relinquish control was enticing. In fact, forcefulness was probably the only way it would ever happen.

Filling the sponge with water, I began to wring it over my chest and back, removing the soap suds and paying close attention to the way it flowed over my nipples which were still drawn tight and hard from my overactive imagination. Pouring a small amount of body wash in my palm, I smoothed it over one of my legs and resting my toes above the water, on the faucet, I picked up the razor and began to shave. As I moved upwards, passing my calf and the curve of my knee, I thought of Hendrix running his hand over me in the same way. What would his touch feel like? If he was truly dominant, could he still be tender? Would he blend the two? I really had no idea what to expect, but I hoped that he would mingle pleasure with pain; the kind of pain that only sparks at your threshold but doesn't ignite it.

Finished with my right leg, I approached the left in the same manner, still in my thoughts, replacing the razor with his fingers. I imagined him using both hands, one on each leg, running them simultaneously up my thighs, parting my knees as he did so. In my thoughts, he was sitting in front of me on the floor, bending his body so that his head came to the level of my navel. He moved one of his hands up my inner thigh, while using the other to spread my leg further away. With his fingers, he began to toy with the juices that were hidden behind my outer lips, using them to lubricate my clit and stimulate it teasingly, with only a breath of a touch that made it feel as if it were actually reaching up for more. My body was opening up to him now, ready to receive him. I thought of him sliding only the tip of his finger inside me and withdrawing it to bring it to his lips and taste the wetness he had drawn out. He smiled, made that delicious Mmmmm sound as he had done at the club, and brought his hand back down to drive two of his fingers inside me. Facing them upward, he grabbed my pubic bone and placing his thumb on the outside, pulled me down slightly so that I could easily lie back. Moving those two fingers in and out of me slowly at first, he soon began pushing them in further, running them in slow circles and feeling the soft skin inside.

I was entirely lost in the thought of this and had started touching myself again, mimicking his imagined movements with my own and becoming monumentally more aroused by this scenario than the one before. In my fantasy, Hendrix withdrew his fingers from me and, parting my legs, forcefully pressed my knees almost to the ground. He didn't waste a second with teasing. He pressed his face between my thighs and began licking and sucking at my clit, then making long strokes up and down from top to bottom with his tongue. Reintroducing his fingers, he moved them in and out of me with deep, long strokes that became harder, almost to the point of pounding. He continued to do this, simultaneously sucking harder at my clit, and I imagined I did something I had never done before. I allowed Hendrix to make me come hard and uncontrollably with absolutely none of my assistance. With the thought of that truly occurring, I continued to stimulate myself, and brought on yet another orgasm, deeper and longer than the last.

I was thoroughly exhausted now but excited and anxious to begin this experiment with him to know if he could truly do to me what I imagined he could. I removed the stopper from the drain and stood up from the bathtub, grabbed a towel, and wrapped it around myself. The stereo was still crooning, but most of the candles had extinguished themselves. I stood in front of the sink and large mirror, looking at myself and seeing that I not only felt satisfied, but I looked it too. This exploration had been a sweet release and had actually managed to calm me quite a bit. I unwrapped the towel and looked at my naked body in the mirror. I wondered if Hendrix would find me beautiful when I was completely naked in front of him, or if Tracy would. He had mentioned sharing with more than one person in a night. What if they didn't find me attractive? No. I couldn't start doubting myself. I had full, high breasts, a toned stomach, and smooth curves, a blend of strength and femininity. I had to stay confident. I loved the thought of him sharing me and oddly wanted him to feel proud to share me, like in my fantasy of him being an onlooker to an encounter he had arranged.

After smoothing lotion over my still tingling skin, I slipped a long Fleetwood Mac concert t-shirt over my head and slid on some panties. Blowing out the remainder of the candles and turning the stereo off, I left the bathroom and my fantasies behind.

Finally, I walked to the kitchen to grab a bite to eat. I realized it had been noon since I last ate, and I was starving. I walked into my small kitchen with black and white tiled floor that felt cold to my too-long-in-warm-water feet. Muted lavender walls held black cabinets which showcased antique green dishware. I had painted my own back splash above the stove, a depiction of *The Scream*, but added a chef's hat to signify my disdain for cooking. Opening the refrigerator, I chose leftover pizza from the night before. There was a multitude of sodas and condiments but not much actual food to speak of. I took a plate from the cabinet, tossed a couple of slices on it, and put it in the microwave. As it was reheating, I thought about Hendrix and wondered what he was doing at this time of night. Did he go straight to bed or have a drink, or call a friend and tell him he had found a prospect today? A friend... I had almost forgotten about his promised call to Tracy. Great, now I would be obsessing over what they were talking about. The only thing I could be certain of was that he was a mystery, and there was no way I could figure him out anytime soon. I would try not to dwell on the imagined conversation he and Tracy were having in my head.

The microwave signaled its completion. I took the pizza and a diet soda from the fridge and went to the living room, which consisted of a lime green sofa shaped like a kidney bean, a purple velvet chaise lounge, and a television that was rarely turned on. The record player that stood alone on the far wall however, got plenty of use. Together, along with the rest of my home, they displayed my personality, which, you could gather by a quick walk through, was confused and unable to decide on a theme. That impression was probably pretty accurate, but the best part of my home was the huge window that stood from the black hardwood floor of the living room to the exposed ceiling, and was separated by steel beams holding the large panes of glass in place. The way it was angled allowed me to see the lights and buildings of the city. I sat there often, gathering ideas for stories or contemplating my last failed relationship, which in turn usually led to writing more stories, so I guess failure to stay in love helped my career. Tonight I sat directly in front of it, so close that I could feel the cold emanating from the glass. I told myself not to write the ending to this story in my head; I wanted the suspense, the excitement of the unknown.

After taking far too long to finish two slices of pizza, I walked back to my bedroom. It housed a wrought iron canopy bed with sheer silver curtains, resembling what you might think a slice of moon reflected water would look like, and the walls were a peaceful, deep cobalt blue.

After pulling back the damask bedspread, I eagerly crawled underneath it. Lying there in the dark room, I closed my eyes and thought of Hendrix, of Tracy, the club, and of all the day's strange events. I felt like I did as a child on Christmas Eve, knowing that the night would surely end if only I could fall asleep, but the more I tried the longer the hours of dark became. I took my Mp3 player from the nightstand drawer, put the ear buds in, and turned on my favorite modern composer, Philip Glass. At some point during *The Illusionist* soundtrack, I finally drifted to sleep.

Three

I awoke to the light of the sun making its journey across the floor to my bed. At first, I thought of what I needed to do and was then quickly reminded that I was on pins and needles. I had the feeling that I should jump from bed and... well, do what? This wasn't my show after all. I had to wait for a man to call me. I guess I had already let him win a little on that one. I did have his number though, but then I didn't want to seem like the desperate girl who couldn't breathe until the phone rang. What did I do every other normal day of my life? Of course, I used the term normal to describe myself very loosely. Maybe I could go for a run or work on my latest project, or just pace the floor until I heard from Hendrix. Definitely not. A run it was then.

Begrudgingly, I sat up in bed, found the ear buds that had somehow migrated underneath my pillow, and threw them on the bedside table. My mind was reeling; I had to zone out and focus on other tasks or this was going to be a very long... What day was it? Thursday? Great, a very long two days until I was supposed to see him.

Bathroom, brush teeth, eat breakfast, program running playlist, change clothes, lace shoes, and go.

Running, to me, was freedom and isolation all at the same time. Hundreds of people surrounded me, moving through the city streets, yet I confined myself inside my music. It was living on another plane for at least three to five miles, it was substitution for loneliness, and it was another form of my control. I could hear my breathing in between songs and see my breath in the cool air. I darted past the few sparse trees left to remind us city dwellers that there was, in fact, still nature out there.

Running until my legs had almost given out and my playlist was about to end, I had just enough steam left to make it home. Leaning into the heavy door of the lobby, I slid my card into the reader and left my ear buds in, so no one would talk to me on the way through the building. I was lost in a song and didn't want to be interrupted. Up the elevator and back to #916.

Two hours had passed, what now? Take a shower, eat some lunch, stare at the phone, put the phone in a drawer, and find something else to do. Write? Yes. I needed to work on my current piece about the need for articles and designs from the past in our modern lives.

I took out my pen and wrote, "Why do we meet strange and intriguing men in vintage stores? Are they better left in the past or should we let them be part of our future?

"Oh fuck this!" I took his card from the top of the dresser where I had tossed it last night, rescued the phone from the end table drawer, and typed in his number to send a text. Inner conflict! I am not like this! I am texting him, that is it!

I thought about what I should say. "Hi, this is Ashton. Um yeah, call me?" That sounds awesome, and you're a writer for crying out loud. Why was I even worrying about this? He approached me and said exactly what he was thinking. I liked his straightforwardness. Why shouldn't he like for me to be the same?

Here it goes: "Hi Hendrix, this is Ashton, remember the girl you want to share with others? I was wondering if we could talk whenever you're available today. Call or text. I'll be around."

Idiot. Of course you'll be around. It's a cell phone.

The phone came to life only a few minutes later with an incoming text: "I'm sorry, have we met? Just kidding. Of course I can talk. I'll be done at the house I'm working on around 6 tonight. Would you like to meet somewhere or would you just like me to call you?"

Wow! That was not the way I thought that would go at all. He was actually very accommodating and not at all perturbed that I texted him before his promised call. I texted back: "Either is fine, your choice." There, he should be happy with that.

Quick response time, I like that. "I would love to meet up with you again, I'll call when I get out of here and we can discuss where to meet. Sound good?"

"Yes Sir :)"

"That was a very good response, good girl. I'll call you soon."

Good girl? Was I a dog now? Oh, who was I kidding? I loved it. Now I had to wait until around six, which as a woman, I knew in male time meant probably more like seven or never.

It was only one o'clock in the afternoon, and the jeopardy theme was playing in my head. This was going to be a long afternoon.

I convinced myself that writing would be the best way to pass the time quickly, and I was right. My phone rang at 6:15, and I hadn't even obsessively looked at the clock since four.

"Hello?"

"Ashton, sorry just got away from the house. So what's on your mind?"

Shit. Punctual and now I'm on the spot. I reminded myself that this was my fault.

"Oh, well nothing serious. I just wanted to get a little more information from you. I know you said we would meet this weekend and discuss it, but honestly this is all a lot for me to process, and I will most likely have an aneurism by then."

He laughed, and the sound of it made me even more attracted to him. "I didn't think you could wait. It's perfectly okay."

"So did you tell me you would call me and set up plans for this weekend just to test me?"

"No Ma'am, I did not. But after talking with you last night, I could tell that you're really not the type to wait on a man to call."

"Well, that's true."

"I know, and that makes dominating you all the more amusing."

"That is yet to be known, may I remind you."

"You are feisty, aren't you? I am going to enjoy spanking

your little ass when you talk to me like that in person."

Silence.

"Ashton? Did I lose you?"

"Only temporarily in thought. I'm here."

"Was it a good thought or a run like Hell thought?"

"Oh, it was good."

"Wonderful. You are going to be a great toy and such a good obedient girl, aren't you?"

I laughed. I could play along with that. "Yes, Sir."

"You'll learn to stop laughing at me when I ask you a direct question. Is that understood?"

Dead serious and a little remorseful. "Yes Sir."

"That's better. Now about meeting up with you tonight. Is there anywhere in particular you would like to go?"

"I'm guessing the proper response here would be, wherever you decide Sir?"

"It's not necessary when I ask you what you would like to do, but I greatly appreciate your digression to my authority. And, for that, I will reward you later, but not tonight."

"Well, that won't drive me crazy at all, thank you. I loved the club you took me to last night. I wouldn't mind going there again."

"No, I think I need to show you what else you might be missing around here. Is there anywhere else that you haven't been but wanted to go?"

"Nothing comes to mind at the moment. I do have a favorite place I go pretty often. It's called International Café. Do you know it?"

"I've been by it a few times but never stopped in. Let's go there, to one of your favorites."

"Sounds good to me."

"Would you like to meet me there or can I pick you up in my car?"

"A ride would be nice." I gave him my address, and we arranged the details. He would be here at eight.

"I'm excited to get to see you again so soon Ashton. Thanks for texting me today."

"I am too, and you're welcome."

"Talk to you soon."

"Okay, bye." I hung up, and immediately my heart started its annoying nervous pounding. People at that café knew me pretty well. I was hoping Hendrix wouldn't make me obey him in public, at least not where I would have to face the same people again.

I made some chai tea, went to the bedroom, and began searching through my closet for something better than the ensemble he met me in. Due to my ever changing attitude about my personal style, I had a large range of choices. Shuffling through a few dresses and skirts, I decided on a simple black silk shirt dress that tied in the center and came to the top of my knees. I unbuttoned a few buttons to show a bit of my cleavage. After all, Tracy wasn't the only one who could invoke lustful thoughts. I slid on some high heeled black boots and styled my hair in its usual controlled disarray.

Seven thirty. Okay, thirty minutes, I can kill that much time. I was hoping that all my excitement was coming purely from the adventures Hendrix had in store for me, for us. With no intention whatsoever of looking at him as a prospect for dating, I would remind myself of this on a regular basis. My problem with love; I always want to be in it. Not this time though, I was in this for pure enjoyment. Hell, I was in it for sex. It felt good to say it to myself. I was truly in this experiment, as he called it, for sex and pleasure only. Maybe I would know what it felt like to think like a man. I looked at myself in the bathroom mirror and said, "You're going to fuck him, fuck whoever he wants you to, and you're going to love it." I smiled and walked out to the living room.

I opened the record cabinet and lifted the lid from the

player. Flipping through my collection, I chose Jeff Buckley's *So Real* album and put it on the turntable. I set the needle to my favorite song "Forget Her," and turned up the volume.

Four

"All life is an experiment."

-*Ralph Waldo Emerson*

Eight o'clock and the intercom buzzed in, "Ms. Rhodes, you have a visitor named Hendrix Larson?"

"Yes, he's expected. Please let him up, thank you."

"Certainly, Ma'am." I hated it when the doorman called me Ma'am, but when Hendrix said it, it gave me chills, and he was on his way up the elevator by now. I tried not to look like I'd been pacing for a half an hour.

He knocked on the door, and I made myself walk slowly to it. When I opened it, my mouth almost fell open. The moonlight streaming in from my room size window was shining on him and highlighting his features. He was wearing black dress pants, a black dress shirt with sleeves rolled up to mid-forearm, a red tie, and black dress shoes. God, he was gorgeous, and he really knew how to dress. I felt much better about being out with him tonight, knowing that I wasn't in jeans and a t shirt.

"You look beautiful Ashton."

"Thanks. You don't look half bad yourself." I smiled, probably blushed a bit too, but I don't think he noticed. He was looking at my living room, taking in my eccentricities. "Would you like to come in, look around?"

"Very much. This is a beautiful place."

"Thanks. I've spent a lot of time decorating it."

"That is one magnificent view you have there. A window like that could get you in trouble with your neighbors."

"I don't make it a habit of walking around naked in front of it, if that's what you mean."

"You may not, but I could definitely pin you up against it

and fuck you from behind. Then all of your neighbors and anyone walking down the street would see your gorgeous breasts pressed up against the glass and the pleasure on your face."

I'm pretty sure he saw me blush this time and smile nervously, trying to recover my thoughts. "Then I would most likely get fined for public indecency."

"I seriously doubt it. Most people would enjoy it too much to turn you in. But, tell me, do you like the idea of that? Me fucking you where we might be seen?"

"A little."

He made a mock frown. "Only a little? What if the people that were watching us were doing the same thing we were, would you like it better then?"

"Possibly."

"So I've decided to go ahead and tell you a few things tonight about what I would like to experience with you and that is one of them. Not the window per say, but in public or in front of an audience of sorts. Would you completely object to that?"

"No, I think I might like it."

"Perfect."

"Do you want to see the rest of my home, or are you just interested in the window fucking?"

He laughed, "Lead on Ma'am. I would love to see it."

We walked through the kitchen. He loved my painting and general decor. The bedroom was his favorite by far and not just for obvious reasons. I was beginning to wonder if he would ever actually use a bedroom for anything he would do with me. He commented on the choice of colors, the bed, and the general ambiance.

"I love it. It's great. Everything, really. I'm thinking mine is very under decorated. I may need your help."

"It's just a hobby, but I'd be happy to give it a shot if you really want me to."

"When you come over this weekend, you can get some ideas. I'm more James Bond in my decorating taste. You know, a bar, cigars, record collection?"

"I might not want to change that. It sounds pretty sexy."

"Time will tell. So let's see what this favorite place is all about."

We rode the elevator down and walked through the lobby doors. He put his hand at the small of my back again. I was beginning to enjoy because it felt better than the normal hand holding I was accustomed to, more of a way to gently lead me than to tug me along.

His car was parked at the curb, a black 1965 Pontiac GTO.

"Holy Shit! Are you kidding me? This is what you drive? Oh my God! It's fucking awesome!"

He laughed hysterically. "Wow! I don't think I've ever met a woman who had the same reaction to this car as I did when I first found it. Of course, mine was internal dialogue, but I love your enthusiasm. I guess this means you're into cars?"

"Some cars, yes, and this is definitely one of them."

"Would you like to drive it?"

"No Sir! If I put a scratch on this car, I'm pretty sure I would jump off a bridge. Thank you though."

He smiled. "Well, there's no need for suicidal tendencies over a car. I would take care of your punishment if you hurt it."

"Maybe I should scratch it intentionally then."

"Mmmm, bad girl tonight, are we? Is that what classic cars do to you?"

I snickered, which I hoped wouldn't get me reprimanded. "Apparently, I mean, they are like porn to me."

"Music to my ears. Though I'm not sure which part was a better song, the love for cars or the indication that you watch porn."

I looked away because I was slightly embarrassed. "Guilty."

"I'm amazed to find a woman that will admit it. Maybe we could watch it together sometime. What do you say?"

"Sure."

"I'm sorry, what did you say?"

A little louder, "I said sure." I realized my mistake the instance the words left my mouth, and he spanked me, right there on the street. It wasn't hard, but it was swift and directly on the right ass cheek. My heart jumped. I inhaled sharply and stopped walking.

He turned to stare at me. "What did I tell you about how to respond to me?"

I was stupefied. I was literally trying to find the best spot on his face to land a solid punch while simultaneously trying to keep from jumping him on the hood of that magnificent car, but I obeyed, reluctantly at first. "Yes, Sir."

"I didn't hear an apology in that. Do I need to spank you again?"

He was dead serious. He looked at me with such an intense gaze that I felt I was being scolded by a parent. "I'm sorry, Sir."

He returned his hand to my lower back. "That's a good girl. Don't forget your place again, or it will be worse the next time."

"Yes Sir." I was so aroused. I could feel the wetness forming in my panties. I wanted to fuck this man so badly that I couldn't even see straight and he without a doubt knew it.

He opened the passenger door for me, the perfect gentleman once again. What a contradiction and I loved it. As I settled into the bucket seat, I felt the slight sting of pain when my ass pressed into it. I stared at him through the windshield as he was walking to the driver's side, still reeling and nervous, and above all else, excited as Hell.

When he got in, his scent filled the car, clean, but musky, with a hint of pipe tobacco and leather. I drank him in, every facet of him, his body, his face, his hands now even more appealing to me that I had felt one inflict pain. More a shock of embarrassment than pain really, masochistically delicious shame that left me feeling like a delinquent child. Yes, I guess I was one twisted girl. Did I want Hendrix to be a Daddy figure now? Definitely not. Probably not. Fuck, I don't know anymore! I shut myself up finally and brought my mind back to the moment. He turned the key, and the car let out the most beautiful growl and rumbled to life. We drove away from the curb, and he turned on the radio.

"Anything in particular you would like to listen to tonight?"

"Am I really allowed to answer this or just say, 'Yes Sir,'?"

"If I ask you a question that deserves an answer more than yes or no, you may answer it however you wish."

"I have no preference right now."

He picked a classic rock station but turned the volume down. I wanted to stare at him and look out the passenger window all at the same time. I was so confused by my feelings. My control freak wanted to jump out, scream at him, slap him, and tell him he was way out of line, but the submissive trapped inside wanted to fall at his feet and accept my desired place.

"So, this café of yours, what's it like?"

I summoned my voice. "Oh, it's beautiful. It's decorated in a mixture of French and Vienna style, Belle Époque period. They have a drink menu that is the size of a book, and you'll be happy they have absinthe."

"Sounds great. I'm glad I'm finally going."

"Me too."

"Are you okay?"

I thought about what I should say. "Actually, yes, Sir, I am." I smiled, pleased with my answer.

"I'm so very glad to hear that."

It was a short drive. After parking the car I wasn't sure

whether I was to remain seated or get out, but knowing how he had behaved so far, I felt staying put was a safe choice. Hendrix made his way around the car and opened my door. He smiled, looking pleased that I had allowed him to use his chivalrous, yet deceiving nature on me once again, and took my hand to help me out. When we stepped into the café, I could tell he was immediately impressed. He seemed the type of man that was into finer things, even with his tattoos that made him seem dangerous. He also projected an attitude of class. He was dressed to the nines, but with a casual roll of his sleeves, he not only revealed a flash of ink, but also a man that didn't fear pain or ridicule, one that didn't abide by social norms, and one that believed in self-expression of the loudest form. In short, he was exactly my type.

The hostess seated us at one of the small tables by the window and handed us the bulky menus.

"You weren't kidding."

"I told you, a book. It's my personal mission to drink one of everything."

"And how far are you?"

"I think as of last week it was seventeen and I have about three hundred left." We both laughed.

"So, what should we drink tonight then?"

"I'll leave that up to you, Sir."

"My, but you are being the exemplary little submissive, aren't you?"

"Yes, Sir, trying my best."

The waitress came to our table. Hendrix ordered a bottle of Shiraz and a cheese plate. I laughed to myself and thought, 'Nothing but finery and domination for this one.'

"Since you are being so accommodating, I'm going to forgo making you beg for information."

"Thank you, Sir." If anyone I knew here heard me talking to him like this, my reputation for being a semi-bad ass was screwed.

40

"I want to dominate you, that's obvious, and I think you're down for that, but let's talk about swinging. Have you ever tried it on any level?"

"No. As I said before, anytime I brought up so much as a hands and oral only threesome, I was shot down. Now, if I mentioned bringing another woman into it, they would actually give it some thought, but I really didn't know how to arrange it anyway."

"Do you think you could handle that, if I arranged it?"

I still wasn't sure that I wanted to admit to my fantasy last night in the bathtub, so I kept it hidden for now. "I think I could."

"Good, because when you come over Saturday night, Tracy will be there, and she is very interested in you."

The waitress brought our bottle of wine and placed the cheese plate between us, such an awkward moment. Hendrix was smiling at me, and I'm sure I looked like he may have just proposed, all stunned admiration and slight embarrassment.

"She liked me?"

"She thought you were stunning, and I couldn't agree more."

"So, is she a lesbian?"

"No, I told you she had something to do with it before. Well, she frequents a club called Inhibitions. Have you heard of it?"

"No, Sir."

He smiled. "I didn't think you would have. It's a swingers club, but not a lot of people know about it. We do a good job of keeping it quiet. Anyway, I was there with an ex-girlfriend who was less than thrilled with my new found sexual expedition. She had agreed to try it, but it didn't last long. One thing I have learned is that if you're going to do it, you should talk about it early on, even if it's just a fleeting thought. It's hard to be with someone for three years and then tell them you want to fuck other women. Even though I gave her permission to be with other men, she just couldn't get comfortable with me being with someone else. Tracy was there pretty frequently. She came over and flirted with my ex and me a couple of times. We finally decided to bring her home with us one night, and let's just say, that's how my ex became my ex."

"Oh, that sucks."

"You could say that, but I'm actually happy it went the way it did. I know now that this is the type of lifestyle I want and I know to bring that out in the open to a woman right away. I don't want to give any false pretenses, hence the reason I approached you the way I did."

"I appreciate that."

"Even though we're not going into this as a relationship, of course. I don't know about you, but for me the relationship thing has become oppressive. I'm honestly tired of it. And therein lies the experiment. That is what you wanted to talk to me about tonight, isn't it?

"Yes, Sir."

"As I somewhat alluded to before, what I'm really looking for is someone who shares my passion for sex that is separate from love, the kind that you go into strictly for satisfaction, and someone who is willing to be dominated by me and by whomever I may choose. To me, dominance is not only about you being obedient for me, but also that you will do as I say even when I tell you to please someone else. After all, a large part of the pleasure I get from dominating is the satisfaction of your submission to me, not necessarily physical pleasure, though I definitely want that as well. I don't want to sound cocky, but I know that I can find women to fuck. That's not an issue. What I want is so much deeper than most people could understand. I'm already getting so much excitement out of seeing you submit to me. Just hearing you say 'Yes Sir' the way you have adapted to it so quickly, drives me mad. I want that power over you, and I believe you want me to have it. Am I correct?"

I smiled. "Yes, Sir."

"So, as I said, Tracy will be over on Saturday, and I would like to initiate you into a little of what I'm talking about. Do you think you will be ready to try a few things this weekend?"

Blessed wine courage. "Yes Sir." I couldn't say no. I was too interested, but I hoped I wouldn't let him down.

"Fantastic!"

We sat at the café for probably two and a half hours, talking about everything from threesomes and orgies to books and cars. I found out he was thirty four and moved to Atlanta when he was twenty-three. I told him about my many moves before finally settling here to write, and though he didn't ask, I decided to give away my age of twenty six. Talking to him seemed easy because I felt no pressure to impress him in the way I normally did with men I was dating. This was what it was, and that was freeing in so many ways. I would please Hendrix in purely physical ways. I knew that I could do that. What I didn't know was if I could wait until Saturday to prove it to him. Would I even get to touch him on Saturday? He may only let me touch Tracy or be touched by her. I was starting to squirm in the seat a little, feeling my arousal at the thought. What would he make her do to me? Would it be like my fantasy? I could only hope.

The waitress brought our check, and I looked over at it begrudgingly because truly I wasn't ready for this night to end. Hendrix quickly grabbed it before I could, placed a card in the folder, and handed it back to the waitress.

"Thank you. I didn't expect you to pay for my part. This isn't a date, after all."

"You're right. It's not, but that doesn't mean I won't treat you with the same respect as if it was."

"Thank you, Sir."

"You're very welcome."

I stood up smoothing my dress down where it had begun clinging to my thighs. Hendrix noticed this and unashamedly watched with a small smile beginning to form. He said nothing about it, probably because he assumed I already knew what he was thinking. Still, I would have liked to hear his thoughts at that moment. We made our way to the door and I told the hostess goodnight.

Walking back to the car, he put his arm behind me. I thought he was going to place his hand at the small of my back again, but instead he reached up and grasped my neck slightly, leading me in a much more apparent position of dominance. Immediately, I had chills running up my arms to my neck where his warm hand was pressed against my skin. When we arrived at the car, he opened my door as he had done before and went around to his side. I sat nervously awaiting him to climb in, not knowing what was about to happen.

As soon as he shut the door, he put his right hand around the back of my neck, forcefully pressing my face to his, and kissed me, deeply and aggressively. I had never been kissed like that. I kissed him heatedly with need and want that I couldn't describe in words. I was worried but also hopeful that he might pull me on top of him and fuck me here in his car with people all around. But he pulled away from the kiss and moved his lips to my neck, placing hungry but gentle kisses along the length of my chin to my collar bone. Unbuttoning my dress at the top, he began kissing my breasts, licking slowly along the curves of my cleavage. This time he grabbed my neck harder and bit the left side of it, not so hard that it truly hurt, but enough pressure that it took my breath away. I gasped and tried to put my hand on his shoulder, but he quickly grabbed my wrist and pinned it to the window behind me. Taking my other hand, he forcefully moved it to rest with the other, so that he now had me pinned by only one of his hands. I was utterly helpless.

The windows began to fog, and his breath was gaining speed.

He took his free hand, loosened his tie, and unbuttoned the top button of his dress shirt. He had a small bead of sweat running down his neck to his collarbone, where I could see a hint of the ink that adorned his chest peeking out. The street lamps illuminated just enough of us that we could make out only shadowed lines and shapes but with the occasional flash of detail from passing headlights.

Kissing me again, but still holding my pinned wrists with his right hand, he began to touch my inner thigh with his left, running it further up until he made his way to the edge of my panties and removed his lips from mine.

Breathlessly, he asked, "May I touch you?"

"Yes, Sir."

He slipped his fingers under the hem of my panties and moved them aside. I was so aroused that when he began to touch my outer lips, I could feel the wetness behind them run out onto his fingers. He let my hands go but grabbed the back of my hair, pulling it somewhat forcefully until my head tilted back, holding me there in that helpless position for only a moment. When he let go, he used both hands to move my dress up to the tops of my thighs. I assumed I was still not allowed to touch him, so I put one of my hands on the dash and the other on the headrest.

Using his fingers now, he opened my inner lips, slipping only one of his fingers inside me. Just like in my fantasy, he put that finger to his lips, but instead of tasting it the way I had imagined, he spread the wetness he had stolen over his lips and kissed me. I responsively licked them clean, and I could see that it drove him crazy. He quickly shoved two fingers inside me now and drove them as far in as he could, practically pushing me into the car door.

"Fuck, you are hot Ashton! God, you know what I want. You're such a very, very good girl."

His voice was somewhat staggered with the thrusting of his fingers. He used his thumb of the same hand to start rubbing my clit. I could tell he really knew what he was doing and that he truly wanted to please me, and that in pleasing me, he was pleasing himself.

He continued to fuck me with his fingers while he buried his face in my breasts, licking and kissing at them. With his free hand, he reached down into my bra and drew my breast up just enough so that he could put my nipple in his mouth and begin to suck at it. With the fingers he had inside me, he began to flick up and down, brushing my cervix as he did. I could feel that I was building to a point of release but wasn't sure that I could actually do it. He was relentless with his fingers; forcing them deeper and deeper inside me, up to the base of them, and then turning them upwards to pull at my G-spot, while at the same time pressing and rubbing at my clit with his thumb.

"Are you going to come for me?"

Barely able to speak, I managed to answer him in a whisper, "I don't know. I'm sorry. It's hard for me."

"You better believe it's hard for you. My cock is so hard right now it may rip through the zipper. But you will come for me Ashton. I'm not asking you. I'm telling you. Come for me!"

I was breathing so hard, my legs straining and flexing with the need to let go.

"If you don't come for me, I'm going to beat your ass, much harder than I did on the street. Come for me now!"

"I'm sorry! I don't know, but please don't stop, please."

"I'm going to pull these fingers out of you and start this car if you don't do what I tell you to do, do you understand me?"

"Yes, Sir." I was getting frustrated. I was so close but afraid to let go. Never had I let a man make me come. I had to help, to touch myself somehow, so that it would be my victory and not his. I couldn't let anyone own me that way.

"Let it go! I'm doing this to you. It's mine! Now give it to me! Do you hear me?"

"Yes, Sir."

"I'm sorry. I didn't hear you. What?"

"Yes, Sir."

"Say it louder!"

"Yes, Sir!"

"What are you?"

"I don't know! What do you want me to say?"

"Tell me you're my little slut and tell me that you'll come for me."

I was caught a little off guard but so in the moment that I let it slide. "I'm your little slut. I'll come for you."

"You'll come for me what?"

"Sir. I'll come for you, Sir."

"Then do it damn it, or I'll pull them out!"

He was literally slamming his fingers in me now, pressing hard on my clit, pinching my pubic bone between his thumb and the two fingers inside me, making the perfect combined motion, even better than I could do to myself.

"If you're my little slut, then why aren't you coming for me?"

"I don't know! I'm sorry." I almost cried as I said this, not out of sadness but out of frustration.

He removed the hand that was fondling my breasts and slapped my face, not too hard but enough to jolt me. I looked right into his eyes, I couldn't believe what he had done, but they were so hungry and intense. It only made me desire him more.

"Don't you dare stop! You will come for me you little slut! Say it!"

"Yes, Sir. I'll come for you."

"Good Girl."

He kissed me but continued his movements. The hand that had slapped me slipped down to my throat, and he closed it around me, cutting off my air for just a moment. In that moment between panic and darkness, I cried out. I was coming so hard I couldn't think. I writhed on his hand, and he pressed harder on my clit. I screamed. I didn't care who would hear me. He released my throat and covered my mouth with his hand, quieting my voice, but not so much that it dulled the sentiment.

I let out another muffled cry. "Fuck! Hendrix, oh my God!"

When my hips stopped twisting, he removed his fingers from me and uncovered my mouth.

"That was a very, very good girl. Such a good little slut, and so obedient."

With the back of my head against the cold glass window, I took a moment to just breathe. I could feel that the seat was wet beneath me, and my chest was drenched in sweat. Hendrix withdrew his fingers from me, lifted them to his face, and ran them under his nose. He breathed in deeply and said, "When I get home, I'm going to jack off to this wonderful smell. You're amazing, so wet and tight, and your scent drives me mad."

"I'd like to watch that."

"What, me jacking off?"

"Yes, Sir."

"I would love to do that for you, but not tonight. You don't get to see my cock yet."

I feigned pouting.

"I said no. Now turn around and put your seat belt on."

Settling back into his seat as if nothing had happened, he started the car and we were off on the short drive back to my condo. I couldn't regain my composure enough to speak, and he didn't ask me to. I could tell that he was still lost in the event, playing it over in his mind. This man must have ultimate self-discipline. He did all of this to me, didn't touch himself, and wouldn't allow me to touch him whatsoever.

We pulled up to the curb in front of my place. After turning off the car, he wasted no time coming around to my door. When he opened it, he helped me out, but before stepping aside, he made sure that my dress was straight and my hair was back to some semblance of its form before we had left. His large hands smoothed my dress to my thighs just the way I had done at the restaurant, while he looked at me with those beautiful dark blue eyes.

We walked through the lobby doors and into the elevator.

When we stood in front of my door, he spun me around and kissed me lightly, not as he had done in the car.

"I had a wonderful time tonight. Did you enjoy yourself?"

"Wow! Hendrix, you have no idea how much."

He ran his fingers over his top lip, closed his eyes, and inhaled. When he opened them again, he smiled. "I think I do have some idea how much."

He leaned into me and whispered in my ear, "When I'm stroking my hard cock tonight, I'm going to be thinking about fucking you so hard that you pass out, choking that beautiful neck of yours, and whipping that tight little ass."

My knees got weak and my still very sensitive clit was pulsing with blood at the thought of this scenario.

He stood up straight. "Goodnight Ashton, until Saturday." Lifting my hand to his mouth, he planted a kiss on top of it. Then he turned and walked down the hall to the elevator. I unlocked the door, and as soon as I was inside, I leaned up against the other side of it, lost in pure and utter bewilderment.

Five

The stars were still out. I had fallen asleep on the couch and was disoriented for a moment. My cell phone glared 3:15 AM. Sitting up, I looked out my window and into the night. What had happened to me? I wasn't sure I could process it yet. How could a man I didn't even know cross a line that I had not let any others cross, even if we had been together for years? Was my control that self-imagined? But I loved it, didn't I? I loved the fact that he took it from me and that it wasn't even my decision. He ordered me to let go, and because I wanted to obey him, I did. The enjoyment of pleasing him through my obedience was almost as thrilling as the physical pleasure.

Heading for the bathroom, I started water for a bath. There was no way I could go back to sleep now. I grabbed a yogurt from the kitchen and sat at the window, eating it slowly. Of course, now I couldn't look at my favorite window without thinking about what Hendrix said. I could imagine him pressing me up to the glass, but what I wasn't so sure of was whether I could have sex with him in front of other people. The fantasy of it intrigued me, but when the time came, could I let go enough to enjoy it? I was worried that I would back away and my time with Hendrix would be over. I wasn't ready to explore my feelings about that situation. After all, I had only just met him. At the very least, I could ride this experience as far as I could.

There were so many questions running through my mind about this weekend. What was going to happen with Tracy? What part would Hendrix play in it? What would sharing him feel like? Could I really watch him do to another woman what he had done to me? How could I fuck another man with him watching? Too many questions to answer right now. I would have to find out through experience, not through words. Words wouldn't work in this scenario, and that scared me too because words were my allies. Most of the time I could talk my way out of anything. I could relay the deepest feelings of my soul to anyone who was willing to read it, but I couldn't find words for how I felt about this. It was beyond my comprehension and therefore beyond that all important grasp I felt I should have on it.

I needed to embrace this excitement as uncharted territory, but that acceptance would take my surrender. That was the real conflict here, my obsessive desire to control my world and everything that happened to me. What kind of life was that really? Isn't the joy of life to experience it, even if it sometimes turns out badly? One of my favorite quotes by Lord Byron hung on my bedroom wall, "The great art of life is sensation, to feel that we exist, even in pain." This was the first time I truly attached the depth of its meaning to a real life event.

Sensation is proof of existence, proof of a life lived. Even pain could be beautiful when it becomes part of the anthology of your life, part of the memories in your mental Rolodex you flip through when life is drawing to a close. How bad could that pain really be when you knew you would no longer have the time to experience what brought it ever again? Then it stands out to you, the sharpness of its impression on your very persona. It becomes treasured and even romantic. What came after because of that moment? Would your life have gone the same way had it not happened? I couldn't let an experience like this pass me by because I was too afraid of what might happen. Good or bad, I wanted whatever this turned out to be to stamp itself on my soul and do with me what it would.

Six

After going to bed somewhere around eight o'clock Friday morning, I didn't wake up again until one in the afternoon. I had that frustrating hungover feeling of too much sleep but very few restful moments. I looked at my cell phone. There was a text from Hendrix waiting for me: "Would you like to discuss tomorrow's plans?" It had been sent at 9:15 this morning. I hope he didn't think I was ignoring him.

I replied: "Sure. I'm sorry I'm just now responding, but I woke up about five minutes ago :/"

I didn't have to wait long before he wrote me back: "Not to worry, I will make sure you are severely punished for making me wait."

I loved the sound of that now that I had a taste of his punishments. That soft, quick slap to my face at the same time as receiving pleasure had given me a feeling of heightened senses. It was like being very cold and plunging your hand into hot water. That shock of opposites took time to reach your brain. In that split second before you felt the difference, hot and cold were one, the same as pleasure and pain could be one. It's only our perception that separates the two, but we wouldn't know how to perceive hot without cold or pleasure without pain. We have to know one side of an extreme to appreciate the other, and Hendrix had definitely given me a new appreciation.

I texted back: "I look forward to it Sir."

I hoped that I had pleased him immensely with my response. A few moments passed: "You are incredible Ashton. I want you to know how much I truly value your obedience. You have no idea how that excites me, but I do intend to show you."

"Once again, looking forward to it Sir."

"Be ready tomorrow by six. I'll be there to pick you up, and that is not a question. It is an order."

"Yes Sir! :)"

He was able to dominate me with only words, and if he could manage that, then I'm sure he could lure other women to his bed easily. At that thought came a flare of jealousy again. I wasn't sure that I wanted to see another woman in his bed, but maybe that was because I hadn't been in it myself. Flicking this thought away as soon as it occurred, I reminded myself that I was not his. He was not mine. We had the freedom to do whatever we chose because we owed each other nothing. Such a freeing feeling, to owe him nothing, yet I still gave him my obedience. Was that not something? Wouldn't I have to trust him immensely to let him dominate me and share me with people I didn't even know? Honestly, I had no idea how this worked and I had to rely on him to show me. That alone was dominance.

For a fleeting moment, I thought of texting him back and telling him I couldn't go through with it, but after the epiphany I had early this morning at that all too familiar hour when everything seems so clear only to disappoint you in normal daylight, I decided to stand by it. To live this life for experience and toss out the notion that I could construct everything to go the way I wanted it to. No, I was going to be taken away by this, outside myself and my limits, and hopefully become someone better for it.

With a new wave of determination, I stood up and walked to the kitchen, fixed some toast and eggs, the first real meal I had eaten since Wednesday, and put a record on, *Gershwin and other Jazz Greats,* then sat on the chaise trying not to stare at my window. Today was the last day of being the me I had known for too long, the control freak. I hoped I could keep this promise and lose myself in pleasure for the sake of pleasure, aestheticism for the body.

When I had finished my much needed sustenance and inner reflections, I decided to go for a run. I changed and once again located my ear buds, this time on the floor of the closet. A centralized location to keep them would be the best idea, but of course, that would be too predetermined for me.

In no time, I was out the door and running to some much needed metal, fast, furious, and charged with energy. At a quick pace, I was doing my best at dodging pedestrians, my urban obstacle course. The city was crowded at this time of day with everyone off to their tasks. I began to wonder how many of them did what Hendrix wanted to do with me. Were there a lot of people who shared each other or hung out in clubs where public sex was invited? That thought gave me a feeling of empowerment, like I was going to be a member of a secret society. I held this thought like a promise that I wasn't actually alone in this, there were others of course, and they had to be new at one time, didn't they? What was I so afraid of? If there was an entire club built around the idea, it couldn't be just a few people. This eased my mind. Smiling, I sprinted the rest of the way to my building.

When I walked through my door, I couldn't help but to immediately check my phone. Several texts had come through while I was out, a couple from neglected friends probably thinking I had been murdered or ran away to Jamaica and one from Hendrix. I read his first: "I'm thoroughly excited about tomorrow night. I can't wait to get this started. Last night was only a small taste Ashton. I hope you're ready."

My hands were shaking from my run, making it hard to type: "I am ready and willing Sir."

He must have been anticipating my response, which made me happy to think of him waiting on my words instead of the other way around. "Good Girl. And I wanted you to know that I made good on my promise last night. When I got home I started jacking off almost the minute I closed the door. I was so hard for you. I thought about all the things I could have done to you in my car, but the agony of not fucking you right then and there made me all the more aroused. Keep that in mind when I tease you, because I will, and you'll beg for my mercy. When you do, remember that the agony of want only makes the getting sweeter."

"I will try my best Sir. I like you telling me about pleasing yourself. Would you mind elaborating?"

"No, I don't mind, but I would rather do it after work, and on the phone, not typing."

"I can wait."

"I know you will, if you want it. You don't have a choice."

"Yes Sir."

"I'll call you on my drive home."

"Thank you Sir."

"Very good girl."

God, he knew how to torment me. The agony of want? He certainly knew how to use words to entice me. This man could not be more perfect. Now to put those words into play. Waiting on him to call tonight and tell me about him pleasuring himself would not be easy.

After I had showered and dressed, I decided to get online and update my Facebook. A great time consuming activity that would hopefully keep me entertained until Hendrix called. Even while scrolling through my newsfeed, all I could do was try to imagine what he looked like while he pleasured himself. What I wouldn't give to have seen his face and body while he was doing it. Admittedly, I have a bit of an obsession with watching a man pleasure himself. There's something about the strain of their body and then the relief on their face when they get that release.

Finally, after another hour of intentionally wasting time, the phone rang.

"Hello?"

"Well hello, my good girl. What have you been up to this fine day?"

I laughed. "Well, if you must know, I went for a run, but other than that have been mostly preoccupied by thinking of you pleasuring yourself last night."

"I do like your mindset. A lot of women wouldn't want to know about that, but then again, you're certainly not like most women."

"I hope not."

Laughter again. "I don't think you could be even if you tried. Now, about last night."

"Yes?"

"Do you want every detail or an abbreviated version? Because I have a rather long drive home today, and I don't know what you might have planned. I wouldn't want you to have to hang up before I finished."

We both laughed at that little pun, "No other plans tonight, so feel free to give me all the details."

"Okay. So, as I told you I started as soon as I got home. Wait, would you like me to start from the time I left you or just when the fun began?"

"Oh, please, if you don't mind, from the time you left me."

"Well, after I got back to my car, I noticed that there was still a little of your moisture on the passenger seat. I reached over and rubbed it between my fingers, then tasted it. I sucked it off my fingers actually. Your smell and taste immediately made my cock start to swell. I wanted to get home as soon as possible. I kept thinking about the feeling of you on my fingers, and God, the way you came. Your body responded to me so well, you obeyed me, and you liked the way I talked to you. I could tell it turned you on so much because every time I made you say 'Yes Sir' or that you were my little slut, you got even wetter. It was like the more I frightened you with my commands, the more excited you got. If I'm wrong about this, please tell me though."

"No, you're absolutely right."

"Good. Because if you liked the way I treated you last night, you have so much more in store. I kept thinking about that all the way home. It felt like it took hours to get there, but when I finally made it, I practically sprinted to the elevator. As soon as I was inside my place, I sat down on the couch and unzipped my pants. I didn't waste time unbuckling my belt or unbuttoning, just unzipped. I pulled my cock out, and it began growing quickly. I teased the head with light circling motions and ran my hand up and down the length of it, still with a light, teasing touch. You do remember me telling you how much I like to tease?"

"Yes, you mentioned that."

"After a few minutes of that, I spit on my hand and grabbed my dick at the base, squeezed it hard and started pumping my hand up and down. I leaned my head back and thought about your tight little pussy while I breathed your scent in that was still on my other hand. That made my cock even harder, so I squeezed it tighter and began pumping it faster, thinking about what I was going to do with you Saturday. I thought about fucking you, like I said up against your window, and about people watching me fuck you. I dropped down to my knees at that point and leaned onto the coffee table, bracing myself with my free hand. I kept the other hand on my cock and started thrusting my hips into it, thinking of it being your pussy and driving my hard shaft into it. I thought about what your ass would look like pressed into me, seeing my cock come out shining with your juices, and then watching me drive it back into you, making your ass bounce off of me with the force of it. Are you touching yourself right now Ashton?"

"Yes."

"No! You don't do that unless you ask me. Do you understand?"

"I'm sorry Sir. I didn't know."

"I know, and that's the only reason I'm going to continue with my story, but from now on you will ask if you can pleasure yourself when I'm with you or speaking to you. In the future, I may even go so far as to make you ask me anytime you want to please yourself because I want to own your pussy. I want you to ask me to allow you to feel pleasure. Now, you may ask me."

"Please Sir, may I pleasure myself?"

"What is it exactly that you want to do?"

I was embarrassed. Was he really going to make me ask for the exact things I wanted to do?

"Ashton, if you don't ask, then I'll have to hang up, because I know you'll be disobeying me."

Fuck, okay I can do this. "Please Sir, I would like to finger myself and play with my clit."

"Good girl! Now see that wasn't so hard, was it?"

"No Sir."

"You may do those things, but I want to know if you feel like you're going to come, you may not come without my permission. Do you understand?"

"Yes Sir." My God, he was amazing! I had never been so turned on over the phone, though I assumed with him, each new experience would top the last.

"As I was saying, I was fucking my hand, imagining it was your tight little pussy. I thought then about making you pleasure another woman with your mouth while I was fucking you from behind. She would be laid out in front of you, so that I could watch her face as you pleased her, and I would be pleasing you at the same time. Do you think you would like that?"

I didn't have to think about my answer, not with the way he put it. "Yes Sir, I would."

"Good because I can't wait to see it. As you were making her squirm with your tongue, you began to finger her, and I told you to make her come. I didn't talk to her at all. I only told you what to do to her. You wanted to please me so badly that you started licking furiously at her clit and moving your fingers in and out of her pussy harder and harder. I could tell she was close, and you were so very wet, but I wouldn't let you come until you made her. I spanked your ass and told you that if you didn't make her come, I would pull my cock out of you and do it myself. This both infuriated and compelled you because you started to suck at her clit and ram her with your fingers. You told her that if she didn't come you were going to punish her yourself.

I interrupted him, "May I please come, Sir?"

"Good girl for asking, but you have to wait until I get to the part in my story where I come."

I didn't know how to hold back with myself. I always did what I wanted. I stopped touching myself, trying my best not to let go, ironically the exact opposite of what I had done last night with him. He knew it, didn't he? He was tormenting me with the conflict of my own control.

"Now, where was I? Oh yes, you threatening her with punishment. That turned me on so much, thinking of you dominating her because she didn't allow you to get pleasure from me. Luckily as you were sucking at her, she started screaming and coming so hard that she was grabbing your head and burying it between her thighs. When she finally stopped convulsing, you turned your face so you could see me and I leaned down and kissed you, licking her juices from your lips. This drove you over the edge and you begged me to let you come. You may beg me now, Ashton."

"Oh please Sir, please let me come."

"You may, but I want to hear you. You came hard and backed your ass into me asking with your body for me to go deeper."

I couldn't stop it now and I wanted to please him by allowing him to hear me, so I moaned loudly and gasped for air, trying to catch my breath, letting out smaller less audible moans in between.

"Good girl, good girl. God I love to hear you come, especially over the phone. As I was saying, you came hard and as I pushed deeper inside you, I began to come too. You ground your hips down onto me, showing me that you like me coming inside you. At that point, I came with my hand, shooting it across the room. All in all, it was a wonderful fantasy, one that I would very much like to act out with you. That is part of the kind of play I'm talking about. I'm guessing that you liked it?

I was so embarrassed from having moaned into the phone. I knew he liked it, but I couldn't help feeling somewhat violated. Never had I let anyone watch me masturbate before, and even though he didn't actually see me, he knew exactly what I was doing and heard me lose control as he had also done last night. Although, I had to admit to him that his fantasy turned me on more than anything I had ever imagined myself. I could only dream of what else he had floating around in his dirty, yet exciting mind.

"Yes Sir. I liked it very much, and if that's what you have in mind, then I am definitely okay with that. The way you described it made it seem so appealing."

"Tell me why you liked it so much."

"I liked it because you made me think about something I never thought I would do and you made me like it."

"No Ma'am. You liked it because I took away your control. You had to do what I said or you got nothing. I made you like it so much that you would have done anything for me to keep fucking you. You made it your mission to make that girl come, not only because you wanted me to please you, but because you wanted to please me. Would you agree?"

How did he do that? Of course he was right, and I saw the way his fantasies worked. The other girl really wasn't a factor, other than the control he had over me, by involving her.

"Yes Sir, you are."

"I thought so. Like I said, I know your type Ashton. You've been looking for someone to absolve you of your control. To make it okay for you to let go, and I promise you, I'm that person."

I was speechless.

"Well, I'm home, and I need to shower, and most likely think about you again while I'm doing that. So I'm going to let you go and leave you to your thoughts. Until tomorrow then?"

"Yes Sir. Tomorrow."

Seven

The phone rang. I dug myself out of the cave of blankets I had created overnight.

"Hello?"

"Hi sweetie! What are you up to today?"

My Mother. I guess talking to her couldn't hurt. It would keep my mind off tonight because I sure wasn't going to say anything to her about it.

"Oh, Hi. Actually, I was still sleeping, but that's okay. I needed to get up anyway."

"Sorry dear. Why are you still asleep at 11 AM though?"

Think of something..."Writing. I was working on a project until late last night. I just needed to catch up on my sleep, I guess."

Of course, the truth was that I couldn't fall asleep after hanging up with Hendrix last night. The way he described his fantasy had left me aching for today to arrive, and finally it had. Now, I just had to make it to six o'clock without going entirely crazy.

"Well, honey, you shouldn't work yourself too hard, you know?"

"Yeah, I know. I was just on a roll and didn't want to lose my train of thought."

I laughed to myself about the train my thoughts were actually on.

"So what are you doing today?"

"Probably go for a run and try to write a little more."

"Ashton, you shouldn't spend all of your time writing. You need to interact with people. Don't be such a recluse."

"I am interacting Mom, I promise." God, if she only knew

how interactive I was going to be.

"Have you met anyone yet?"

"You know, I'm not constantly looking for someone. I'm just fine on my own."

"I know you are honey. I don't doubt that a bit, but I worry about you not getting out there again after this last breakup."

"Don't worry about it, Mom. Really, I just need a little time off. I'll meet the right guy eventually."

Or I could meet a sadistic James Dean wannabe, who was going to make me fuck other people.

"Alright, Ashton, I'll stop harping about it. I'm sorry. I just care about you."

"I know you do. I love you."

"I love you too. I hope you have a good day. And get outside!"

"Okay, Mom, I promise, I'll get out today. Talk to you later."

"Bye sweetie."

Ugh! That was awful. I kept trying not to bust out laughing while I was lying to her. I couldn't tell her the truth. She would probably try to have Hendrix arrested or me committed. Maybe I should have myself committed for agreeing to this craziness, but no matter how I tried to convince myself that I should back out now before I got in too deep, I just couldn't. I wanted the experience too badly. At the very least, I could go through with it tonight, and if I hated it, I would never have to do it again. He did say that I could quit at any time.

When I began to think about Hendrix all my fears scurried away. I wanted him. I wanted him badly, and if sharing him with others was the way to get him, then I would endure it. I would do it, and I would love every fucking minute of it!

It was almost noon, and that meant six very long hours until Hendrix would be here to pick me up. Would he text or call me at all before I saw him? I hoped that he would, but at the same time, not hearing from him would probably... how did he put it? Make the getting sweeter? I liked that, and I thought about the "getting", about what that would entail exactly, but I had to convince myself that I couldn't know what was going to happen. I couldn't, and that was part of the thrill. I had to stop trying to construct an escape plan in my head. Let go, just let go and let it be, whatever happens, happens. That's the way it had to be in order to enjoy it, and I was going to stick with it.

Having nothing more distracting to do, I thought instead of running, I would take a walk through the city. No pedestrian dodging today. Sitting down at the computer, I made up a playlist. A different playlist for every occasion was a must. I was one of those people who believed that music was the soundtrack for your life. For instance, I could play a song and remember moments in so much detail that I felt like I was there again. In fact, some of my favorite songs were terrible, but because of the memory they invoked, I loved them. What songs would stay with me after this part of my life was over? What song would pinpoint Hendrix in my life? I didn't want to think of him as someone I would have to remember, to assign him to my mental scrapbook, complete with song lyrics and the taste of certain kisses. I felt an inkling of remorse. Maybe I wouldn't have to. Maybe we could go on with this arrangement forever if we wanted to, as long as neither of us every wanted to marry someone, or have children, or any kind of postcard picture life. I shook the idea from my mind. Stop Ashton! Just go walk! I popped my ear buds in, actually finding them in the same place I left them, and was convinced this was a turning point in my life.

Walking through the Little Five district was a smorgasbord of culture. You could buy anything from a vase costing hundreds of dollars to a voodoo doll. It also housed one of my favorite stores in all of Atlanta, The Junkyard. It was the biggest vintage/retro/hodgepodge store I had ever been in. Passing it I thought, "What if I had been there on Wednesday?" I probably never would have met Hendrix. That reminded of his pick up line, "Of all the vintage stores in all the cities, in all the world, you had to walk into mine." Even before he knew anything about me, he got me, and that was the rarest of finds.

I walked on for about two hours, eventually making my way past the International Café. All I could do was smile and walk home faster.

Three o'clock. Okay you have to eat, do that. I did. Get a shower. Check. Get frustrated over your wardrobe and say you have nothing to wear. Absolutely. Now, really pick out what you're going to wear. Trying.

Five o'clock. I had finally decided on a blue party dress. Not quite cocktail but not casual either. It was strapless and came just above my knees. As I got ready, I sang the song about the devil in a blue dress in my head and smiled because I knew most people would see me that way, especially Hendrix. I did my makeup a little darker, cat-eyed my eyeliner, and put some effort into neatly disheveling my hair, instead of its usual complete discordance.

It was 5:45 PM. I had to calm my nerves somehow. Remembering I had some airplane whiskey bottles in the freezer, I got one out and poured it into a rocks glass. While I was trying my best to only sip at it and not shoot it for insta-courage, I thumbed through my records and settled on Bon Iver. I put the record on and set the needle down.

Six o'clock on the dot, and the intercom buzzed. I almost yelled at it to tell the doorman to let him up before he even got the words out of his mouth. Instead, I finished the whiskey and listened to the man.

"Ms. Rhodes, you have a visitor. Hendrix Larson."

Breathe. "Yes, thank you, he's expected, please let him up."

Breathe, breathe, this is not Lamaze, just normal breaths, breathe, count to ten, don't pass out.

He knocked. I answered.

"Ashton, you look stunning."

"Thanks, as do you." He was wearing gray dress pants with a dark blue shirt and a muted silver tie.

"No, thank you. I'm glad to see that you want to dress up for me, or is it for Tracy?" He smiled, already knowing the answer.

"It's all for you, Sir."

"Yes it is, and you are all for me, aren't you?"

"Yes, Sir."

"And I will do with you what I please, won't I?"

"Yes, Sir."

"Now, be a good girl and gather whatever you need to bring. You have five minutes."

"Yes, Sir." I took the needle from the record, put the cover on the player, grabbed my purse and phone, and stood in front of him.

"Good girl, only three minutes. You will be rewarded for that."

"Thank you, Sir."

"Now lock your door and come downstairs with me."

I did, and we walked out into the hall, but he just stood in front of me. "What? Did I forget something?"

"I should say you did."

"What? Please tell me."

"You forgot your manners. Now get down on your knees."

"Are you serious? There are people in the hall."

His voice was low and commanding, stern without yelling. "Get on your knees, now."

I did, but I was scowling at him. Luckily though, the onlookers had turned the corner and we were alone again.

"When I told you to lock your door and come downstairs, you didn't respond. You did what you were told, but you didn't acknowledge me."

I looked down at his feet. "I'm sorry, Sir."

"I will make you sorry if you ever do that again. Do you understand me?"

I was actually scared, but I was also wet and thinking about what he was going to make me do down here on my knees.

"Look up at me and say that. And tell me you won't ever forget again."

I looked up at him. He had never seemed as attractive to me as he did right now. He had the look of a dictator, a disciplining Father or teacher, but he had lust in his eyes, not anger. His excitement was evident, as was the impression that that this was what he got off on. Power.

"Sir, I'm sorry. Please forgive me. I'll never forget again."

He stared down at me and offered his hand. Taking it, he helped me to my feet.

"Good. Now are you ready to go?"

"Yes, Sir." I couldn't have had a more ridiculous grin on my face when I said it.

"Good girl." He smiled approvingly and led me out the door to his car. Of course, he opened the door for me and then went to his side.

When he turned the key, the radio came on immediately. He had been listening to The Black Keys, one of my favorite bands.

"Oh, I love this band."

"Great, because we'll be listening to them for the ride to my place."

I wondered if he was going to be the dictator all night or if he would lighten up. I liked it, but I didn't want to feel too oppressed.

"Yes, Sir."

"You do look beautiful tonight Ashton."

"Thank you."

"Are you nervous?"

"Yes, Sir."

"It's okay, I'll allow you to be, but I promise you're going to have a good time tonight."

I felt a little better and smiled at him. "Thank you."

He looked at me briefly and returned the smile. "I'm sure I will be the one thanking you before the night is over."

"I would like that."

We were quiet the rest of the way. Both of us were intentionally focusing on the music and I was trying to contain myself.

He parked the car in the underground garage but didn't open his door to get out.

"I want to talk to you for a minute before we go in. Tracy is here already. She is not going to do anything that you don't want to, nor will I. You can leave if you want to, whenever you want to, and I will take you home. I want you to enjoy this. If you don't, it's not worth it. Everyone involved should enjoy it, and if at any time someone doesn't, we stop. Sometimes, you may be in a situation where saying stop could be taken as playing along, so I want you to remember the word, 'Mercy.' That will be your safe word, okay? If at any time you really want to stop what we're doing, in any situation, say it.

"Yes, Sir." What a fitting word.

I was shaking now, literally shaking, because I was so nervous and excited. I thought I may be sick or have a laughing fit. I wasn't sure. I just wanted to get up to his condo and put these anxieties to rest.

He got out of the car and came around to my door. As usual he helped me out, and as he took my hand, he spun me around to look at me from all angles.

"Quite a Devil tonight, aren't we?" He winked at me and closed the car door.

"Yes, Sir. I had hoped you would make the connection"

"Of course." He smiled.

Alright, this was it. We were getting into the garage elevator and heading to the lobby. We walked in, and the doorman waved at Hendrix and me. The place was exquisite. I knew he had good taste, but this was beautiful beyond words. Marble floors, modern chandeliers, plush mod furniture. I couldn't wait to see what his place looked like.

My heart began to pound as we stood in the elevator. He pressed the button for the twelfth floor, and we were on our way. As we waited in the confined space I could feel the tension building between us. My hope was that he would turn and attack me, press me up against the sides of the elevator, but most likely there were cameras, and he wouldn't want to get evicted.

After a whole agonizing minute the elevator finally dinged and the doors opened. When we stepped off, I could no longer feel my feet. In fact, I felt a bit lightheaded, and I was convincing myself not to pass out. We walked down an ornately decorated hallway and arrived at door #1223. When he withdrew the keys from his pocket and turned them in the door lock, I think my heart actually stopped for a moment.

Tracy was sitting on a large black chaise, much more modern and sophisticated than mine. His whole living room was modern sophistication. That's the only way I could describe it. White floors with a giant, black shag area rug in the center of the living space and a fire place that stood between this room and the bedroom. The kitchen was stainless steel and limestone, pure class from top to bottom. My God, if he thought I could ever decorate this place, he was crazy. My kind of crazy. I grinned at the thought.

My instinct told me that from the moment I walked in the door, there would be no more formalities. I was here to be his obedient submissive and he was my, I guess, Master, but he hadn't made me call him that. I might feel a little like Igor if he did, and accidentally laugh when I said it. Yeeeess Maaaaster. Yes, entertain yourself, Ashton. Think about anything than what you're still thinking about. It wasn't working. I gave up.

"Ashton, you've met Tracy."

Tracy stood up and walked towards me. How could this girl look any more like a Barbie doll? She was flawless, and I was jealous this time. The waitress garb was one thing, but this was insane. She was barely wearing a long black dress that was slit from ankle to hip. When she walked, you could see the edges of her panties, and the top was cut all the way down to her navel, barely hanging on to her breasts, just enough to cover each nipple. Silently, I was resenting the fantasy I had before of pleasuring her.

She came to stand in front of me. "Hi Ashton."

"Hi Tracy." I might have said that with a little disdain, but I hoped it would be passed off as nervousness. I heard faint music playing… Was it Sinatra? Tony Bennett? I couldn't tell, but it was definitely one of the crooners. James Bond style, indeed.

Hendrix began his reign. "Ashton, tonight I will be instructing you on a few things."

"Yes, Sir."

"Oh, Hendrix, will you let me play with her too?"

"Tracy, you'll have your turn, but for now, Ashton is all mine."

What the Hell have I gotten myself into? I had the Barbie asking to play with me and Hendrix saying I was all his. I was so confused.

"Drink this." Hendrix handed me a glass of dark red wine.

I felt a little like Alice, afraid that I might be shrunken, but I accepted. "Thank you, Sir."

I did as I was told, but took only a few sips before he told me to set it down on the coffee table. As I did, Tracy stared at me, sizing me up and down. I felt like I was being ogled by a man but still so much different.

"Wow, Hendrix, you really have her trained well, don't you?"

"Yes, she is an exemplary woman, isn't she?"

"Definitely. I love the way she looks, so cute and edgy."

I felt like I didn't exist. They weren't talking to me but about me, right in front of me, intentionally making me feel unimportant. I assumed it was part of the game, so I continued to play for now.

Hendrix sat on his oversized black couch, and Tracy sat on the floor next to the coffee table. It was an odd picture, him on the couch, her near his feet. Where would I fit into this?

"Ashton, take off your shoes."

"Yes, Sir." I slid them off and held them in my hands, unsure of what he wanted me to do with them.

"Good girl. You may set them near the door."

I did and walked back to where I had been standing.

"She minds so well Hendrix, and she is so eager to please you."

"Isn't she though? Come here Ashton." He beckoned with his fingers as he had done to Tracy in the restaurant. I could tell this was meant to be demeaning, but not in a rude way, more to show that he was in charge.

I moved to the couch and sat down on his lap with my back facing him and both of my feet on the floor.

"Such a good girl." He put one of his hands on my arm and ran his index finger along my shoulder to my neck. I instantly got chills, and I knew he noticed them. I felt warmth on my neck and realized that his lips were hovering right above my skin. He kissed me then, but very lightly, and as he was pulling away, he nipped me with his teeth, just the slightest little bit of pain. My clit began to swell. I closed my eyes and stayed with the sensation.

"Ashton is very turned on by mixing a little bit of pain with the pleasure you give her. Aren't you?"

"Yes, Sir."

"Tracy, are you enjoying watching me tease her?"

"Oh, yes."

Why didn't she have to answer him respectfully? He didn't

say anything to her about her responses. It seemed very unfair, although it did make me feel special in a weird way, like he was prepping me for something more important. I was so conflicted. I wanted to obey him, but I couldn't help feeling very uncomfortable with Tracy just sitting there looking at us. I also wasn't sure that I wanted her to do anything but sit there because my jealousy was starting to get the best of me.

Hendrix started to unzip the top of my dress, just down to where my bra strap should have been. "May I unzip this further?"

"Yes, Sir."

He slowly pulled the zipper down. I could feel more and more of myself being exposed. It was such an odd feeling, I loved that he was undressing me but felt that I should not be undressed in front of Tracy. He began kissing the back of my neck and running his hands to the front of my dress.

"May I touch your breasts?"

I was aching for him to touch me, everywhere, but I was embarrassed to feel that way in front of Tracy. "Yes, Sir."

He flipped the top of my dress down. Since I wasn't wearing a bra, my breasts fell out, and I felt utterly exposed. I wanted to cover myself, but I wanted him to touch me, but more than anything, I wanted Tracy to go away, so that I could have him to myself.

"Oh, she has gorgeous breasts." Tracy reached a hand out to touch me, but Hendrix must have shot her an intimidating look because she stopped mid-reach.

"Yes, she does, but you have to wait, Tracy. You can only touch her when I give my say-so."

"I'm sorry Hendrix, you know I'm not used to being submissive."

"I know, quite alright, just keep it in mind for tonight."

She didn't answer, but nodded in approval. If she wasn't used to be submissive, then I assumed that meant maybe she had her own submissives. The dynamics of this game were too confusing to follow, especially being in this uncomfortable position.

Hendrix cupped my right breast, then began caressing it, squeezing it firmly for a while, seemingly almost lost in what he was doing. "Now, Tracy, would you like to touch them?"

My heart fluttered. I wasn't sure how to feel. I was nervous and excited but afraid.

"Of course."

Tracy rocked up onto her knees and moved close to me. My breath was unsteady and I wasn't sure I could keep myself from leaning away from her when she reached for me, but I held my ground. Lightly, she put her hand on my left breast, ran her thumb over my nipple, and then cupped my breast with her palm. She moved it up and down in her hands, feeling the weight of it, almost inspecting it. I could hear Hendrix's breathing pick up, and it excited me. He put his arms around my waist and moved me back just slightly.

His voice was smooth and low right next to my ear. "Do what you would like Tracy."

She could tell that I was very uncomfortable and looked up at me, giving me a knowing smile, as if to say everything was okay. I remembered then that she was no virgin to this lifestyle and she must know what she was doing. Perhaps I should give her more credit and a little trust. Truthfully, I didn't think Hendrix would make her do something to me that he thought I would really dislike.

Tracy brought her face down to my breast and softly placed her lips on my nipple, kissing it at first, and then sucking it into her mouth. It was an intense feeling, her red lips covering my nipple while at the same time Hendrix held me around my waist. I was easing up a little more. She started flicking my nipple with her tongue and teasing it into a hardened state. The feeling of a woman's mouth at my breast was entirely different than that of a man, so much gentleness and softness. Her hands felt tiny and smooth to me, the complete opposite of Hendrix, but the sensation she gave me was the same.

Hendrix was breathing heavier now. He pulled me all the way back into him, and I could feel his hard cock under his pants. This was it. This is what he wanted, to be turned on just by watching Tracy pleasure me. Feeling his hardness against my lower back made me ache to be touched elsewhere.

"Tracy, I'm sure Ashton would like to be pleasured in another way. Would you like to oblige her?"

My heart was beating in my throat. I didn't know what to say. I was so very turned on and wanted the relief so badly, but I didn't want to say yes to having a woman please me.

"Absolutely."

"Mmmm, thank God. I can't wait to see this. Push her legs apart and look up her dress. Describe what you see."

She took her delicate hands and placed them on the insides of my knees, gently spreading my legs. The way I was sitting on Hendrix's lap had me tilted slightly back, and I knew she would be able to see my panties clearly.

"Oh, Hendrix, her panties are dripping wet."

Hendrix pressed his cock harder into my back at the mention of that. I could tell he wanted the relief as badly as I did. His hands still held me around the waist and I knew now, it was so that I couldn't get up.

"Move her panties aside and slip you fingers into her. Give her some pleasure but not too much."

I was in absolute agony. The feeling of Hendrix against me, my lips exposed to Tracy, and now he had said she couldn't give me too much pleasure. Oh yes, he loved to tease. How could I forget?

Tracy slid her hand up the inside of my thigh and over top of my panties. She pressed a finger onto my clit, which made me jerk slightly. Hendrix held me tighter. She ran that finger in circles making my clit stiffen and ache. Still keeping up with that motion, she slid my panties aside with her other hand. All the while, my dress was still in place. I knew Hendrix couldn't see anything, but he could feel my body react to her touch.

She moved my panties further aside and slid one of her slender fingers down from my clit and over the outer lips, but not inside. Then, turning her hand palm up, she slipped two fingers inside me. I thought I would climax then, but I was conflicted with the feeling of allowing her to do it. It wasn't so much the act of what she was doing but the whole scenario. I was held down for her to tease me while Hendrix got harder and harder not doing anything to himself. He truly was turned on by the power he had over me, and I was in agonizing pleasure from him controlling the situation.

Tracy was still moving her fingers inside me, tormenting me by avoiding my clit, which was begging for attention. Subconsciously, I strained my hips to make her touch it, but she wouldn't. That was her stipulation: she couldn't make me come. Hendrix moved me down onto his chest. I slid partially down his leg, and this brought me closer to Tracy.

"Lift her dress."

With her free hand, she pushed my skirt up to my hips, finally exposing to Hendrix what she was doing to me.

"Fuck." It was more of a sigh than a word really. Hendrix was obviously very aroused by what he was seeing. He slid me down further, so that my pussy was over the end of his knee and my face was at his lap. He unzipped his pants and pulled out his cock. I finally got to see it. My God, it was huge, at least eight inches in length and very thick. It was almost purple from the amount of blood that was pumping into it.

Tracy was watching all of this, and I knew she had to be aroused too. I didn't know what was going to happen next. I was on the verge of coming, Hendrix was ready to burst, and Tracy hadn't asked for anything.

"Ashton, put your mouth on my cock."

At last, I would get to feel it. I didn't care how. I just wanted it. I began licking around the head and down the length of his shaft. I was slightly sideways, so I couldn't get my mouth over top of it. He realized this and moved me off of his lap to lay me on the couch. Tracy never stopped what she was doing. He stood over top of me now, his hard cock pointed at my face. He grabbed the back of my head and drove my mouth down over it and began pumping his hips. His strong hands were on either side of me. All I could see, taste, or smell was him, filling my mouth and senses.

After only a few minutes, Hendrix stopped moving and pulled himself from my mouth. He stood up and unbuttoned his pants, sliding them down along with his boxer briefs. I could see all of him now, and I wanted it inside me so badly. I wondered if he would move Tracy aside now and take over. Instead, he offered Tracy his hand and helped her stand.

"Tracy, lie down on the floor."

She did as she was told, and he came over to me, helping me up in the same way. When I stood I could feel my wetness run down my thigh. I was hoping he was going to have me to himself now, but instead he guided me down to the floor to sit on my knees at Tracy's feet.

"Lift up Tracy's dress."

"Yes, Sir."

"Now, Tracy gave you a lot of pleasure didn't she?"

"Yes, Sir."

"I want you to show her the same kindness, but I want you to make her come."

I couldn't do this. It was one thing to hear it in his fantasy, but entirely different when I was right here experiencing it. I hesitated to answer him.

"Is there a problem, Ashton?"

"No, well, maybe, Sir."

"Are you trying to tell me that she gave you pleasure without complaint, but you aren't even going to try and touch her?"

"No, Sir. I mean, yes, Sir." I was getting flustered.

He grabbed my arm, bent me forward, and placed three swift, sharp slaps to my ass. He looked into my eyes for a brief moment. I could tell that he was looking to me for permission to keep going, and that little bit of control he gave me, even though it was silent, made me want to please him by doing anything he wanted.

Satisfied with my knowing acknowledgment, he continued.

"Tracy, ask her to please you. Ashton, you answer Tracy with the same respect you give me."

"Yes, Sir." I bowed my head and looked at my hands on the carpet.

"Ashton, please make me come. Touching you really turned me on. I didn't want to stop."

"Yes, Ma'am."

When she asked like that, I felt very guilty for feeling so selfish. After all, she hadn't asked for anything in return until Hendrix made her.

Hendrix looked at me and put his hand on my head, almost petting me. "Good girl."

I was shaking. I was so nervous but so aroused. Slowly, I moved Tracy's dress up to her thighs and then to her hips. Hendrix came to stand behind me. He was hovering over me, his cock still rock hard and waiting to be relieved.

"Go ahead."

"Yes, Sir."

I could see her panties now, what little there was of them. She was wet, and it turned me on, knowing that it was because she had been playing with me. I moved them aside the way she had done to mine so I could see her. This was the first time I had ever really looked at another woman like this before. She looked different than me but not too different, just subtle things, like smaller outer lips and a lower set pubic bone.

"Tracy, tell her what to do to you."

"Ashton, I want you to use your fingers and do what you would to please yourself."

"Yes. Ma'am."

I began by touching her clit. It felt slightly smaller than mine and hidden under a bit more flesh, but I began to rub it as I would my own. Tracy started to breathe heavier and closed her eyes. Hendrix was behind me. He knew that I wanted to turn around and look at him to see what he was doing, but I knew he would never allow that. The sound of his breathing told me that he was pleasuring himself. I touched Tracy's outer lips, opening them slightly with my finger, and she moaned.

Seeing her so excited and hearing Hendrix behind me was pushing me to the edge, and I was no longer as apprehensive. I slid my fingers into Tracy then and began to move them in and out at a steady pace. She moved her hips along with my motions.

"Ashton, will you please me with your mouth?"

"Yes, Ma'am." I didn't even have to think about it. I wanted to do it. I wanted to please her now. Keeping my fingers inside her, I leaned down to her and began to lick at her clit. As soon as I saw how she responded to me, I wanted nothing more at that moment than to make her come.

She was moving her hips faster now, begging for my fingers to go deeper. Licking at her with quick, light strokes, she moaned louder, and I could tell she liked everything that I was doing to her. Soon, I felt her start to tighten around my fingers and more juices flow down to the bottoms of them. I knew what was happening. She was going to come. I was going to make her come. She moaned loudly. Her juices flooded my hand as she clamped down on my fingers and she moved her hips to press her clit harder against my mouth; her body was practically convulsing.

As I was watching all of this take place, utterly amazed that I had given a woman so much pleasure, I heard Hendrix moving faster, pleasing himself with his hand. I could make out the sound of his hand hitting his lower abs and the friction of his flesh under his tight grip. I didn't dare look at him, but the sound of it filled my imagination.

Her breathing slowed. "God Ashton, you're amazing."

"Thank you, Ma'am." I sat up and withdrew my fingers slowly from her.

"Now Tracy, you may give Ashton what she wants."

What? Hendrix wasn't going to do it? Was he really going to just stand there and watch us? I looked over it him with what I'm sure was a dumbfounded glare.

He continued to stroke himself, unaffected by my questioning look. In fact, he moved slower, more teasingly, especially now that he knew I could see him. Tracy asked me to sit on the edge of the couch, and I wasn't nearly as nervous this time. She parted my legs like she had done before and slid my panties completely off. Hendrix was standing so that he could see everything Tracy would do. The strain in his face told me that he was purposefully holding back. She moved my legs further apart and slid her fingers inside me again. Then, she pushed my skirt up and moved herself to the side a bit so that Hendrix could get a full view, an especially explicit picture now that Tracy had her fingers inside me.

"Hendrix, are you sure you wouldn't rather be the one to make her come?"

She was tormenting him, and he liked it. I could tell the anguish of his decision made him want me even more.

"Make her come!"

She smiled. "Oh, I will."

She quit teasing him then and moved back in front of me. Eagerly, she began to lick at my inner lips, running her tongue around where her fingers entered me, and pulling the wetness from inside, drawing my clit into her mouth, and sucking hard. It wouldn't take much. My arousal was too great to hold back.

Hendrix was standing closer now. He wanted me to watch him and to imagine it was him fucking me. I did so without effort. I couldn't look anywhere else, and while I watched, I was mentally focused on what Tracy was doing. The mixture of the two was devastatingly arousing. I was right on the edge, my legs tensed, and I leaned my head back, not wanting to look away, but unable to accomplish the task of using my muscles any longer. All the energy in my body was going toward one place.

"Oh my God!" I was screaming. I couldn't help it, but my screams were quickly muffled by Hendrix's cock. He stood over my chest and shoved it into my mouth. I felt like he was going to choke me, but I liked the feeling of being filled with him. I felt him tense up and hot liquid pump into my mouth. Tracy removed her fingers from me. The enjoyment of making him come was overwhelming, but I loved the way he intentionally tormented himself. He was right, it made the end result even better. It took great control on his part though, but that's what I liked about him. Well, that and quite a few other things.

When he had finished, he stood up and offered Tracy and me his hands. We both stood, but it was me that Hendrix brought down beside him to sit with on the couch. She remained standing, picking up the forgotten glass of wine and taking a few drinks while she looked at us both, not with any jealousy, only with admiration and thanks.

After several silent moments and enough time for us all to recompose ourselves, Hendrix was the first to speak. "Tracy, thank you so much. I'm so glad you got Ashton over her fear."

She laughed. "My pleasure Hendrix, and Ashton, I really enjoyed you." She straightened her dress and walked to the bathroom.

"Tracy will be leaving in just a minute." Hendrix stood and pulled his pants back on, then handed me my panties and helped me zip up the dress that was still around my waist.

She came out of the bathroom looking just as stunning as she had when I'd walked in. Hendrix stood up from the couch and gave her a quick hug.

"I'll see you soon Hendrix, and I hope I see you soon too, Ashton."

He walked her to the door, and she was gone.

"Well? Was this a good introduction?"

"Yes, Sir."

"I'm glad you enjoyed it. I know I did."

I wanted to ask him why he wouldn't have sex with me, but I assumed that was out of line. I wanted to ask him a lot of things, like what he had done with Tracy in the past because they were obviously very close. Why did she leave right away? I really wasn't in the mood to hear those answers right now, so I stayed silently smiling.

"Stay here tonight. I'll sleep on the couch, and you can have my bed."

"Are you sure? I don't mind getting a cab if you're too tired to drive."

"Ashton that was an order, not a question. I told you before that if you want to leave, I will take you home."

"No, Sir, I don't. I would like to stay."

"Good girl."

Hendrix got up to gather the blankets and pillow for the couch. I felt bad taking his bed from him, but I also liked the idea of sleeping in his sheets. I wasn't exactly sure why he wanted me to stay, but I was happy that he didn't want to get rid of me right away either.

He returned to the living room with blankets stacked in his arms. "You don't have to go to bed right away or anything. I don't want you to think that I'm kicking you off the couch. I'm actually not very tired at all."

I had a mean thought of him not really doing anything to get tired since all he really did was shove his dick in my face. I wasn't sure why I felt somewhat betrayed by the fact that he didn't have sex with me. Knowing that he liked to tease, I was sure this was one of his games to make me want him more, and it was working.

"That's fine. I can stay out here if you would like. I'm not very tired yet either."

"Would you like some tea or anything to eat?"

"Sure. I am a little hungry, thanks."

"Me too."

He went to the kitchen and took some vegetables from his refrigerator, along with a wedge of cheese, and some hummus. Once again, I was surprised by his taste because it was so like mine. I walked into the kitchen with him. "I love hummus. How did you know?"

"You just seem like the type."

"I wasn't aware there was a type for hummus affection."

"Generally the hippie types like it." He laughed. "Or the courageous purveyors of cultural foods, which is where I would stick you on the spectrum of hummus affection."

I laughed. "Then you would be correct, Sir."

He boiled water on the stove and poured us two cups of Indian Spice tea, also one that I loved, but I chalked that up to being in the range of cultural foods. He carried the tea and the plates of food to his small breakfast table near the window. I could see the lights of the city from here, but it was so different from the view I had. His suggested wealth and class with a solid view of the Fox Theater and the niceties that Midtown had to offer, whereas mine displayed all the weirdness and artistic expression that was Little Five Points. Sometimes, we seemed so at odds, and then at others, we were one and the same.

"So tell me, did you really enjoy everything that happened tonight? Was there anything that you would have changed or wish you wouldn't have done?"

"I was surprised at how much I enjoyed certain aspects that I never thought I would."

"I'm glad. Was there nothing that you would have changed then?"

"Maybe one thing." I was embarrassed to tell him what it was.

"Will you tell me, or do I have to order you to?"

"No Sir, I'll tell you. I was a little disappointed that we didn't actually, you know…"

"No, I don't know. Tell me."

I knew he wasn't naive and that he loved to make me say things that made me uncomfortable. "I guess I wanted to have sex with you."

"You guess?"

"No Sir, I know that I did."

"Do you think that I didn't want you?"

"I'm not sure. I'm not sure of anything really. This is all new to me, remember?"

"Oh yes, I remember. I'm going to tell you now that you are very wrong. Most certainly I want to have sex with you Ashton. But like I told you, I like to prolong my wanting you. It was very, very hard for me not to bend to Tracy's whim when she was teasing me about taking you for myself. She knows that, and she did it to build my interest all the more."

"Can I ask what the story is behind you two, I mean besides the part about your ex-girlfriend?"

"Yes. I can explain that if you would like."

"I would."

"Did she make you uncomfortable, or jealous, or uneasy? I don't want to put you in a situation where you really don't want to be. Remember that you can say the safe word at any time, no matter what."

"No Sir. I liked everything. I really did. I was surprised at how much I enjoyed it actually, but I was a little jealous."

"That's perfectly natural. You can't ignore the fact that we are human and prone to feelings of jealousy, but that's the great part of this lifestyle. You can learn that jealousy has no bearing when you are thoroughly open and honest with each other. You may feel that pang at first, but soon after, you'll know that there is no reason to be jealous. Jealousy comes from the feeling of ownership, of thinking someone is going to take what is yours, but if none of us feel that we own the other and we always have open and honest lines of communication with each other, there really is no reason to have those feelings. It takes time to master, so it's normal that you felt that way, but I'm very glad that you were able to get past it and enjoy yourself."

"Me too, and that makes sense now that you explain it that way."

"Believe me, when I was with my ex, I had to get through those same feelings. See, she never had a problem in fucking other men, but when it came to me touching another woman, she couldn't handle it. She never let go of that feeling of ownership over me. Of course, we were dating, but women tend to have a much harder time with jealousy than men do. I got over it by telling myself that if she wanted to cheat, she would, and if she wanted to leave, she would. There was nothing that I could do to change her mind if that's what she truly wanted. The best thing I could do was let her explore herself and her fantasies, so that she could feel that she wasn't threatened by me. Of course, I wanted the same treatment, and like I said, when I finally got the chance to bring Tracy back home with us, all Hell broke loose."

"Why didn't she see that she was being unfair?"

"She knew she was, but she just couldn't get past the jealousy. It can consume you if you let it. It took quite a while for me to come to the realization that she was never going to get past it."

"You said, finally got Tracy home with you two, is she the only one you have shared with anyone?"

"No, after my ex and I split, I continued to hang out at the club. As a single male, I had to be invited by another couple or be picked up at the bar. I couldn't roam the club looking for prospects, which is one thing I really enjoy about that club. People are very polite, and they respect each other and the couples that are together. They don't try to cut in or badger you. It's not a cheesy pick up line bar. It's a true culture of people who see that sex can be just for pleasure and that love is something else entirely. Anyway, there were several couples that liked to bring me in on their fun and several women that liked to be taken together by me."

I was trying my best not to get jealous. "Sounds like fun."

"It is fun, but you don't mean that, I can tell, and it's okay. I'm sure you have it in yourself to get past the jealousy. If I'm wrong, I'll be shocked. You don't seem like the type that wants to be owned. Though you like to be dominated, but that's another thing entirely."

"How so?"

"Being dominated isn't about someone owning you. It's about having the freedom to relinquish control to someone else. To have the ability to let things happen to you rather than to plan everything. Of course, the sub always has the true control. You know that, don't you?"

"How is that? I'm the one getting my ass beat." I laughed

"Because you know that at any time you can call it off. You allow yourself to be dominated. I don't force it upon you. You take the pain, which makes you a strong person. If you weren't, you would never be able to do it. Doms are in control when their subs allow them to be. It's a wonderfully contradictive relationship, really."

"I hadn't thought of it like that before, but it makes sense."

"Like I said, this is an experiment based on personal boundaries and social norms. You will be pleasantly surprised at how many people are into this lifestyle. The ones that have success with it have probably the best marriages I've ever seen. And the ones that stick mainly to the Dom/Sub play have a great relationship as well. They understand each other in ways that many couples could never dream of. By combining the two with you, and us being purely physical and platonic, I think this will be the best of both worlds."

"I hope you're right, but why do you think that the swingers, as you call them, have the best marriages?"

"Because they realize that they don't own each other and that they are still human beings with sexual desires that don't just disappear because they got married. They actually enjoy watching each other with other people because they can see them through another person's eyes. They can see what they saw the first time they had sex with them. They feel that they are so lucky to be with that person, and they want to share them to show the other people how good they have it. I've never had that experience myself of course, but I have many friends who have and explained it to me. It sounds right on track, but I'm not ready for a total commitment right now, as you know."

"No, of course not. I understand that and fully agree. I like knowing that this is not a weird and sick thing that only a few people do. It makes me feel better to know that there are actually a lot of people out there that are as crazy as me, and you I guess."

He laughed, "Oh yes. You have no idea, but I can't wait to show you."

"I'm excited."

He smiled and looked at me over his cup of tea. My mind was going a hundred miles an hour with thoughts of married couples sharing each other and how that worked and how they got over the jealousy. Could I ever get used to seeing Hendrix with other women? I hadn't even seen him with Tracy, and I was jealous. I didn't want to feel jealousy. He wasn't my boyfriend; he wasn't my anything... well except I guess you could call him my fuck buddy, although we hadn't actually had sex and that term just didn't do him justice. I reminded myself that letting go of my feelings of jealousy, was all part of the game. If I wanted to stay and play, I had to drop the norm and go with the flow. Why did other girls have to be in constant competition with each other anyway? When did all that begin, and why couldn't we choose to ignore it? I had always thought of myself as distinct from most girls, but that stupid age old feeling of competition amongst each other caught me, just like any other ordinary woman. I could be better than that, and I decided that I would be, no matter what the circumstances.

"Would you like to wear one of my shirts to bed? I guess I should have told you to bring some clothes, just in case, but maybe I wanted to keep you naked as long as possible."

Would that devious smirk of his ever get old? I doubted it. "Sure, I'll take a shirt. I think I'll make you wait to see me fully nude."

"You are a bad girl, aren't you?"

"I can be."

He walked to his bedroom, and I sat at the table admiring the city and the fact that I found myself in the position to stay at Hendrix's overnight. Maybe I would see him in the morning and get a glimpse at some sort of imperfection because I had yet to find any. Thankfully, I always carried my makeup in my purse, so I didn't feel bad knowing he would see me first thing tomorrow. My hair would be another issue. Hopefully I could get to the bathroom and tame it with water before he saw me.

Hendrix walked out holding a white under shirt that probably wouldn't fall past my hips. He held it up for me, "Will this work? If I can't see you naked, at least I can watch your beautiful ass walk around in this."

"Hmmm, I guess you got me, or I could just sleep in my dress."

"Or your panties."

"I'll take the shirt."

"I thought you might."

Standing up from the table, I took the shirt from him and smiled. While I was walking back to the bathroom, I thought of how much I actually wanted to see him sans clothes. I had gotten a brief glimpse of his thigh muscles and of course quite a bit more, but I was dying to see his chest and shoulders, the tattoos he had been hiding from me. I could only hope that he would leave his shirt off when he slept.

After folding and leaving my dress on the bathroom counter, and adorning Hendrix's very short white shirt, I walked back out to the living room, where I found him lying on the couch, not in a sleeping position, but in that sexy sideways lean, propped up on his arm and resting his head in his hand. He was a dead ringer for the suave bad boys of the fifties, but his tattoos made him a more modern version. I wasn't sure how I was going to stand him not taking me then and there. His shirt left enough of my panties showing that he could easily make out the shape of my outer lips and see any wetness that could accumulate there.

"Perfect, exactly the length I had hoped it would be."

"You know, just because you like to torment yourself doesn't mean that I want to be teased as well."

"May I remind you that you do not make the rules here, Ma'am?"

"I thought you said as the sub, I had all of the control?"

"Ah, that is the catch twenty-two, isn't it? You may have the control to tell me to stop, but if you do, then everything is off, isn't it? I mean, our relationship is based on me being in control, so if you decide to stop, it wouldn't be much fun. Such a conundrum." He smirked

"A beautiful one, Sir."

"Such a good girl. Now, why don't you come over here and give me a kiss and then go to bed. Do you have everything you need in there?"

I walked over to him. "No Sir."

"What do you need?"

"You, in the bed with me, fucking me. I want you Hendrix. I don't want to wait."

"That's too bad Ashton. I need you to wait. Believe me, I'm aching to fuck you so bad I can hardly stand it, but I keep reminding myself what I have in store for us and that waiting is best."

"But I don't know what you have in store for us. Maybe if I did, it would be easier for me to wait."

"I doubt it. In fact, it would probably make it worse."

I sighed. "Fine."

Hendrix sat up on the couch and grabbed my wrist. He spun me around, and I thought he was going to set me in his lap, but instead he spanked me, hard.

"Don't you dare disrespect me again! Did I not give you a fair enough warning earlier this evening?"

I was biting back tears, not truly of pain but shock. "Yes, Sir. I'm sorry Sir."

"That's better." He ran his hand softly over the mark he had left on my ass. His cool hand felt like ice to the hot skin he had created. It was an evocative opposite, making me want the punishment again, just so that I could feel the difference. He moved his hand away and leaned into me, placing his lips where his hand had been. He licked the spot lightly and gave just a few gentle kisses, then gripped my hips and brought my ass closer to him. Using his teeth he pulled my panties down to just beneath his hands so that my ass was fully exposed to him. Unsure of what he was doing, I soon felt his tongue licking lightly at the top of where my panties had stopped. He used his hands and spread my cheeks apart.

"Bend over and put your hands on the ground."

I was scared. I wasn't really one for anal play, and I was seriously hoping it wasn't his intent. "Yes, Sir."

"Don't move your hands from that spot. Do you understand me?"

"Yes, Sir."

He slid my panties beneath my hips, and they fell to rest around my ankles, but the t-shirt he had given me still covered the upper half of my body. He began giving me quick and sharp little nibbles on my ass cheeks, and placed his tongue at the top of the separation. He gripped my hips firmer now and tugged me back slightly, I kept my hands planted as he had told me. I knew that my ass as well as my open and wanting inner lips were completely exposed to him now, and being in this position made me feel so very vulnerable. Maybe he had decided there had been enough teasing and was going to take me from behind. I loved the idea of him not being able to stand it any longer. I thought of him gripping my hips tightly while he drove his hard shaft deeper and deeper into me.

Instead of my fantasy, I experienced something I never had before. He began to lick at the tighter opening above my pussy, not going inside it, but flicking it with his tongue. I felt a new sensation, like the excitement I felt the first time he touched me in his car but different. An excitement that was fear of the unknown and the possibility of what he could do. I had tried anal sex before, but it never went well. The men that I had tried it with were always too eager, too forceful. Ironically, it seemed like the only time they wanted to be forceful, but the way Hendrix was teasing me, gently coercing me to feel pleasure from what he was doing, was turning me on, and I briefly thought that maybe with him, I would enjoy penetration.

He stopped momentarily. "Do you like it?"

"Yes, Sir."

"Good. Because I love doing it. Would you like to be fucked there?"

"I don't know, Sir."

"Have you ever tried it?"

"Yes, Sir."

"Then why don't you know if you would like it?"

"Because the times that I have tried it, I didn't enjoy it."

"Then your answer should be no, shouldn't it?"

"No, Sir, because I like what you're doing."

"Well, I can do this without fucking you."

"Yes Sir, but I may like it with you."

"I hope you do. We'll have to add that to the to-do list."

He spanked my ass then and didn't return his mouth to where it had been.

"Stand up."

I was not happy, but I did as I was told.

"You may go to bed now."

Had I done or said something wrong? I was confused. I thought that he was priming me for something. If not sex, at least his fingers, but nothing? I knew that the disappointment was visible on my face.

"Don't look at me like that. I told you I'm not going to fuck you yet, not even there. This little scene started as a punishment remember? What kind of lesson would I teach you if I let you have what you wanted?

"I guess none, Sir."

"That's right. Now go to bed."

As I turned to walk away, I could feel his eyes following me, but I didn't look back. I got into his bed and smelled his scent throughout the sheets. It enveloped me and made my desire for him palpable. Turning to my side, I looked out of his large window. I thought of how many other things I may have disliked before, that might be pleasurable with Hendrix. Being told what to do was definitely one of them, and touching another woman was certainly one. It all came down to him being the catalyst, having the control over me, and allowing me to feel free. I pulled the sheets up to my face and fell asleep while breathing him in.

Eight

"Yes, Wednesday will be fine. See you then. Bye." I heard Hendrix's voice speaking to someone, presumably on the phone.

Sitting up from his bed, I made my way to the bathroom as quickly as possible, to make sure I didn't look like a complete train wreck. The result wasn't too bad considering everything I had been through last night. Making some quick improvements, I shimmied into the dress I had been wearing not so long ago. It felt scratchy and uncomfortable, something I didn't notice in the least yesterday. Wednesday? Who was he meeting? Probably just business. He did go to his client's homes after all. It was none of my business anyway was it? So I wasn't going to ask. I found some toothpaste and did a quick finger brushing and walked to the living room. I looked at my phone on the way, 11:45 AM. Wow! I had really slept in. How long had Hendrix been awake?

When I walked out into the large room, Hendrix was sitting at the breakfast table where we had sat and talked last night. He was on his laptop and was nursing a cup of something, coffee I assumed.

"Good morning, sleeping beauty."

"Hi."

"I see you've changed already. Are you wanting to leave?"

"Yes, Sir. I need to get home."

"Okay. Do you mind if I finish this email first?"

"No, Sir, that's fine."

"Thank you, Ma'am."

I smiled, even though I was slightly, okay maybe a little more than slightly curious about his phone call, but I couldn't resist his charm.

"Would you like something to eat, some coffee, anything?"

"Sure. I'll take coffee, thank you."

He got up and poured me some. I met him in the kitchen.

"Would you like anything in it? There's cream in the refrigerator and sugar or sweetener on the counter. Help yourself."

I doctored the drink the way I took it, sweet and practically white with cream. He had sat back down at the table and continued to type while I stood in his kitchen watching him. I thought it was a bit ironic, seeing his morning routine only days after we had met. We weren't dating or had any inclination towards a relationship, but if I was a girl he had hopes of more with, I'm sure I wouldn't have seen this for weeks or even months. It's strange that the promise of nothing makes you more comfortable to the visions of daily life. Instead of placing that person on a proverbial pedestal, you see them as they are and you feel you know them better, like a friend instead of a lover.

That thought gave me an idea of what Hendrix was talking about when he spoke of married couples being happier or more open to one another as swingers. Maybe if you could watch your spouse with another person and not get jealous, you could see them as a friend or perhaps even just someone you wanted to sleep with, someone you didn't judge and who didn't judge you. I thought about my past relationships and how much I tried to change them to suit me or vice versa, when really I should have taken them at face value. Maybe we become blind to the face value when we're trying to see them as the perfect partner. Love shouldn't be blind; it should have eyes wide open.

"Done. Let me put some shoes on and I'll be ready."

When he stood from the table, my eyes took him in. Ruggedly handsome, he had already formed his hair into that cool pompadour (how did he do that anyway?) and was wearing dark jeans that fell to the middle of his naked feet and a plain white t shirt that made it easy to see his tattoos underneath. It also clung nicely to his shoulders, stretching the fabric as he lifted his laptop off the table. Damn! Still deprived of seeing his naked chest. If I would have only gotten up sooner, maybe I could have caught him still sleeping. Something told me though, that Hendrix was probably an early riser and since I was lucky to get in bed before two in the morning most days, an early riser I was not.

I mentally shook myself out of a sleepy gaze. "Okay, thanks."

As Hendrix walked away towards his bedroom, I finished the coffee and sat the cup on the counter.

He appeared in the living room now wearing his black shoes with white trim that always gave him a look of playfulness, yet the rest of his features were so dominating, once again the contradiction that I loved. "Ready?"

"Yes, Sir."

We walked out into the hall and got on the elevator to take us to the main lobby. It was even more beautiful in the daylight, sun glinting off the marble and filling the room with a luscious glow. We didn't talk on the way to the second elevator that would take us to the garage. I felt a little awkward having spent the night with him but not with him, not to mention all the flashbacks of last night starting to pop up in my mind. We arrived at the floor he was parked on, and he opened my door for me as usual.

When he sat down and started the car, he didn't turn on the radio. "Is there anything wrong?"

"No, Sir. Why do you ask?"

"I'm just surprised that you were ready to leave so quickly after getting up."

"No, no, I'm fine really. I don't normally stay with other people. They usually stay at my place, so this is a little out of the ordinary for me. Well obviously the whole thing is out of the ordinary for me, but you understand right?"

"Yes, Ma'am, I do. That's fine. I just wanted to make sure that I didn't make you feel unwelcome. I'm sorry that I was on the computer when you got up. I was just finishing up a bid on a job I was offered, and I had to get it to the owner today so he could make his decision first thing tomorrow."

"Oh, I understand. Please don't feel like you have to

apologize or explain anything to me. It's none of my business, anyway."

"Ashton, just because we're playing this game together doesn't mean that I won't treat you with the utmost respect. In fact, I respect you even more for what you have agreed to do with me. It takes a very strong minded woman to do what you're doing, and I admire that."

I blushed because that was probably one of the nicest compliments I had ever received. "Thank you."

"No, thank you."

We both smiled at each other, and he backed out of his parking spot.

Once we reached the street, he turned on the radio, classical music today, relaxed and contemplative, a very Sunday type of music.

The ride was short. Not all of the church crowd had left yet, so the streets weren't too overwhelmed with cars. It amazed me how short a distance it was between our condos, and to think, he had lived there longer than I had been in my place. How we hadn't met or seen each other in passing all this time was a mystery.

Hendrix pulled up to the curb at my building and came around to open my door.

"Ashton, it has been a pleasure....in more ways than one." He kissed my hand as he helped me from my seat and walked me to the lobby door.

"I'll call you soon. Are you free on Wednesday?"

Wednesday? Now I was far too curious. "Yes. Why?"

"Wednesday nights are newcomer's night at the club. Would you like to go?"

"Who else is coming?"

"I invited Tracy along if you want to go. If not, then I'll be going with her but only to get in. She has other plans there if you won't be with us."

So he was going whether I went or not. The idea made me a little angry. I thought of him having sex with another woman when he wouldn't have sex with me. I wasn't sure what to say.

"No. I don't think so, not yet."

"Are you sure? It's a great night for you to go. There should be quite a few new people there."

"I'm sorry, Hendrix. I just don't feel like it yet."

"Okay, I respect your decision. I won't force you into it. Maybe next time you'll be more up for it."

"Maybe."

He looked somewhat crushed but wasn't going to say anything about it, then opened the lobby door for me, but didn't follow me inside.

"I'll talk to you very soon."

"Okay, thank you."

I walked inside and got in the elevator. When the doors shut and I was alone, tears began to well up in my eyes. It didn't matter how much I was trying to think differently. The fact that he would go to the club without me was infuriating. He had already told me that he went as a single man and would be with several girls at once. How could married couples do it? He and I weren't even thinking of dating, and I was jealous. I wanted to overcome these feelings so badly. I wanted to work on it and to build armor to it. The elevator doors opened, and thankfully there was no one waiting to get on. Heading straight for my door, I walked inside.

The tears that were threatening to spill over had subsided, thankfully, and I felt more like myself when I saw my living room, my things, my life. When I was home, I felt very little of the worry that had been plaguing me. The comfort of knowing that I still had everything that was me and I didn't owe him anything made me more aware of how uncomfortable I had been this morning with him. Was it because I spent the night or maybe it was only because of the phone call? Shedding the shoes and dress, I stepped into the shower.

The warm water was calming my nerves and I thought about what harm it would really cause with him going alone to the club. Why did I care what he did? So what if he had sex with other girls? He was waiting to do it with me for a reason and that made me more desirable to him. Maybe that was his plan, to make himself wait for me and only me, but why?

I stepped out of the shower and dried off. With the towel still wrapped around me, I put on an album by Animal Collective and poured a bowl of cereal. Sitting by my window, I felt much more self-assured, not like a timid girl that cared what Hendrix did in his free time. Maybe I would go with him after all, or I could make him wait and wonder if I was going to back out altogether. He did say I truly had the control. Maybe I should try it out on him.

A text came through from Hendrix. "Thank you for staying with me. I really enjoyed your company and of course everything that we did."

"Me too, and you're welcome."

Always the gentleman, albeit a sadistic, dominating one, but a gentleman none the less.

He didn't send me anymore texts that day. Most of my time I spent watching movies, French erotica, my favorite. As I was watching one of them about prostitution, I began to think of marriage and infidelity, why it happened, and how it could be prevented. Finally, I began to understand the concept of sharing each other with other people. Maybe if you allowed each other freedom, then there would be no reason to stray in secret. After all, was it really the act that hurt the other person or the lies they were told? For me, I imagined it would be the lies. I could handle the idea of my partner having sex with someone else, but being lied to, humiliated, and degraded in that way seemed far worse than a sexual act. If as a swinger, the sexual acts were condoned, even coveted, there was really no reason for lies.

It seemed men typically strayed to have what they couldn't get from their wives. Why did a wife decide not to do certain sexual acts with her husband? Normally, she did them when they first began dating, but after years of marriage, she found them repugnant. What would make a woman see her husband so differently? It was sad that married couples became separated by their lives. It happened so gradually that before they knew it, they were resenting each other. I had never been married, but I knew that I didn't want that to happen. How could you stop it? How could you keep passion and love alive over the years?

I had seen many of my older friends who had been married quite some time acquire more and more material things. A bigger house, a better car, more clothes, shoes, jewelry, and for their husbands, more extracurricular activities. It was like the more expensive the item, the greater the sentiment of apology, even if they didn't realize it as that. What was it that diminished the ability to express your love or your passion? How could years together not make you more familiar with what the other wanted, rather than more annoyed by it? This was why marriage wasn't on my to-do list, as Hendrix would most likely put it. Truthfully, I was scared of losing the passion, and I felt immense passion for Hendrix, even though we hadn't slept together yet. My passion was derived from the feeling of freedom he gave me and the way he wanted to please me without asking that I belong to him.

I had three days to make a decision whether or not to go to the club Wednesday night. I wasn't going to make it right now. Maybe if I slept on it, things would seem clearer in the morning. I went to bed around midnight, and I didn't even need an Mp3 player to fall asleep.

Nine

A rainy Monday. Things did look different this morning but not necessarily clearer after all. Atlanta was not the prettiest city in the rain. I decided I would take a cab to the outskirts and visit my friend Stephanie. I hadn't spoken to her since meeting Hendrix, and I desperately wanted to fill her in.

No texts this morning, and it was already nine o'clock. I assumed I wouldn't see any from Hendrix today or at least not until this afternoon. I think I may have put up too big of a front yesterday, and it spooked him enough to keep his distance, which was my intent, but now I regretted it a little. Always a mouse and never the cat in the game it seemed. I wanted to be chased and putting up obstacles helped the chase last, though I was often too good at making my obstacle courses insurmountable. I kept telling myself that these walls were the way to find the one I was really looking for, someone that could climb them, no matter how high, but why did I need to do this with Hendrix? This arrangement was only a game, making him chase me would only eliminate me from it. There were plenty of other players he could choose from. I thought about texting him after talking things over with Stephanie and telling him I was in for the club this week.

I got dressed, ate a small breakfast, and called for a cab. Stephanie lived out near Druid Hills, but it wouldn't take too long to get there at this time of day.

The intercom buzzed. "Ms. Rhodes, you have a cab waiting for you."

"Thank you. I'll be right down."

Grabbing my purse, laptop, and Mp3 player, I locked the door behind me. A jolt of recollection hit me when I walked out into the hallway, remembering being on my knees in front of Hendrix there. The elevator was already at my floor, thankfully, because the cabbies here started charging the moment they pulled up to your building.

The rain was coming down hard when I walked out the door. I didn't like umbrellas. I liked to feel it wash over me, true untamed nature even in the midst of industrialization. I opened the door of the cab and settled into the back seat.

"Where to, Miss?"

"North Druid Hills Road please."

"Sure thing."

I texted Stephanie on the way, forgetting that not everyone had the luxury of drop-in visits like I did. She was a stay-at-home mom of two though, so I assumed she would be home, whether or not she had time for me was up in the air. Even if she couldn't see me today, I could stay in the area and do some writing. A little change of scenery couldn't hurt.

"Hey Stephanie, guess who? Yes, I am still alive, and I'm on my way to your area. Are you free for some company? I have a lot to tell you."

It took her several minutes to text back but finally I received an answer. "Sure! I've missed you. Can't wait to hear about what trouble you could possibly be causing now. :) See you soon!"

Great, I needed some time with her, away from the sexually charged atmosphere I had been living in. It was beginning to feel surreal and I needed some grounding. I put my ear buds in to avoid any strange conversations with the driver and chose Norah Jones. Perfect rainy day music.

I didn't hear him, only caught him glancing at me in the rear view mirror and some lip movement. I popped an ear bud out. "I'm sorry. What?"

"What is the address?"

"Oh, sorry, it's 4035."

In just a couple more minutes, we were there. I didn't know how Stephanie was going to take all this. She wasn't a reserved woman by any means, but she certainly wasn't as adventurous as me either. We had definitely had our disagreements in the past, and while I greatly valued her opinion as an outsider to the craziness I was usually experiencing, I also knew to take it for what it was, an opinion. Gratefully, after several years of knowing each other, she didn't take offense to me not adhering to her advice and just let it roll off of her as another one of my loveable and flawed character traits.

"Twenty-seven dollars, Ma'am."

I handed the driver $35, thanked him, and got out of the car, actually remembering everything I had brought with me. I practically ran to the house to avoid looking like a drowned rat when I got to the door.

Stephanie was standing behind the storm door waiting for me. How had I let four months pass since visiting her? Time slipped away so quickly now that she had two children and a husband, and I had a busier writing career. However, no matter how much time passed, she still greeted me with a welcoming hug. I wasn't the hugging type, especially not with other women, but with her, it just felt normal, and I was thankful for that.

"I've missed you so much, I'm sorry I haven't been out here for so long."

She laughed. "Oh, Ashton, you know I understand. You're a city girl, after all."

"I may be, but I should still visit my best friend more. Maybe you can bring the kids along and come to my place again." She had only been once since I had known her. It wasn't exactly a kid friendly zone, and it kept her on her toes the entire time she was there. Plus, I think it made her a bit jealous of my lifestyle, and I had to admit that at times I was jealous of hers as well.

"Maybe. It's pretty hard to get anywhere right now. A three year old and a one year old are not exactly the best traveling companions."

"I could only imagine."

We walked into her kitchen, and she started some tea for us. Her three year old crept cautiously around me. I knew he remembered me but not enough to jump into my arms. The one year old girl was already down for her nap.

"So what have you gotten yourself into? You know you're like my reality TV fix."

We both laughed. "I think we might need to wait until James takes his nap."

"Oh, that good, huh?"

"Or that bad, haven't decided yet."

"Oh, boy."

We sat in her living room talking of PG things including her husband and my writing. Finally, her son began to wind down, and she carried him to his room.

"Okay. We *might* have an hour and a half before he wakes up, so spill it."

"Well, first of all, don't freak out until I get to a stopping point, okay?"

"I'll try my best. Man, this must be good."

"It's… interesting."

I told her all about how I met Hendrix, his incredible good looks, the jazz club, the date at the International Café, and the phone call about him pleasuring himself. She looked like she was in shock.

"Stephanie, are you okay?"

"Um, yeah, what? Are you serious? This guy just picks you up in a store and now you're dating?"

"Well, no, not exactly." I had left out everything about the arrangement to let her settle in to the idea of Hendrix, much like I had been doing. Maybe if she understood how great he was, aside from the strange sexual fantasies, she would give him more credit when I told her the rest.

"What do you mean, not exactly? What aren't you telling me?"

"A lot actually. We're not dating for one."

"So you're just fucking him then?"

"Actually, I haven't slept with him."

"Okay, but you are fooling around with him, obviously."

Fooling around, good terminology, because I often felt like a fool for doing any of this. "Yes, you could say that. We have an arrangement going on or an experiment, you could say."

"Go on."

"He's a swinger. You know a couple swapper, open relationship, whatever you want to call it."

"Okay, but if you're not a couple, then what does that have to do with you?"

"He wants me to join him as his submissive. You know, like he's the Dom, I'm the Sub?"

"Like the book I read?"

I laughed. "I suppose but not as far-fetched." I forgot that her only real experience in the life of BDSM was her favorite book series she just finished this year.

"I'm confused. Not saying it's terrible, but I don't get it."

"He wants to control me sexually, and get me into the swinging clubs with his friends and tell me who to have sex with and, I guess, watch him have sex with other women."

"What the fuck?"

"I know it's strange, but it's kind of exciting. I mean, we've already vowed no relationship. This is purely for pleasure."

"But how does that work? How can you not have a relationship with someone who is going to control your sexual life in every single way?"

"Because, for one, I need to learn to separate the two, love and sex. Why can't women experience sex for sex instead of always trying to attach an emotion to it? Men do it all the time. You know I'm different and I like to go against the grain. Well, this is my chance to really push the envelope. I want to experience this, for better or worse. It's exciting."

"I guess so. Have you done anything besides what you've told me?"

"Yes. I went to his place Saturday night, and his friend Tracy was there. She's already been a part of the lifestyle for a while, and he kind of initiated me into it with her."

"So you actually watched him fuck her in front of you?"

"No, no, I didn't. He made me pleasure her and her pleasure me while he watched."

Stunned silence. I could tell she was between disgust and curiousness.

"Stephanie, it was actually pretty fun. You know I've never been attracted to women, and I've never done anything like that before, but with Hendrix instructing me and Tracy having experience in it, it was a brand new level of excitement."

"Well, what was it like?"

"You mean being with a woman?"

"Yeah, of course. What did you think I meant?"

"Oh you know, what his place was like, his fashion sense, that whole thing?"

We laughed. Thankfully, she was taking this pretty well, and I could tell it did interest her, whether she wanted to fully admit to it or not.

"Smart ass! You know very well what I meant."

"I know, I know. It was a little weird obviously. I was nervous, and scared to say the least, believe me. I thought of backing out, but I was too excited to see how it would go, how it could be in his world, so to speak, that I did what he told me. Tracy was soft and small, nothing like being touched by a man, but as a woman, she knew just what to do to me and I to her. That was fun. She was different than me, you know physically, but she didn't taste bad or anything."

"Oh my God. I thought you were maybe just talking about

fingering, but you mean you actually ate her out?"

"Yes. Hendrix made me, but she did it to me too."

"Holy shit Ashton!"

"Is that an excited holy shit or a disapproving one?"

"It's a 'Whatever it's your life, live it' holy shit, but I could never do it."

"I would have never thought of it if it wasn't in this context either, but with Hendrix it's so exciting, so new, and so fun. I'm thinking of going to the swinging club with him this Wednesday."

"I'm just worried about you, Ashton. You've had such a hard time with relationships here lately. I don't want to see you hurt again."

"It's not a relationship, so it's okay. It's just sex."

"If you say so, but I know how you are."

"How's that?"

"You're going to end up falling for him, and you're going to be crushed. You wait. The first time you see him have sex with another woman, you're going to lose it. I don't care how much distance you think you have from your emotions. It's ingrained in our DNA, and you can't outrun that."

"I know. I expect to feel some jealousy. He even warned me about it. He has felt it before with an ex-girlfriend, but he told me it can be overcome. You just have to keep telling yourself that it's just sex."

"Well, I hope that you can do that. He sounds gorgeous and exactly your type, except for all this kinky sex shit."

"It's really not all that weird. There's tons of people who are into it."

"Then why is this only an experiment? Why can't he have a relationship with you and have this lifestyle?"

"Because he's done that before and it didn't work out, and this is different. I'm also his sub, not a girlfriend, so I have to obey him, and without the emotional attachment, it's easier for us both."

"I'm sorry to be such a Devil's advocate here, but he's been in this lifestyle and knows what he's doing, you haven't. You have to rely on him to teach you, and if you think that isn't going to create an emotional attachment, I think you're mistaken."

"You may be right about that, but I've already decided that I don't care. I want the experience. I just have to tell myself that I'm not going to feel hurt by any of it. I decide if I'm hurt or not. No one can hurt my feelings without my permission, right?"

"If it were that easy to decide whether or not you would be hurt, why would any of us ever choose to be?"

"I guess because we didn't think about the possible outcome beforehand? I'm not sure exactly, but even if I do feel hurt somehow, I've already decided that I don't care."

"I care about you, Ashton. I want you to be happy. I know your definition of happiness is something other than mine, but I don't want to see you hurt again. You're a strong woman, and I know you can take care of yourself, but you don't need to unnecessarily put yourself in a position to be devastated."

"I know, and I don't want to see you hurt either. I'm so happy that you have a family and children and all the things that mean happiness to you, but those things aren't the happiness I'm searching for right now. I want the memories of experiences that I didn't turn down when I'm too old to have the choice anymore."

"I understand, and I admire that about you. I do. Just be careful."

"I will."

Stephanie's daughter was waking up, and her husband would be home in a couple of hours. She had things to do, and I had a taxi ride's worth of thinking ahead of me.

"Well, I should be going. It was great catching up with you. I promise I won't let so much time pass until I see you again."

"Good. I miss you, and as much as I protest your decisions sometimes, I do like hearing about them, and I'm glad you share

105

them with me."

We stood up from the couch and she leaned in to give me another hug, again I was thankful. I didn't want to admit that sometimes I needed that reassurance of comfort.

I called the cab company and it didn't take long for them to arrive. After giving Stephanie another quick hug, I dashed out of her door, down to the cab. She stood at the door waving as I looked out of the car window and gave a wave in return.

"The International Café please."

"Yes, Ma'am."

Why did he have to call me Ma'am right now? I was so conflicted in my attraction and reminders of Hendrix. Stephanie was so right. I tried to deny it when I was with her, but she couldn't have been more spot on. Hendrix had the upper hand. I had no idea what I was doing, so he had me by the proverbial balls in this situation. She was right, wasn't she? About choosing to be hurt. It's not like I had ever chosen to go into something knowing I would be hurt, but that's what made this different, wasn't it? I knew that the outcome could never be anything more than pleasure, so why even bother with the what ifs? I had to listen to music and work on my story just to calm my mind for a bit. Multitasking always helped center me. Weird, I know.

Walking through the door of the café, I had a conflicting feeling of nostalgia and familiarity. What was I thinking bringing him here? Now every time I walked into my place, my escape, I had to think of him and that night. Damn it! I'm already thinking of him as if we're through with our little escapade, and we haven't even really gotten started. I shouldn't let Stephanie scare me. I have this under control, damn! Out of my control, I mean, which really means, I'm in control. Fuck!

The waitress came to my table, and I ordered an absinthe. I liked the way it made me feel, more of an elevating high than a nauseous low. Besides, I was determined that I could have this drink without it symbolizing time spent with Hendrix. Kind of a cleansing by fire thing, but I wasn't cleansing him from my life, at least not yet, just making sure that my enjoyments weren't caught up with him. So far, I had enjoyed every minute I was with him, and I had never had so much pleasure. Whether I liked it or not, he was part of my life now, no matter how it began or how it would end. Would it be the same for him, was I a part of his life in an inescapable way? I wasn't sure what I wanted the answer to that question to be, but the good news was it had stopped raining.

Ten

"It is only by way of pain one arrives at pleasure."

—*Marquis de Sade*

On my walk home from the café, I received a text from Hendrix.

"How has your day been?"

I didn't know how to answer that. I had been having an existential romantic/sexual conversation with myself over absinthe for the last two hours. Do I call it quits now, or do I wait until I start to get hurt? Why do I have to get hurt if it's my decision? These thoughts were exactly the reason I wanted to be a submissive. I wanted the control taken away, forcefully if necessary, and with me, it was.

I texted back and hit send quickly before I changed my mind, "It's been good. How about you?"

"Normal day. Always feels strange to have such normalcy after so much debauchery, don't you think?"

"I don't know that I've ever had too much normalcy plaguing me."

"Haha! You are probably right about that. Have you thought anymore about Wednesday?"

I wasn't ready to answer that yet. "Not yet. I haven't decided. I'm sorry."

"That's perfectly okay. Knowing that you haven't decided means there's still a chance it will be yes."

"There may be. Can I ask you something?"

"Of course."

While I was thinking of how to word my question, I made the walk through my building and into the living room. "I've been having some doubts about all of this, and I know my problem is control. I was wondering if you could help me with that, you know, in a way I would enjoy?"

"You mean today?"

"If possible. If not, I understand."

"Are you kidding Ashton? Do you really think I could pass up an open invitation to punish you? How about nine this evening? I'll pick you up."

"I was hoping you couldn't. :) Yes, Sir, that would be great."

"Good girl."

"I'll see you at nine then."

"Yes, Ma'am, you will, and you had better be ready to leave the minute I get there."

"Yes, Sir."

Maybe a little dominance would cure my jumpy imagination. I could not let the fear of what could be change the here and now and become instead, what could have been. It was wonderful that all I had to do was ask Hendrix if he would "punish" me, as he called it, and he leapt at the chance.

I showered, grabbed a quick dinner because I assumed he would not be taking me out to eat, and dressed comfortably in jeans and a tight, black V-neck t-shirt as I also assumed, or rather, hoped that I wouldn't be wearing them long.

He arrived promptly as usual. The intercom buzzed and I figured by now the doorman thought we were officially dating. Boy, was he wrong. He knocked on the door, and I felt a little less nervous than on Saturday but only minutely. The fear of doing sexual things with a woman had at least passed, but Hendrix was still more of a mystery to me than the uncharted territories of another woman's vagina. I opened the door, and to my surprise, he was dressed as casually as I was, though still strikingly handsome.

"Get your things and get out here. I'm not coming in."

I guess he was starting right from the top. "Yes, Sir." I

reminded myself that I initiated this, I asked for it, so I couldn't choose anything specific. This was all in his hands.

I gathered my purse and phone but nothing else. This time I was not planning on spending the night. I walked out into the hallway in seconds flat and locked the door behind me.

"So you're ready to run from me this soon?

"Only somewhat, Sir."

"Well, we'll have to change that, so I'm going to show you what I do to girls who want to run from me."

That sounded a little over the top scary, but I played along. "Yes, Sir."

He grabbed the top of my arm, not too hard, but hard enough to assert dominance and led me to the elevator. When we got inside, there was another man standing against the wall. Hendrix took his hand from my arm. He instead ran it across my shoulders and moved it to the small of my back, which I thought was pretty polite and helped to remind me that it was just a game. The man was headed to the lobby as we were, so he was with us the whole ride down. Luckily, no one else got on. Around the third floor, Hendrix decided to move the hand at my back down to my ass and give it a hard pinch. I bit my tongue, but it was difficult not to cry out.

Finally, the doors opened, and Hendrix returned his hand to the small of my back, but only as we were walking out of the building. As soon as we cleared the doorman, he grabbed my upper arm again.

"Why do you want to run?" He was asking me as he was leading me to his car. This seemed like a very bad beginning to a horror flick. I definitely had goose bumps, but they weren't from fear. I enjoyed this. If that made me a freak, so be it.

"I'm afraid, Sir."

"Of what? Getting fucked too hard, getting too much pleasure, too much attention, what?"

"None of those things. I'm afraid of what will happen to me

when you get tired of me."

He opened the car door for me. When he made it to his side, he had a changed air about him, not quite so domineering but still in charge.

"Who says you won't get tired of me?"

"Nothing, Sir."

"That's right. Remember this is mutual. If either of us decides it's over, it's over. I'm not going to ruin the fun we're having by filling my mind with hypothetical situations."

"You're right, Sir."

"So why did you want to be controlled tonight? Punished, it seems, is more fitting."

"I went to see a girlfriend today and told her about us. She brought up some things and it spooked me."

"What kind of things?"

"Nothing I didn't have an answer for and haven't already thought through."

He grabbed my chin with one hand and pulled my face close to his. "I said, what kind of things? Now answer me!"

"Yes, Sir." He let go of my face. "She said that I would get hurt and that I couldn't control being hurt, no matter how hard I tried to look at this as just sex."

"Do you feel like it's more than just sex or, we'll say physical, because we haven't even had sex yet?" He lightened the question by laughing slightly.

I felt silly even thinking it when he put it that way. "No Sir, I don't."

"But then why did it scare you?"

"Because this is all new to me, and I'm afraid I might end up attaching to you just because I don't know what I'm doing."

"You are attached to me, Ashton. You're my submissive. That is a relationship, not a dating one, but a relationship none the less. When I say I don't want a relationship, I hope you know I mean dating, not that I'm going to treat you like you're less than human or something."

"I do, Sir."

"So fear of attachment is irrelevant then. What else are you afraid of?"

"Not pleasing you. Not being able to handle going to the club. Not being able to see you with other women."

"Those are legitimate fears, and hearing that you are afraid of not pleasing me turns me on more than you realize. After all, that is your job as my sub, to please me."

"I'm glad that I'm getting the right picture then, Sir."

"You are. Now, I've dispelled all of your fears so far. Any others?"

"No, Sir, I think that's it. Thank you."

"Ashton, even if we were a married couple, you couldn't know the future. You ask, what if I get tired of you. That could happen to anyone, anytime. Marriage, the boyfriend/girlfriend status, that doesn't give you any more security really. It's all designed to make people feel like they're in control of the other person, but they're really not. It's always a choice, just as this is your choice, remember?"

"Yes, Sir, you're right."

"Now, let's stop all this talk because I have some punishment to inflict."

He started the car, and we were off, but I had no idea where we were going, and I didn't dare ask. He made so much sense. I shouldn't have listened to Stephanie. She was married, she had no idea what this was between Hendrix and me, and she'd never done anything like this in her life. I loved her for her concern, but I felt stupid having spent most of the day worrying about something I shouldn't have even questioned.

"We're going to the club."

"What?"

"You heard me loud and clear. We're going."

"You mean Wednesday?"

"No, tonight."

"No! I can't. I'm not ready, and I'm dressed in jeans and a t-shirt. I don't want the first time I go there to be seen as a woman with no sex appeal and shown up by all the beautiful girls you're going to fuck!"

He pulled the car over to a dimly lit curb and looked at me, his eyes probing mine and his hair falling just over his right eye. I couldn't meet his gaze. I was afraid of the disappointment or the anger I would see there, but more importantly, I was afraid of how much I wanted him in that moment.

"What did you just say to me? Who do you think you are, talking to your Master like that? You asked for a punishment and I'm giving it to you." He was genuinely frightening in a very attractive way. "It will do you good. I'll get you over all these silly fears, and they'll be out of the way so we can really explore things together. Now apologize!"

Despite being inexplicably drawn in by his authority, I felt ashamed, and tears began to well up in my eyes. I thought of using the safe word, but I knew the night would be over if I did. He was most likely right, forcing me into this may be the only way I would ever do it, and underneath the fear, I really did want to go through with it.

"I'm sorry, Sir." I began to cry silently. I knew even in the dark that he could see the tears running down my face. Great, now I was dressed like crap and would have smeared makeup. This was not the way I wanted my first experience there to go.

"I know you mean that. Now dry your eyes."

He turned to face the steering wheel again and drove away from the curb. I spent the rest of the way to the club staring out the window. I was seventy five percent dreading this, but the other twenty five percent wanted it badly.

When we finally rounded a turn, I was surprised at what I saw. The club was a brick building with black double doors and a small plaque on the door to the right reading, "Inhibitions". I had expected it to be flashy, lit up in neon or draped in string lights. But this was demure and made it even more interesting, fitting for the secrets that went on within. I remembered that Hendrix said not many people knew about it, now I saw why.

We pulled into the small parking lot that had infrequent overhead lamps, plenty of neglected shady spots. But Hendrix pulled into a space directly beside the base of one of the lights, so that it shown down on the car like a spotlight. He turned the engine off and got out of the car, not giving me a word of instruction, so I stayed put.

He was at my door in a heartbeat, opened it and held out his hand, I took it, but instead of his usual gentlemanly grasp, he practically snatched me straight up from my seat. Moving me back slightly, he shut the car door. "Turn around and put your hands on the roof of the car. Then spread your legs shoulder width apart."

I didn't dare disobey. I heard the sound of him unhooking his belt buckle, and in one quick pull he had stripped it from its loops. No longer than I had heard that sound, than I felt the belt across my ass.

"One! Now you count the rest!"

Really? I couldn't do this. It was time to say it. My hands gripped at the roof of the car with the intent to fight.

He whipped me again. Instead of bolting from my position, I held firm. The second one was swift, but thankfully my jeans took some of the sting from the pain.

"Count them, Ashton!"

I was biting my lip, trying not to cry out the word, and I felt the belt again, a bit harder than the last. My hands were starting to sweat and slide slightly on the roof of his car, even in the cool night air. The feel of the sweat made me think of placing my hands on his chest when it was drenched in sweat from fucking me. Obviously that hadn't happened yet, but it was a fantasy and it was the perfect image to keep in my mind right now. I had to focus on the sexual side of this pain, like the slap to my face he had given me, it was shocking, but it exaggerated my pleasure.

"You are a stubborn girl, and you are going to get it harder and longer if you don't do as I say!"

God, he sounded hot when he was commanding. This was what I wanted, wasn't it? What exactly did I expect my punishment to be, a few slaps on the wrist? That's not what I was after; this was. I had an epiphany then, in the midst of the pain and humiliation, because I knew there were probably onlookers, not that they were going to try and stop him. We were at a sex club, after all. I knew what I had always wanted, and it was happening. This was the moment I had been telling myself to enjoy, and I was close to overlooking it, stopping it, and controlling it. Instead, the pain brought me front and center. It grounded me into feeling the moment, and it was blissful actually, a meditation almost. I felt free from myself, and I screamed, "Two, three!"

"Yes, good girl, good girl!" I could hear the smile on his face when he said it, he was breaking me and he loved it and maybe I loved it too.

He whipped me again, harder, and I didn't hesitate. "Four.... five....six, seven!" I was getting sore, and it was hurting. I wanted it to end, and I dreaded it ending at the same time.

"Have you learned your lesson?"

"Yes, Sir!" Tears were streaming down my face, but I was smiling and felt that the world had been lifted from my shoulders.

Again I felt the sting of the belt. "Eight....nine!" No, he couldn't stop. He had to stop, or I was going to drop to the ground, but I didn't want this feeling of floating, or possibly ecstasy, to leave me.

"I'm not sure that you have."

I barely choked out, "Ten." It was hard, and it was final.

"Put your feet together and stand up straight, but remain facing the car."

I obeyed and then I heard something. It was clapping. The imagined onlookers were real, and they were enjoying the show. I heard one man come up to Hendrix and tell him what a wonderful sub he had and how much pain I could take. Then, he asked him if he would be bringing me into the club and if I was going to be available.

"No, not yet. She's being trained, and she's not ready."

The man told Hendrix he understood. He was very polite as Hendrix had said that most people were here, but I was confused. Did he mean that I wasn't ready to be shared or that I wasn't ready for the club? I heard the small crowd dispersing and saw them look back at me as they passed. I felt humiliated and I wanted to climb into the car. I wanted to keep the feeling that I had when I was being whipped, when they looked me over, but my true nature couldn't be hidden.

"Turn around."

I did, and I was sure that I looked like crap. If I looked in a mirror, my mascara would probably resemble an inkblot test, and the doctor would tell me what I saw in it meant that I was emotionally damaged and too fucked up to be cured.

When I saw Hendrix standing there with his belt still in hand, hanging to his calf, and the glimmer of sweat on his forehead, I didn't give a fuck what I looked like. He was my Master, my imprisonment, and my release. He had just given me something that no one ever could before, complete and utter loss of control, and I wanted to smother him with gratitude.

His voice was low and smooth, "Get down on your knees."

"Yes, Sir." The pavement was cold to my overheated body. My ass felt like I had been sitting in a wood-burning stove, and I was thankful that he let me perch on my knees instead of having to sit on the welts I was sure were there.

He held out his right hand, palm down and brought it close to my face. For a moment, I thought he was going to pet me on the cheek with the back of his fingers. "Kiss my hand, the one that caused you pain. Show me your respect."

I kissed his hand with one gentle press of my lips, but it meant more than I could ever show him in this way.

"Look up at me."

I saw his face framed by the parking lot light. I couldn't make out his features, only the shape of him. He seemed like a warrior or a God to me, bathed in light, fresh from battle and still wielding his weapon. I wasn't sure if I was allowed to speak, but I took my chances.

"Thank you, Sir. Thank you."

He took a step forward, just enough that he was no longer in a shadow, and I noticed that a small smile began to emerge. "Good girl. Now get in the car." He opened my door and it hurt when my ass hit the seat. The door closed, and he was in and starting the car before I realized he had even made the trip around to his side.

He didn't look at me when he spoke. "We're not going into the club"

"Can I ask why?"

"Because I never said we were going in. I said we were going to it, and we did."

"Yes, Sir." He really knew how to torture me. That's not normally something you look for in a man you want to have wild, passionate sex with, but in my case, I guess it was.

"I'm taking you home now."

I was disappointed. I wanted more, so much more of what he could give me. Unless, of course, he was taking me home to have his way with me sexually, but I doubted it and I couldn't even pretend to know what he was thinking. There's no way that I could have guessed what he was going to do tonight, and maybe even he hadn't planned it all, but it was by far one of the best "dates" I had ever had. I laughed to myself thinking what my dating criteria would be from here on out. "Yes, Sir."

His normal low and soothing voice was coming back. "Do you feel less in control now?"

"Very much, thank you."

"You really enjoyed that, didn't you?"

"Yes, Sir,"

"I'm glad. I enjoyed it, I believe, even more than you did. Put your hand on my lap."

Placing my left hand on top of his pants, I could feel the massive bulge he was concealing. He was so much harder than he had been the other night, and it gave me far more pleasure as well to know that what he had been doing to me caused him this much arousal.

"Don't take it out of my pants, but stroke it."

I softly rubbed my hand up and down the length of his shaft, and after a few minutes, I pressed a little more firmly. We were barely two blocks from the club, and he pulled into a dark parking lot.

"Keep going." He leaned his head back on the headrest and closed his eyes. Low moans were starting deep in his throat. I could see the tension building in his face while his hands gripped the steering wheel.

I didn't pick up speed but kept the same slow but firm stroking over top of his jeans.

He groaned low, his head still lying back, eyes closed and mouth opening. "Fuck yes."

The denim became wet with his come. I had no idea how much it would turn me to know he would come right there in his jeans. I was wet beyond belief. I thought I may come just from watching him.

He lifted his head from the seat, released the wheel, and directed his gaze towards me, that languid, lids half-open gaze that pierces you somewhere in the lower belly and stirs your arousal. "Do it. Make yourself come. I know you want to, but don't you dare put your hands down your pants."

There were people walking by, but the windows were probably too dark for them to see what was really going on. I moved my fingers to my lap, feeling my pubic bone through my jeans and began to rub my clit. I wasn't sure if I could do it, if I could masturbate in front of him. On the phone was one thing, but this was different. Although, after what he just did, I could probably muster the courage and I didn't think he would give me the choice at this point. I pushed harder, moved my hips in rhythm with my hand, and closed my eyes. Within a minute's time, I was coming. Hendrix covered my mouth. My eyes shot open at his touch and he stared into them. I had never had a man stare into me like that when either of us were climaxing. It made it seem more real, like I was more present and not off in some dark world with only pleasure attached to nothing.

He spoke low into my ear, "Good girl."

I felt somewhat ashamed, but not in an entirely negative way, more like getting caught when you wanted to be. I sat up straight and Hendrix repositioned himself to drive. He pulled out of the parking lot and continued heading for my building.

"Do you feel sufficiently punished now?"

"Yes, Sir."

"And are you satisfied as well?"

"Very much, Sir."

"Good. Now, I don't want to hear any more of this nonsense about wanting to run or being afraid. Are we clear?"

"Yes, Sir."

He pulled up to the curb nearest my building.

"Obviously, I can't get out of the car yet. Hopefully this will be dry by the time I reach my place, but right now, it's far too noticeable."

"That's fine. I don't mind letting myself out."

I opened my own door, and when I turned to shut it, he leaned over to look up at me. His dark blue eyes shadowed by the roof of the car and the streetlamp's projection of light above it, how could I ever deny him anything he asked? "Let me know about Wednesday."

"I will." I closed the door and walked into the lobby. The elevator ride to the ninth floor was creeping along. All I wanted to do was get inside and look at the evidence of my experience, written in bright red across my skin.

When I made it through my door, I went straight to the bedroom mirror and slid off my jeans. There, staring back at me, were six separate, long red welts; the other four must have met up and merged with them. I could tell that, by tomorrow, they would most likely be bruises. If I did go to the club with him on Wednesday, they would make nice accessories for me to show off.

What would it really hurt if I went? I wasn't sure that I could watch him with another woman, or several women for that matter, or if I could have sex in public, but if it were with him, if I would finally get to feel his strong arms wrapped around me, holding me as he was impaling me with his cock, I wouldn't care if there were millions watching. I could do this. I would do it. My mind was made up. I removed my phone from my pocket and texted him. I wasn't going to talk myself out of this.

"Hendrix, I'll go Wednesday. I want to."

It took him no time to text back. "Wonderful! I can't wait. That was a quick decision."

"You helped me get over my fears. I'm excited."

"Good. Now I know all I have to do is a little public punishment, and you'll be putty in my hands."

"I think you're right, Sir."

"You're even better than I imagined. I can't wait to see how much you enjoy the club, but I would like to pick you up around six, so we can go to dinner first. Is that okay?"

"That would be wonderful. Thank you, Sir."

"Great. I'll see you then. Try to get some sleep and don't let yourself go crazy trying to get through tomorrow."

"Easier said than done. It's going to crawl by."

"I know. All part of the fun, Ma'am."

120

That was it. It was done, and I was going. No backing out now. I was better than he imagined? My face lit up at the thought, and he was taking me to dinner first. Dinner and a sex club, just my kind of night out.

After a quick shower and a bite to eat, I went to bed. I was actually pretty tired. It seemed that thoroughly exhausting my stubborn will took a lot out of me. In fact, I felt like I did after a very hard run, the kind of exhaustion that leaves you feeling better off than you were before.

Lying in bed, I found that I had to turn to my stomach because my ass was just too sore to put pressure on. I wasn't upset about it by any means though. It only added to the sense of contentedness that I was beaming with.

Eleven

I awoke in the same position as I had fallen asleep, face down, ass pulsating with pain and heat. Though, this morning the stinging sensation had evolved into what felt like a sunburn and a bruise combined. Being careful, I sat up on the side of my right hip, swung my legs down, and touched my feet to the floor. Without putting any unneeded pressure on the welts, I stood up. As soon as I had my balance, I walked to the mirror.

They were still streaked but now more purple than red. It looked as if some of the swelling had subsided, but it was now replaced with hickey-like marks from where the belt managed to break some of the capillaries. Beautiful really, a lovely compliment to my milky skin tone. After a few minutes of slowly turning and noticing all the ways I could see them from each angle, except for directly head on, I walked to the bathroom. The cold, hard toilet seat proved to be a struggle, and I decided that a hot shower might be the best remedy. The thought of sitting in the bathtub made me cringe.

First, I needed coffee and food. I was starving and had a pain hangover. I couldn't wait to tell Hendrix my new found terminology. A pain hangover, as I had dubbed it, was the feeling of lightheadedness and bliss coupled with pure satisfaction, and some part of your body thudding with dull pain. I could definitely go for some more of these hangovers, much better than those inspired by alcohol that only left you with half-remembered moments of joy or stupidity. Of course, I was always glad for half-remembered stupidity, but a pain hangover left you with none of the forgetfulness and all of the recollection. I never wanted to forget how I had felt in those moments of absolute surrender to the moment and to my Master.

I did like thinking of him as my Master, not in the comedic way I had before, but in a true and honest form, where I looked to him for my next move, my answer, and my salvation. The act of succumbing to someone else, leaving myself at his mercy, was making me a better person. Even the mundane things in my life, like making the bed, brushing my teeth, and the things that would always be there, were becoming more enjoyable because I was looking at them from another standpoint. Not that they were any more fun really, just that the act of living was becoming more enjoyable because I was letting go of the me who was always in control, and, ironically, the more of myself I relinquished to him, the more freedom I felt.

The coffee finished brewing, and I sat in front of my window drinking it, watching the steam rise and fog the small portion of the glass above it. I only ate toast this morning because I was afraid that my nerves would get the best of my stomach and instigate an upheaval. I did, however, have to find something to pass the time today and running was a great time-killer. It was so sunny outside that it gave the impression that the temperature could be well into the nineties, but by the feel of the cold glass, I knew it may be fifty at best. I was also unsure of the stability of my glute muscles to carry my legs any faster than a slow jog, but I had to get out of the condo or I would go mad with anticipation. Hendrix wouldn't be coming to get me until six o'clock the next evening. I would make a list of things to be done and that I could do to pass the time somewhat productively.

Mental List: Eat, dress, run, shower, dress, eat, do makeup, do hair, write, listen to music, talk to friends and family, eat, write a little more, do your job for crying out loud or you won't be able to afford your thinking window anymore. Shit, what was I writing about? I'm not even sure that's what I want to write about anymore. Fuck, I need to get my mind on track. What was I doing? Oh, yeah, run, no I already said that. Well I could run again tomorrow morning, but for today, what else can I do? Sleep, shower, listen to music, think of a possible replacement for current writing subject, run... fuck this!

It was a bad idea to let my inner dialogue direct me, as it had no clear direction either. I would do what I did best, improvise. A run first it was. After depositing the coffee mug and plate into the dishwasher, I made a direct line to the bedroom before I had time to sidetrack myself.

Getting dressed, I was careful to pull my running pants on

slowly over the welts and even tied my shoes while standing. The playlist for the day was dance, pop, and metal music with definitive beats to help propel me when my body began protesting. My ear buds were once again where I had left them, more proof that I was becoming a better person. Perhaps, Hendrix could even come up with a punishment for me losing them. Then, I could lose them on purpose. I smiled at the thought. After brushing my teeth, I popped on some sunglasses to disguise my lack of makeup, and walked out the door.

Once I stepped out of the lobby, I realized that I had been off on my estimate in temperature. It was probably only forty, and I was freezing in nothing but very breathable running pants, a thin t-shirt, and tennis shoes. True, this weather would not have been cold to many other people, especially not at the end of October, but to a girl who had spent the last five years in the South, it was. I would have to run extra fast to improve my condition or let the cold take over and numb my throbbing ass. It was a toss-up, but I opted for actual running.

It was surprising that I only felt searing pain on initial take-off. After that, there was just a slight reminder when I would take a quick turn or leap off a slightly taller curb. Thankfully, there were very few people out today. It was already afternoon and most of them were back in their buildings for the rest of their nine-to-five life. I felt sorry for them. I'm sure a lot of them actually enjoyed their work, but I could never see myself living that kind of life. Working in a box would ruin me or improve me based on individual consensus. Hendrix would definitely agree on ruin because it would most certainly do the same to him.

He really was an amazing man, not just in looks but in overall style, attitude, character, and whip-wielding strength. He knew how to psychologically dominate me, and that was far better than using sheer brute alone, that wouldn't tame me. I would never succumb to it, not willingly anyway, and it took my own will to make the transformation I experienced last night. Hopefully, that would be only a first of many more self-realizations brought on by Hendrix. Then, I thought about what Stephanie said and that I would fall for him because he gave all of this to me. No, I wouldn't. I knew, like he had confirmed, that I would have an attachment, but that didn't mean it had to be an attachment based on love and need.

After the first two miles, my tender behind had ceased to exist, and I was able to run more freely. The sidewalks stayed relatively sparse of pedestrians, and the Mp3 battery was holding up nicely, so I decided to run towards Midtown, Hendrix's neck of the woods, which was an idiom that made me laugh since we obviously lived in a very large city. I was determined to make it a long run today. I may even go towards Pastimes, the vintage store I met him in, and Blue Rhapsody, just to reminisce. It had been a week, tomorrow, since I'd met him. That reminder made me check my thoughts and almost halted me in my tracks. Was I really allowing all of this to happen to me in a week's time? How could I make such uncharacteristic decisions with someone I had only known for not even a week? I needed to distance myself a little or Stephanie's predictions would come true. No matter if everything we had done up to this point had been only physical in nature, it was changing me emotionally, and I needed other influences, so that I didn't let Hendrix be in the forefront at all times. I turned around before I hit Midtown and headed back to Little Five.

I made the way back to my building with some pounding metal on in my ears to drown out the thoughts in my head. I wasn't going to back out of the club, not now, I wasn't even going to see less of Hendrix, but I needed to temper my desire with something outside of it all.

Once I was back in the condo, I peeled off my clothes and started the shower. The hot water felt like ice on my freezing but sweaty skin. I soon began to warm up though, and the nice memento began to sting again as the now bruised welts came to life. I let the water run over my face and kept my eyes closed, thinking of what I could do the rest of the day that wouldn't keep me locked in a circle of Hendrix. It finally came to me: shopping. I didn't really do a lot of it, at least not the kind that girlfriends fawn over and make special excursions for the simple task of buying a dress. No matter how I had tried throughout my life to fit in with other women, it just never happened. Today, I was not going to shop for anything that could be specifically for Hendrix or the club. I was going to shop for casual Ashton clothes that I could wear at

anytime and anywhere.

I finished showering and stepped out. The water must have been hotter than I thought because as soon as my skin hit the air I saw a thin wisp of steam rise from my arm. Wrapping the towel around myself, I hurried to dry off, put warm clothes on (skinny jeans, a thin, long-sleeved purple sweater and brown knee-high boots), and turn up the heat like I had neglected to do this morning or last night. After remedying the situation, I called the cab company and set up a pick up time. I put on makeup, fixed my purposefully unfixable hair, and walked out to the living room in just enough time to hear my doorman buzz the intercom.

The cab was waiting at the curb, and I had a flash of Hendrix's black GTO sitting there instead, the quick spanking he gave me on the sidewalk, and the passion that occurred in his front seat later that night. I walked to the cab and climbed in the back.

"Peachtree Center Mall Please."

"Yes Ma'am."

I cringed at the words that now seemed to belong only to Hendrix and wanted to tell the driver not to call me that, but instead sat back and stared out of the window.

When I arrived at the mall, I knew exactly where I was going and what I was looking for. I also was not the type to spend hours walking and window shopping. Get in, get out. That was my task, but today I might just walk a little slower and take my time, because the longer I spent doing anything, the faster it would become tomorrow. I was here to take myself out of the Hendrix frame, and by reminding myself of that, I was inadvertently making him more apparent to my train of thought. Deciding to get some lunch, I stopped at a restaurant with a bar. Having a glass or two of wine might help or hurt the situation, but it was yet to be determined.

Eating at a restaurant alone wasn't my favorite thing to do, but I didn't feel all that embarrassed either. After all, I did quite a lot of things alone. Why couldn't I do this? I ordered a glass of a cabernet/merlot blend and a salad. It was always amusing to me how a restaurant that existed outside of a mall could be exactly the same as one in it, but with a stark difference. People were dressed in sweatshirts and jeans, carried loads of bags, and just looked frazzled. Whereas, the same restaurant in the outer mall world, people were calm, friendly, dressed nicely, and generally happy. What was it about shopping that strained people's minds, bodies, and tempers so much? I would never understand because I would never become one of them. If I was certain of nothing else in my life at this moment, I was sure of that. I sat there people watching and imbibing, gradually becoming more detached from my previous thoughts, when I was startled by a man in a business suit standing next to me. I thought it was one of the waiters at first, but they were not wearing charcoal gray, lightly pinstriped suits worthy of Wall Street. I looked up at the man. He was tall, stout, and had a very authoritative look. I assumed that I had done something wrong. Perhaps my hair was offensive to someone across the room, and he was going to throw me out. Instead, he held out a glass of wine similar to the one I was drinking.

"I wanted to buy you a drink, but I thought you looked very fascinating, and I would rather bring it to you myself to get a better look at you. I hope you don't mind."

This had never happened to me before. Could he read the deviousness on my face? Was my ass showing, taunting him with the purple welt lines? A suit was buying me a drink, in a mall? What was the world coming to? "Well, thank you." I refrained from using Sir. Hendrix had gotten me so accustomed to it that I thought of calling every man who addressed me that, but that would almost seem disrespectful, ironically.

"May I sit down or are you in a hurry?"

"No hurry. Yes you may." What was I doing?

"My name is Tag Davidson."

Tag? Really? "I'm Ashton."

"A very unique name for a very unique woman."

"Tag is quite unique too. Is it short for something?"

"No. Unfortunately, my parents liked it just the way it was. You have no idea how often people say, 'You're it,' after I tell them my name, so thank you for refraining."

I laughed. I surprisingly hadn't thought of that. I was out of it today. "That's a great one, but it must get old."

"You have no idea. So, Ashton, what brings you to this wonderful mall on such a beautiful day?"

"Boredom, mainly."

"How could a woman as beautiful and interesting as you possibly be bored?"

"It happens, believe me. I don't think beauty has anything to do with boredom."

"Perhaps not, but it should at least have something to do with you having an over-abundance of company."

Ah, typical male flattery. I loved that Hendrix didn't use this tactic on me, and really two men hitting on me a week apart? This was strange indeed. He was attractive, nothing like Hendrix, but attractive in a contrary way. The way that makes you blush and feel that you have overstepped your boundaries just by looking him in the eyes, which were a peculiar shade of hazel. His hair was very business appropriate but was a nice shade of light brown, a good compliment to his eyes.

"How do you know I don't have company meeting me here any minute?"

"I don't, but then again, I'm not doing anything I wouldn't mind them seeing, so there's no concern on my part. However, if you would like me to leave, I will understand."

"Oh, no, I'm not meeting anyone, just being a smart ass. I apologize."

"No apology necessary. I admire a witty woman. I do, however, have a meeting of mine own to attend very shortly, which is the reason I'm here. I wanted to take the opportunity to introduce myself before leaving in the off-chance that you may be interested in having dinner with me sometime. You don't have to answer me now. I'll just leave you with my card, and you can call me if you decide."

"Thank you. I'll definitely think about it."

"It was very nice meeting you, Ashton. What was your last name?"

"Rhodes. It's Ashton Rhodes."

"Very nice. I will hopefully be seeing you again, Miss Rhodes. I hope you have a wonderful day."

"You too and thank you for the drink." We shook hands and he turned to leave. I couldn't help but watch him walk away, business suits did have a nice way of framing a man's ass and shoulders. He was such a contradiction to Hendrix and of course, me and my contradictions....

After he was out of sight, I snapped out of my trance. What the fuck just happened? A man, not a guy, a man in a business suit came up to me in a restaurant in a mall, no less, and bought me a glass of wine, sat down with me in just enough time to hand me his business card, and invited me to dinner. Am I in a parallel universe? Why was he in a mall for a business meeting? I looked at his card for a clue. Right there in bold black ink, it said, "Tag Davidson CEO Davidson Enterprises." Davidson Enterprises owned this and about a hundred other malls around the country. Wow! He's a CEO, in a suit, and inviting me to dinner. Me, who looks like your typical confused artist wondering the fringes of society and opposed to all conformity. Maybe he liked contradictions too. Maybe he was a lot more than meets the eye. I was immediately singing the theme song from Transformers in my head. Transformers, more than meets the eye, hmmm hm hmmmm." Tag could never handle me. Nevertheless, I put his card in my purse, finished my wine, and paid the bill. I walked out of the restaurant even more confused than when I entered it.

I thought about texting Hendrix and telling him what had just transpired, but I decided to keep it to myself. If I was determined to break out of the Hendrix cycle, I needed my space and my secrets, and I was sure Hendrix had plenty of his own. I spent the rest of the afternoon looking for new clothes that I found interesting, which were very hard to find in the corporate shopping world, the top forty of clothing, if you will. After a weary search, I ended up with two pairs of jeans, several t-shirts, some of which were cropped 80s style, and a new pair of heels that could be worn to the grocery, as I reminded myself that I was to buy nothing to wear on special Hendrix occasions. Maybe I could wear them on a date with Tag. No, stop that right now. Don't even entertain that thought. After tomorrow night, you'll be damaged goods for a man like him anyway. Maybe I liked the idea of being damaged goods because I had a pretty good idea of what the damaging entailed.

I called a cab, and after hanging up, I received a text from Hendrix. "Hello good girl. What have you been getting yourself into today?"

"Shopping."

"Thrift store?"

"You'll never believe it, but actually, the mall."

"What???? You at a mall? I would like to see that. In fact, are you still there?"

"Yes, just called a cab."

"Well, call them back and cancel. I'll pick you up."

"Yes, Sir." Just like that, I was back in his world, whether I wanted to be or not. He was irresistible, and I was a firm believer in giving into temptation. "Where should I meet you?"

"How about the ice cream shop near the center entrance?"

"Sounds great. How long?"

"Twenty minutes give or take. I'll text you when I'm getting off the exit."

"Thank you, Sir."

"You're more than welcome, Ma'am."

I walked around for a few more minutes. I was overly excited to see him and it was such a surprise. A little guilt began to creep up from my secret encounter earlier, but I wasn't going to let him in on it. I needed my separateness, at least in some aspects. Besides, Hendrix didn't want to date me. The only thing he wanted form me was obedience and the willingness to accompany him in public sex clubs. What would I do when this was all over? Leave myself with no prospects and be lonely? Definitely not, and even if I would be damaged goods to a man like Tag, there were plenty of other people who would be into the types of things I was. Really, how did I know that Tag or numerous other men like him weren't just as wild as Hendrix? They might just not show it on the outside. I should stop judging men by their cover.

"Taking the exit now. Should be there in five."

"Yes, Sir. I'll be there."

Walking into the ice cream store, I sat down at one of the small benches near the wall. I saw his black GTO pull up at the door.

"Do you want me to come in or would you just like to get in the car?"

"I'll come to the car. I see you."

It was chilly outside and the moon was already out. Hendrix got out and opened the door for me. As soon as I saw him, I forgot about everything else. He was my Master. I couldn't betray him, even if I wasn't dating him. For right now at least, he owned me.

After he got into the driver's seat, I told him about Tag.

"Well, you're just having a good month, huh?" He smiled and that wasn't what I expected.

"You're not upset at all?"

"Why would I be upset Ashton? We're not dating. You can do whatever you want to do when you're not with me."

"What do you do when you're not with me?" Damn it! I didn't mean to ask that. It just slipped out of the place in my head where I was holding it for a much later or never discussion. "I'm sorry. I have no right to ask that. I'm still learning about all of this, and I'm sorry."

"It's okay. I know this is all new for you and I don't mind answering. Right now, I mainly just work, and when I'm not working I'm making blueprints or preparing bids for jobs, which is still working, but when I'm not doing either of those, I've been with you or sleeping. I'm not dating anyone if that is what you were getting at."

"You really didn't have to answer me. It's none of my business."

"It's okay. I don't care if you ask, but I promise you, I'll always tell you the truth. And, honestly, if I was dating someone, we wouldn't have this arrangement."

"But then why would it be okay for me to date someone?"

"Like I said, you can do whatever you want, but I'm fairly certain that if you started dating someone right now, you would have a hard time hiding what you're doing in the interim. How's your ass looking by the way?" He gave me a devious smile as he was pulling out onto the interstate.

I laughed. "Well, you're right about that. It looks like a bit of purple and red tiger striping, thank you very much."

"You say that sarcastically, but I know you mean it."

"Yes, Sir, I do. Let me ask you, I may have marks to prove my other hobbies, but you won't, so you could date other people. Why wouldn't you?"

"Because I don't want to, plain and simple. I'm not looking for that right now. I have all that I want at the moment."

I couldn't help but smile at that. Even if it meant not a chance in Hell at a relationship, it still sounded romantic in a twisted way. "Okay."

"Now, if you're done interrogating me, would you like to go to my place for a drink, maybe order a pizza?"

I liked the thought of him not being able to wait until tomorrow, just as I couldn't. He was a man, so he would never admit that was the reason for him coming to pick me up. "Yes, Sir. That sounds great."

"So what did you buy?"

"Not much. Some jeans, a few t-shirts, and one pair of

shoes."

"You don't really seem like the mall type to me."

"I'm not. I just needed a change of scenery."

"There's plenty of better looking scenes in this town."

"You're right. I learned my lesson today." Which was that I should take a break from shopping, period, because apparently I had "hit on me" written across my forehead while doing so. I had never been the type of woman that men approached easily, and now look what had happened. One was already coercing me into fondling a woman and being whipped in a public parking lot, and the other was a starched shirt yuppie. What was next, a rodeo clown?

"Maybe I should teach you another lesson."

"What's that Sir?"

"The proper way to suck my cock while I drive."

"Oh yes please. I do want instructing on that, Sir."

"Now, before you get your greedy little mouth on it, I'm telling you that I don't want to come, got it?"

"Yes, Sir." He really was too much about the teasing sometimes.

He grabbed the back of my head by my hair and pushed my face to his lap.

"Undo my pants."

"Yes, Sir."

"Don't speak. Just do as you're told."

I refrained from saying 'Yes Sir' and unbuttoned and unzipped his jeans. I could see the shape of his cock growing underneath his black boxer briefs.

"Take it out."

I obeyed. The light coming in from the moon and the illumination from the dashboard made it seem somewhat secretive and hidden, revealed only to me. Though I knew that wasn't true, for now it was and I wanted to stay with that thought. It wasn't fully hard yet, which was fine, because I hoped I would get to feel it grow in my mouth.

"Lick it, gently with only the tip of your tongue."

I ran my tongue around the head and down the bottom side of his shaft. Every inch that I moved down, I felt it grow almost simultaneously.

"Yes Ashton, very good girl."

Bringing my tongue back to the head, I flicked it lightly, back and forth. It wasn't only a tease for him. I was dying to put it all the way in and to feel the smooth, hard skin on the walls of my mouth. I had always enjoyed giving oral pleasure, and now I could add that I enjoyed giving oral pleasure to women as well, thanks to Hendrix.

"Do you want to suck it? You can answer."

"Yes, Sir."

"How badly do you want to suck it?"

"Very badly, Sir."

He reached over to me, slid his free hand down the top of my jeans, into my panties, and ran his fingers over my soft outer lips. His hand glided over them easily, spreading the wetness he had coerced me to produce. Bringing them back out, he approvingly looked at the moisture on his fingers and put them in his mouth. That was all I needed to dive my head down to his cock, devouring it like I was starving.

He grabbed the hair on the back of my head and pulled me up quickly.

He only made quick glances in my direction, because he was driving, but I could still see the look of authority in his eyes. "Did I tell you that you could do that?"

"No, Sir. I'm sorry."

He tucked himself back into his boxer briefs and at the first red light we came to, he zipped and buttoned his pants.

"I'm sorry, Sir. Please, I'll be good. Don't make me stop. I want to please you."

"Part of the pleasure I get is from you behaving me and, of course, in having to punish you, which I will be doing when we get back to my place. Until then, you just stay over on that side of the car and keep your hands on your knees."

Even though I did what he said, I wasn't sorry for what I had done. As I sat there with my hands resting firmly on my knees, I thought of what my punishment would be this time. We weren't far from his building now, so I would know shortly.

He didn't speak to me for the remainder of the ride but, as usual, opened the car door for me. As he said, he would be polite in public, but as soon as we got to his condo door, he turned into the Dom again.

"Take your clothes off."

"Yes, Sir, but I really need to use your restroom. I had several glasses of wine in the restaurant at the mall."

He didn't waiver. "I said take your clothes off."

I did, but I hoped he would at least give me a human moment, a time out, and then I would come right back to him. "Please, Sir, I want to play along, but I really just need to pee."

"Go to the kitchen."

Was he fucking serious? He wasn't going to let me go? This was just mean, and I got the safe word ready in the back of my mind. I walked into his kitchen, stepping on the cold tile, briefly remembering the sound of my heels on it the morning after I had spent the night.

"Bend over and place your hands on the sink."

I stayed where I was and looked at him with pleading eyes. "Hendrix, I really need to use the restroom first. Please, I have to pee!"

He looked as stern as ever. "Bend over Ashton, now!"

I couldn't believe him. This was it; I was done. He found

my line, and he crossed it. "No!"

"What was that?"

"I said no, no Sir, if you prefer, but no!"

"Why? Why won't you bend over and hold onto the sink? You let me whip you in public, but you won't bend over for me here in my own kitchen?"

"It's not that I don't want to bend over. It's that you're not letting me go to the bathroom. Why won't you let me?" I was starting to get upset. I knew he could hear it in my voice, but I really didn't care.

"What do you think is going to happen if I don't let you go?"

"Obviously, I might lose control in front of you."

"And do you think that would make me disgusted with you?"

"Of course! I would be disgusted with myself!"

"Bend the fuck over and put your hands on that sink, immediately!"

He didn't say whether it would disgust him, but I didn't care. I knew how I would feel about it. "No, Hendrix." I didn't use the safe word yet. I wanted to see if he would give in to me, but I knew that was wishful thinking.

He grabbed my arm, spun me around, and spanked me swiftly and very hard, right across the marks he had left the night before, and I cried out in pain. It felt like the welts were being opened. He waited only a few seconds and proceeded with another round of spanking, not as hard but faster.

"Please, stop!" I was crying now, but something inside me wouldn't let me use my safe word. There was a curiosity that wouldn't leave me. Did he want me to lose control in front of him? Would that get him off? I knew it wouldn't do a damn thing for me, but how would it excite him? How many other women had done that for him, or, more likely, had he ordered to do it for him?

He yelled at me again. "I will not stop until you do what I have been telling you to do, and I will continue to punish you until you do as I say! Now, either you are deliberately bating me to inflict more pain upon you, or you're forgetting what we have discussed!"

My voice was shaking, "No, Sir. I haven't forgotten."

His voice was low and stern, but also devilishly sexy, "Then you want the punishment, and part of that punishment is that you are not allowed to leave this room. Do you understand me?"

"Yes, Sir." I could hold it. I knew I could. He could spank me and torment me all he wanted, but I wouldn't lose control in front of him.

"Good. Now bend over and grab that sink!"

He finally got me to do as he wished. I grasped the cold sink, bent over, and looked at my feet. I realized this was the first time I had been completely naked in front of him. The other night with Tracy, I left my dress on, though it was pulled down from the top and lifted up from the bottom, it was not entirely off. I stood there in what in any normal relationship would have been a pinnacle, the first time he saw me naked. It would proceed a raucous love making session or a mutual worshiping of our bodies, but instead I was here, ready to pee myself, grasping Hendrix's sink, and staring at the floor. I still had not even seen him fully naked; I hadn't even seen him with his shirt off for that matter. In the midst of my thoughts, I felt a finger sneak its way slowly between my thighs, opening and entering me, then turning downward to press on my G-spot, which was also directly in front of my bladder. No, he wouldn't make me. I would hold it. He could do anything, but he wouldn't break me, not this way.

"Does that feel good?"

"Yes, Sir." It did feel good. The feeling of a full bladder intensified the pleasure he was giving me, but not just the physical feeling. It was the setting, him displaying his ultimate control over me. Even though I knew I wouldn't bend to his will this time, I could still enjoy the position of dominance he had. How humiliating would it be if he made me lose my control? Terrible, it would be terrible, and it wouldn't happen.

"Still have to go?"

"Yes, Sir. Why are you tormenting me like this?"

"Because I can and because you want me to."

"No, I don't."

"Oh really? Then why haven't you made it stop?"

He had me there. I could have stopped it, but I didn't. He was right; I did enjoy the torment. I would use the safe word if it came to the point I knew I couldn't hold out any longer. That was my fail safe. He could torment me all he wanted until that point. Sliding another finger inside of me, he pressed harder against my G-spot and started to wiggle them back and forth. My bladder was being provoked to empty, but I felt that I still had a long way to go before I would make him stop. Truth be told, I liked the fear it gave me, the fear of losing control over my own body, and the fact that he didn't seem the slightest bit worried about it happening.

He began pushing harder and wrapped his free arm around my stomach, pulling me into his hard chest and torso, while I was still grasping the sink. His legs spread out on either side of me, so that his feet were locking me in, until I had no hope of a physical escape. Continuing to torture me, he bent his fingers sharply, hooking them more, so they had an unfair advantage against my G-spot. I was on the verge of coming. The sensation he was giving me was unlike anything I had ever felt before. It was a feeling of intense pleasure and absolute dread. I was so fearful of what could happen, but I had to keep my mind on my own task, while he was trying to tear it away from any other thought, besides that of the pleasure he was giving me. He pushed harder. I could feel my bladder shift and move with each stroke of his fingers. The pressure of the fluid ready to leak out excited the nerves in my clit to the point it felt as if his tongue was licking at it.

"Do it, Ashton."

"Do what?"

"Whatever you feel."

He was relentless now. I could feel his hard shaft pressing into my bruised and sensitive ass, his strong arm around my stomach, and his fingers working furiously to make me come or lose control, whichever he was wanting, maybe both. I poised the safe word on my tongue, ready to scream it at just the right moment.

"Don't hold back with me. Do it!"

"I can't."

"Your body can. You won't let it. There's a difference."

"Why do you want me to do this?"

He growled in my ear, "To prove to me that I have ultimate control over you, that I can make you do anything I want, and because I will reward you with more pleasure and more satisfaction than you have ever known. Tell me, what you're feeling right now."

"Fear."

"Is that all you feel?"

"No, Sir. I feel fear and pleasure."

"Do you think that pleasure is better or worse because of the fear?"

"I don't know."

"Well, then, let me take away the pleasure."

He removed his fingers with a jerk, and I felt lost. Now, I only felt the sense of urgency I was fighting against and my legs were trembling. He was still holding me as he did before, but the thought of losing control with him so close was so overwhelming that I couldn't fathom it.

"No, Sir, please. Give it back, please."

"See, you dirty little girl, you like it don't you?"

"Yes, Sir."

He pushed his fingers back inside me, harder and more unforgiving than before.

"You like to be dirty. You like to push the limits, don't you?" He was speeding up his movements.

"Yes, Sir."

"You want to piss on this floor, right in front of me, don't you?"

"No, Sir, I don't!"

"Yes, you do. It gives you a thrill to think of doing something so taboo, so socially unacceptable, and especially in front of me, especially while you're receiving pleasure. Am I right?"

I didn't know what to say. When he explained it that way, it excited me. My reason was going out the window, and I was succumbing to the feeling of the moment, the way I had done when he whipped me.

"Do it!"

"I can't, Hendrix, I can't!"

"You can. I'll make you."

He snatched a dish towel from the stove handle right next to us and removed his fingers from me only long enough to wrap it around my eyes. His arm left its hold around my waist to tie the towel, but was back in an instant and his fingers went back inside of me. Everything was dark. All I could do was hear him and feel, at a greater intensity, everything he was doing to me. Pressing down hard with his fingers, he hooked my G-spot, pulling it towards my pubic bone, and he continued to pull and to agitate until I could no longer take it.

"Do it, Ashton, do it! I want to see it."

I felt slightly less fearful now that I had the blindfold on. The total darkness, the idea of not knowing what was happening gave me courage, or at least would give me the advantage of not seeing what could happen.

He gave one last hard tug to my G-spot, and I gave in. The hot liquid burst from me. He pulled his fingers out and stepped back while my shame ran from me and splashed on the tile floor. It

140

ran down my thighs, but I could not see what I was doing or where Hendrix had gone, though I heard him near me. It seemed like an eternity that it was draining from me, the sound of it torturing me because I couldn't make it stop. Even amidst my mortification, I could hear his belt buckle being undone and I was aroused, especially now so, that I thought of Hendrix being excited by what he had made me do. The buckle hit the tile floor.

The splash of fluid finally ceased, and I began to cry, silently. I felt Hendrix's hand on my back and then at the top of my left arm. He led me out of the kitchen and onto the shag rug in the living room. When he removed the blindfold, my tears had dried as they emerged, and hopefully, he wouldn't know that I had been crying.

As soon as I could see again, my eyes were fixed on the sight of Hendrix, naked, moonlight glinting off of him. He was more magnificent than I had dared to imagine. His musculature was made by working hands, not created in a gym. The tattoos I had been so curious about were beautiful, complimenting the ridges in his chest and shoulders. His cock was rock hard, and he was stroking it, holding the makeshift blindfold in the other hand.

"Ashton, I know that was hard for you, but as you can see, I enjoyed it, and you have proven your absolute surrender to me. Now, you will be rewarded."

I could only hope he meant what I thought he did. "Thank you, Sir."

After using the towel to wipe my legs dry, he picked me up and laid me on his couch.

He stroked my hair back into place from where the blindfold had adhered it to my forehead and ran his fingers down my neck to my chest and over my breasts. "Such a good girl."

I felt as if I were being worshipped, which was very opposite from the way he normally made me feel.

"Tell me, good girl, do you want to be fucked?"

"Yes, Sir."

"By me?"

"Oh, yes, Sir."

He grabbed my legs and spun me around on the couch, so that he was on the floor in front of me and I was splayed out before him on the cushion, my feet on the floor, much like I had been in front of Tracy, but now, at last it was Hendrix staring at me, fully naked, fully erect, with his hungry hands all over me. I couldn't' believe what I had done, but the excitement it had obviously produced in him made it worth it. He ran his hands up my thighs, grabbing my hips and pulling me closer to him. The skin of his hands was slightly rough, solidifying the vision of him sweating in the sunlight while he worked, making me all the more attracted to him. On his knees, the couch was the perfect height for him to impale me, and he had lined my hips up with the end of the cushion. If I looked over my stomach, I could see his hard shaft, large, pulsing with blood, and ready to enter me.

"How badly do you want it?"

"Very badly, Sir."

"Then you shall have it, but only because you were such a good girl, and you deserve it."

"Thank you. Sir."

"Will you obey me, whatever I ask of you?"

"Yes. Sir."

He moved in towards me and I could feel the tip of his cock barely start to part my inner lips and hint at penetration.

"Will you let me watch another man fuck you?"

"Yes, Sir." He pressed the head in only a little bit further, just enough to allow the wetness to coat the tip, enough so that when he was ready, he could slam it into me without resistance.

"Will you pleasure women when and where I ask you to? Will you let me watch you please them and they please you?"

"Yes, Sir."

He pressed a few more centimeters into me, right on the threshold of passing into me completely, right at the opening where so many nerve endings jumped at the feeling of his hard cock finally touching me there.

"Will you allow me to fuck you in front of other people, even if there were hundreds watching us? Would you let me?"

"Yes, Sir." He was turning me on so much with his questioning and his teasing. The desire for him to drive into me the rest of the way was maddening. I was envisioning scenes to go along with the things he was asking me and in the moment, they seemed like the sexiest, most erotic encounters that I could ever dream of. Why had I given them a second thought as to whether I could or would do them? Of course I would. With Hendrix, I didn't think that there was much I wouldn't do with him or for him.

"Would you let me join in with you, if another man were fucking you? I could fuck you at the same time he did, fill you up, maybe even add a third man to make sure that there were no areas of you left open?"

"Yes, Sir! Yes, Sir!" He pushed passed my threshold now and plunged deeper and deeper inside me, until he reached my cervix and held himself there, grabbing my hips.

"And will you watch me fuck another woman while you're pleasuring her and then, of course, I'll fuck you while she's giving you pleasure? Can you do that?"

"Yes, Sir!" The way he described it made it seem easy. Why would I feel the least bit of jealousy from what he had just told me? It sounded immensely erotic.

He slid back slowly away from my cervix, back until the head of his shaft passed my threshold again. He didn't pull it out all the way, just enough to make me think he was going to and then rammed it into me with an alarming force that shook my body and made my head spin. Beginning to do this faster, he took shorter strokes as he picked up speed, but each time ramming me hard and leaving me reeling. I felt drunk with pleasure and the pain of him bruising me with each thrust. It was a high, the mixture of pain and pleasure, like nothing I could have imagined.

Suddenly, he pulled out, then flipped me over, and moved

me down so that my knees were on the floor in front of the couch. I was bent over, face on the cushion, but my hands were pinned behind my back by only one of his. The other stayed at my hip, his fingertips gripping my flesh.

"Do you like it hard Ashton? Rough, the way I'm giving it to you, is that what you've been wanting?"

"Yes, Sir!"

"Can you take it harder from behind?"

"I want to, Sir."

He slammed back into me, reaching my cervix immediately. Grabbing my hands harder and gripping my hip deeper with his fingers, he began to pump in and out of me with a ferocious rhythm. My whole body was vibrating with each of the rebounds off of my cervix. He was large, not so large that it was impossible, but large enough to perfectly fill me and his girth was enough so that he stretched me every time he entered or reentered me. I loved the sound of his hips colliding with my already sore ass and knowing that he could see the marks he had given me last night.

Letting my hip go and unpinning my arms from his other hand, he grabbed me at the fold of my elbows, one in each hand and pulled back, so that my chest and face came off the couch. My back was arched and my arms were being used as reins to hold me in this position and to drive himself deeper and deeper into me. I felt suspended, weightless almost, and wholly lost in the rhythm of his motions. He was breathing so hard now. I could feel sweat collecting on the small of my back, and he made the most satisfied, guttural grunts when he slammed into me. Pure male, brute strength, and animalistic fervor. I was a captured animal, and he was a wild beast bent on ravaging me without care.

He continued without slowing and without fatigue at the same intensity, driving me hard into the couch. Without warning, I was hit with an orgasm that rocked through me with blinding waves. I felt nothing but that. No couch, no floor, not even Hendrix. All I felt was wave after wave of the most immense pleasure. My eyes rolled into my head, and my senses dulled. The only thing that existed was this ocean of pleasure. Was that me screaming? I couldn't be sure if the sound was coming from me or if it was only in my head. I had all but blacked out. I felt that I was in another world, that world that you enter right before passing out when everything is surreal, and you feel that you don't belong to your body.

It seemed to go on forever, but eventually the waves became softer, and I began to come back to reality. All feeling returned. Hendrix had brought my hands back in front of me and lifted my upper body from its bent position, but we were still on our knees. He had me crushed to his body, locking me in his grasp. I had been rocking on top of him this way, and he was undulating with my movements. My knees in front of his, my ass pressed into his hips, his arms pinning my arms to my chest, and his lips on my neck. I felt his hot breath rise up to my hairline, and it caused me to shiver.

It amazed me that he could keep going. He had the stamina and power of a racehorse, and his body mimicked the muscular definition of one as well. He lifted his arms from their protective grasp and used my arms to lift me off of him, but he quickly turned me and laid my back on the rug. I was excited that I would get to watch him over top of me, my fantasy coming true. No matter how good it felt to be fucked from behind, the visual enhancement of seeing a man, an attractive man, over top of you was far more gratifying. Although, after what he had just done to me, I wasn't sure anything could be better.

Throwing one of my legs over each of his shoulders, he pushed my knees towards my chest with the weight of his body, folding me. He didn't spend time teasing. He pressed his cock into me, not hard, but slowly, so that I felt every inch of it. His hair was wet with sweat, pieces of it falling over his eyes which were fixed on my face.

"God Ashton, you feel incredible."

"So do you."

"You really came hard, didn't you?"

"Harder and longer than I ever have. Thank you, Sir."

"No, thank you. I'm impressed that you could take it. No woman has ever been able to handle me fucking them that hard, certainly not from behind." He covered my mouth with his hand. "Now shut up. I'm not finished with you."

Normally, I would never let a man get away with telling me to shut up, but in this situation, he could say worse and I wouldn't give a damn. It only added to the excitement.

I watched his body as he began fucking me hard again, his abs flexing with each thrust, his shoulders tensing from holding himself above me. I loved the view of my legs on his shoulders and the look of pure satisfaction on his face. He lifted himself up now and took both of my legs over one of his shoulders but kept them straight in the air.

"Now, hold your legs up, and don't let them fall, no matter what I do."

"Yes, Sir."

He kept one arm wrapped around my legs and the other pressed into my shoulder, pinning me to the floor. There was no way that I could push him off of me. I was strong, but he was much stronger. I had the thought then of him forcing himself on me and wondered if that dark fantasy could be played out, maybe even with several men. With Hendrix, I was sure it could be; with him it seemed even my deepest and darkest fantasies would be accepted and even enjoyed.

He opened his eyes and looked into mine; they were lustful and passionate. I wondered how any woman could ever deny him or leave him if they had the choice. I couldn't think of anything this man could do that would force me to make that decision, if it were mine to make. He parted my legs then, bringing them down to the floor, so that my heels rested on the carpet, and I could see his body fully. I looked around his right shoulder, watching his hips and ass rise up and down as he continued to move inside me. His body was covered in sweat, and his muscles had been straining for so long that his veins were starting to bulge. He placed his hands beside my ears, positioning his face right above mine, still keeping his body suspended over me. Then closing his eyes, he lifted his chin up, and tilted his head back.

"Mmmmm, God Ashton, fuck." It wasn't a scream it was a moan turned into words.

He was close to coming, and I couldn't wait to feel it. His cock was stiffening even more than I thought it could, the veins in his neck were bulging further, and his face was turning red.

He opened his eyes then, starting into mine. "Where do you want it?"

"All over me."

He pulled out of me then, positioned his cock over top of my pubic bone, and shot load after load of his hot come all over my stomach and breasts. A little landed on my chin and bottom lip.

He rocked up on his knees. "Don't touch it. I want to look at it."

"Yes, Sir." I said it carefully as to not accidentally press the come on my lip into my mouth.

"Lick it off."

I did, slowly, so that he could see my tongue as it trailed over my bottom lip and lapped his come onto it. I let it stay on my tongue then because I wasn't told what to do with it after licking it off. I was learning to behave, more than I ever thought possible.

"Hold it there on your tongue until I tell you to swallow it."

Holding my tongue slightly out of my mouth so that he could get a better look at it, I let it roll back, but caught it by tilting my tongue downward.

"Oh, you bad little girl. Are you taunting me with insubordination?"

I shook my head yes but gently. I didn't want to get in trouble, not right now. I just wanted to let him know that I didn't fear the thought of being punished. Instead, I actually relished it.

"Swallow it."

I did and made a face as if I had swallowed a rare and

exquisite delicacy.

"You are an amazing woman, Ashton."

"Thank you, Sir. You're pretty amazing yourself."

"I'm serious. You are more than I ever expected you to be. It's a very pleasant surprise."

"The feeling is mutual."

He stood and extended his hand to me, helping me from the floor. Thankfully, I had forgotten about the kitchen until just this moment and wasn't sure what I should do. I certainly didn't want him cleaning it up. "Hendrix, let me clean your kitchen."

"I will allow you to, only because I know you're very disturbed by it. I'll bring you some towels."

"Please don't watch me do it."

"Now what fun would that be? I want you to stay naked and get on your hands and knees to clean it, like a good servant. It's either that, or I'll clean it myself while you watch."

"No, I'll do it, Sir."

Was he so into constant mortification that he had to continue to demand it even after he had fucked me? I knew the answer to that and I was quickly learning that being Hendrix's sub was a full time act. It wasn't just something he wanted at certain moments; it was what he expected every time I was with him. That was our arrangement after all. I had never expected him to be so thorough, not when I agreed to it originally, but I was reminded more and more how happy I was that I took him up on the offer.

I was reluctant to walk to the kitchen, so I stood in the living room while he went for towels. He was back with three of them very quickly and handed them to me. This was the part I was going to detest, but I would try to keep in mind the amazing sex we just had and clean the kitchen as fast as possible. I didn't plan on letting him get too much pleasure from me being degraded.

"Now, go clean up your mess."

"Yes, Sir."

As soon as I rounded the wall that had been separating me from my shame, I felt my heart sink. All of the fear I had before rushed back into me, and Hendrix stood behind me making me all the more uncomfortable.

"Get down on your knees and clean it."

"Yes, Sir."

I laid each towel out, and thankfully, it was just the right amount to cover it all. I let them sit there absorbing my humiliation.

"Don't be so embarrassed, Ashton. Can't you tell how much I liked it?"

"Yes, Sir, but enjoying it in the moment is one thing. Seeing it afterward is different."

"Kind of like getting drunk, fucking someone you know you shouldn't have, and then waking up beside them in the morning?"

"Well, yes, actually. It's exactly like that."

"But even when we're ashamed of what we've done, it doesn't change the fact that the good parts of the experience we had remains the same, does it?"

"No Sir. I suppose not."

"And don't you think that maybe a big part of why people do those things they regret later is actually because they like the idea of feeling guilty or ashamed?"

"I wouldn't think so."

"So feeling ashamed doesn't turn you on? Being whipped in front of other people in a public place didn't turn you on? Doing what I forced you to do in front of me didn't turn you on?"

"Yes Sir, it did."

"Then why punish yourself for something that brought you pleasure?"

"I don't know."

He leaned on the counter, resting on his elbows and

forearms, so relaxed while I was so on edge. "Because you think that's what you're supposed to do. I'm giving you the freedom to stop thinking about that, remember? You listen to me now, and you have no business feeling embarrassed or ashamed for something I've made you do. I've taken the guilt away for you."

"Yes Sir, thank you." He was right, and I was happy that he was. He did things to me I didn't even realize. He was more than a Master and more than an incredibly handsome man. He was a manipulative, sexy, mind-fucking Adonis. He had actually made me feel okay about cleaning up my own pee from his kitchen floor. Anyone that could do that deserved a lot of credit. Oddly enough, amidst this crazy scene, I had a flash of sadness, thinking I didn't know what I would do with myself when he was done with me, but I played his words over in my head like a self-help audio book. Telling me that I shouldn't dwell on the future, to enjoy the present, and I did, immensely.

He bent down, opened a cabinet, and held out a garbage bag for me. "Just toss the towels in here."

"Yes, Sir."

He tore some paper towels from their holder on his counter and handed me a bottle of cleaning spray. "Wipe the floor with this."

"Yes, Sir."

"Now, throw those in here too."

"Yes, Sir."

He tied the bag and just like that all physical trace of my coaxed surrender was gone.

"Don't get dressed yet."

He was still naked, and I was hoping that by his request he was hinting at more fun to be had. I stayed where I was on my knees until he reached his hand out for me to take and helped me stand.

"Such a very, very good girl. I'm so proud of your obedience."

150

"Thank you, Sir."

"You should be ready for tomorrow night now. Wouldn't you say?"

"I think so."

"I'm sure you'll be fine. In fact, I think you're going to be so much more than fine. You won't ever want to leave."

"That remains to be decided."

"Yes it does. Now come here."

He led me to his couch, sat down, and pulled me down beside him. This was awkward, sitting here in his home naked next to him. Sure, that seemed reasonable. This was awkward, but not any of the weird escapades he had put me through? What was happening to me? Though I had always been more comfortable with sex than I had ever been with true intimacy, and I certainly didn't expect to feel that with Hendrix. Maybe this was intimacy to me. Maybe it didn't have to be some prescribed list of shared experiences or touching moments. It might be that it was simply this, a Master and his obedient girl sitting next to him after a very well-played game. Wouldn't that be fucked up? To know that all this time, I had been searching for this Holy Grail, light at the end of the tunnel, be-all end-all relationship, and really all I wanted was to be owned and controlled by someone who knew what he was doing.

He moved me into a sideways hug. "Stay here tonight."

"I can't Hendrix. I need to go home if I'm going to the club with you tomorrow."

"Why? I have to go to work early. I can drop you at your place on my way."

"I just need to go home."

"As you wish, Ma'am." It wasn't said in a sarcastic way, more of an obliging acknowledgment. Either way, I knew he wasn't all that happy with my decision. I remembered his promise that he would always take me home if I really wanted to leave, so I was sure that it was bothering him that I had made my wish known against his desire. I had given him enough today, and the sensation of the moment was leaving me feeling confused, and when I was confused I ran, but I wasn't running this time. There was nothing to run from. I was only making my independence known, and I truly did want the night to myself in preparation for tomorrow.

"In that case, you can get dressed now."

"Thank you, Sir."

I located my clothes before heading their direction, and Hendrix followed because his were discarded not far from mine. We dressed in silence, and I was feeling regretful for my decision, thinking that I may have wounded him in some way. "You're not disappointed, are you?"

"Not at all, I'm just reflecting. You know you always have the final say, and, well sometimes it's hard for me to stop owning you."

I smiled because I didn't have a clue how to respond to such an unexpected admission.

He finished dressing at the same time I did. "I'm ready to take you home whenever you're ready to leave."

"Thank you, Sir. Just let me slip my boots back on and I'll be ready." I took my time putting them on just to give myself a few minutes to change my mind if I needed to, but I knew I should hold firm. I didn't want him to think I was drifting from our agreement in anyway, and if I decided to stay, I was afraid he might think it was because I would miss him. I couldn't miss him; that was out of the question. "I'm ready."

He opened the door into the hallway for me and we walked to the elevator. I felt strange in a way that I couldn't put my finger on, and I wasn't sure if it was him who made me feel that way or if I had changed something between us that caused the unease. I also wasn't sure if he was feeling it too or if it was all in my mind.

When we walked outside, the city-streaked sky seemed more ominous, a place without atmosphere surrounded entirely by buildings. I had the all too familiar feeling of suffocation, and I knew what I wanted to do, but I kept calm by assuring myself it was all in my head. Hendrix had done nothing to invoke this fear; all he had said was that it was hard for him to stop owning me, it was only our game, and I had no reason to get so mentally bent out of shape.

He opened the car door, and I climbed inside. The local jazz station he set the radio dial to aired Duke Ellington throughout the small space, reminding me of Blue Rhapsody. I couldn't fathom that only a week ago I had first met Hendrix and that I was feeling this ridiculous about possibly being suffocated by him. I shook the thought and laughed to myself, knowing that the only kind of suffocating he would be doing to me would be erotic asphyxiation.

"Hey you, over there, where are you right now?"

He broke me from my daze, and I laughed. "Honestly, I was thinking of you choking me."

He laughed, and I knew the tension between us disappeared. Whether he had ever felt it or not, it was gone for me. "You never cease to surprise me, Ashton."

"I hope I never do, Sir."

"I don't think you could ever be predictable. That's what I like about you, among other things." He looked over at me and smiled, a warm honest smile that put me at ease. Soon, we pulled up to my building, and he parked so that he could let me out of the car properly, unlike last night. When he came to my side and took my hand, I felt electricity when he touched me. Even though, sharing our bodies with each other today meant nothing in the way of commitment, it made me familiar with his skin and his touch, and I couldn't control my senses the way I could my heart. I wondered if he felt it too but when I looked up at him, into his eyes, I knew that he did.

He walked me to the lobby but didn't ask to come up, and I didn't invite him. It was time to go before my trembling body begged him to share himself with it again.

"Goodnight Ashton. I'll pick you up here tomorrow at six, and we'll have dinner like I planned."

"Yes, Sir. I would like that." I stepped into the elevator and watched him walk away as the doors were closing. When I made it to my door, I walked straight to the window. "Fuck!" What are you thinking, Ashton? This guy wants to fuck other women, he wants to share you, and he wants to control you! This is not someone to suddenly develop feelings for. It's just sex, remember? Just two bodies fucking, no love, no taking him to meet Mom. Just sex. Now drop it!

After I felt I had thoroughly convinced myself that my future love life did not depend on a handsome, voyeuristic sadist, I went to the bedroom, stripped off my clothes, and started the shower. I was ready for tomorrow. I wanted to know what I had been missing all this time, in this club that had been hiding from me the entire time I lived in Atlanta. I was ready for Hendrix to show me and to share me, but right now, I was my own woman, and I needed to be alone to remind myself of that. I had my life, my things, and my career. I was Ashton Rhodes, and I didn't need a man to feel complete. I had everything I wanted and I had earned it all on my own. No one was going to take that from me. I may lend my body and my temporary obedience to Hendrix, but he would never truly possess me.

Twelve

"Hello?"

"Hello, good girl."

"Hi."

"Everything okay? You sound a little down. I thought you would be bursting at the seams with excitement."

"Oh, I will be. I just wasn't awake yet. It takes me at least fifteen minutes to reach bursting capacity."

He laughed. "I should have guessed. I'm sorry I woke you."

"Don't be! I'm glad you called."

"So are we still on for tonight? I didn't scare you off yesterday, did I?"

"Not at all, of course. I want to go."

"Great. Is there anywhere in particular you would like to have dinner?"

"No, you can decide."

"Okay, I'll think about it and let you know. Are you sure you're okay about yesterday?"

"Yes. I'm good, really."

"Oh, Ashton, you are far more than good. You are phenomenal."

I blushed but thankfully he couldn't see that over the phone. "As are you."

"Well, then we mutually agree. About tonight, I want you wearing a dress, something short, and no panties, understand?"

"What will you be wearing?"

"That's for you to see when I pick you up, and you didn't answer me."

"Yes, Sir."

"That's better. You know, I love your obedience, but I enjoy your independent spirit too."

"If you enjoy it so much, then why are you so eager to break it?"

"The same reason that you're so willing to allow me."

"And why is that, do you think?"

"A mutual desire to experience the opposite. I know you don't see the other side of me, but in my job, I'm very eager to please my clients. I cater to them and am pretty over the top when it comes to making sure they're satisfied. You are overly independent and want to make sure everyone you meet knows it."

"And what's wrong with that?"

"Absolutely nothing. And there's nothing wrong with me wanting to bend over backwards to please my clients, but each of us wants that taken away. It's like a vacation from our usual persona, but I think it's also what is deep inside us and wants out. Have you ever studied Jungian psychology?"

"I've read a little about it, here and there."

"Then I'm sure you're familiar with his concept of archetypes, namely the Shadow?"

Who would insight a psychology lesson at eight thirty in the morning? "Yes Doctor, I believe I've read about it, but what does that have to do with us?"

"Quite a lot actually. I think your desire to be controlled, or rather to have your control taken away, is part of your shadow self, the part that you don't want to admit you have but desperately want satisfied."

"Hendrix, you amaze me. How do you expect me to grasp all of this when I haven't even stepped out of bed yet? We just talked about my bursting capacity, remember?"

He laughed. "Ashton, you know you're probably the wittiest woman I have ever met. You really make me laugh, and that's saying a lot."

I didn't know how to respond. That was the best compliment, I think, anyone had ever given me. Of course, I liked to be told that I was pretty and smart and so on, but to be told I really knew how to make him laugh, that was something personal, something secret almost. Men had such a shell around their emotions, and I had broken into his. "Thank you, but why is that saying a lot?"

"Because I don't laugh much. I'm pretty serious most of the time. Running my own business has made me very responsible, and I guess I've grown up too much, if you know what I mean."

"That's a good way of putting it, and yes I understand. I'm glad I can make you laugh."

"Me too. It's not just laughing that you make me do, it's a lot of things, but that's for another discussion at another time."

"Makes sense. Bring out Jungian psychology right now, but not that."

"Of course it does. It's easier to talk about when I'm analyzing you."

"Would you like me to analyze you then?"

"I think you would do a good job of it, but honestly, I don't want to hear it. I'm your Master, remember? I don't want any lines getting crossed."

Just like that, we were back into our roles. "Yes, Sir."

Even though he cut me off from my response, I knew I had touched on something deep within him. He needed me, just as much as I needed him, to feel like my other side was being fulfilled. We all have an inner desire, a secret self, the shadow, and he had brought mine into the light. I knew I was doing the same for him, whether or not he would say it out loud.

"I'll pick you up at six. No panties, short dress. Oh, and I want you shaved."

"What?"

"You heard me. I know you keep a nice trim, but I want to see that beautiful little pussy completely bald."

"Yes, Sir."

"Good girl. I'll see you tonight."

I hung up the phone while my mouth was still trying to form a word. I had to shave, have no panties on, and wear a short dress? God, he was great! Now, I was bursting with excitement. In fact, the less choice he gave me, the more freedom I felt.

Throwing the covers off, I planted my feet on the floor. This was going to be an interesting day, possibly the most interesting of my life, and I had a feeling buzzing in my stomach that told me, after tonight, it would only be getting better.

First things first though, food. I knew I would be far too jittery to eat much at dinner with Hendrix. Well, honestly I would be too busy making sure that I had my dress far enough down to avoid flashing everyone. The more I thought about that, the more it aroused me. Hendrix was fun, not just riding a roller coaster fun, but fun to the core. It made me a little sad to think of him as being too grown up to laugh that often. I mean, he had the ability to look at life as a game. He was using something that many people take so seriously, love, sex, dating, the whole charade, and removed himself emotionally, making it something easier to analyze, or at least something very unique, and I got to play a role. I'm sure a lot of women would detest being part of his little experiment, but not me. The more time I spent with him, the more I felt like I wasn't just a player, a chess piece, but that both of us were the board, the other people were the pieces, and we cared nothing about what went on above us.

Walking into the living room, I saw that the sun was clinging to every surface it could hold to. I caught a glint off the record player and took it as a sign that I should turn it on. I wanted to go with my instincts today, all day, so I was turning off my nay-saying, inner dialogue as of now and practicing for the free-flowing, uninhibited Ashton that I wanted present at the club. If I could get her to stick around for the rest of my life, that wouldn't be bad either.

In the record cabinet, I ran my hand along the sleeves of my most treasured memories and let my touch do the choosing. Today, it seemed I was meant to listen to Michael Jackson....wait, no, let's try that again. I wasn't ready. I started over. This time, no matter what I landed on, that was it. It was Ray Lamogntane. Much better. Removing the record from its sleeve, I placed it on the turntable and let the needle land where it wanted. I liked this choice-free feeling, and I wanted more of it, but I wanted Hendrix to provide it. The record contained one of my favorite songs that spoke of making love and all the girly thoughts that I didn't normally entertain, but never the less, I had a brief fantasy of making love to Hendrix under a tree in the rain. I pushed it back and thought instead of what we would actually be doing, fucking in a club, surrounded by other people. All in all, I felt it was a good trade-off for not having to experience heartbreak. Lovemaking was, after all, something for lovers, and lovers were something he and I could never be.

I ate a bowl of cereal while sitting on the kitchen counter. It was nine thirty in the morning and I had to fill my day. I didn't feel like running. Instead, I had the urge to write. I thought again of changing the topic, but I had already made it far enough into my current work, that backing out now would be a waste. After finishing the cereal, I jumped down from the counter, and walked to the couch where my laptop was resting. I had been working on titles and arrived at "The Art of Living with Posthumous Eras." I liked it, which probably meant that my editor would say it was too obscure, but I didn't care.

I wrote for about an hour before I changed records. This time my fingers landed on Spoon, a great Indie band that wasn't associated with Hendrix in anyway, thank God. I continued to write for the length of that album as well.

It was now almost noon, and I had made some real progress on my work, somehow dragging out of my mind worthy insight on the subject. I hadn't heard from Hendrix again, and I didn't plan to until he was at my door. My heart leapt at the thought. Each time I saw him, he managed to fill me with more and more excitement until I felt that I really was ready to burst. Well, he would see me ready tonight. In fact, I would be so ready to burst that I would probably just explode when he touched me and melt in his hands. I laughed out loud and thought of the old M&M commercial about melting in your mouth. The limitless possibilities of my dirty mind never ceased to amaze me. I might just have to remember that one liner for Hendrix. It would go well with Tracy too since I had felt her melt in my mouth. The nerves of my clit perked up at the thought. Was I actually wanting to pleasure her again? The question was already answered because I was thinking of the feeling of her soft, wet inner lips on my fingers and mouth, the sounds she made, and the way her body moved when I touched her. I still needed to imagine Hendrix there with us, even if he wasn't doing a thing. I needed the permission he gave me to want her.

Before I let my imagination run too wild, I removed the current record from the turntable and ran my hand along the shelf one last time. Massive Attack. Perfect. Sexy and transcendent. I practically had to drag the words from my mind on this go round of writing, but I managed to eke out enough to satisfy me for the day. By the time the record ended, it was nearing two o'clock. That left me four hours to get ready. I had one to shower, do my makeup, and get dressed. The other three I would probably spend pacing, trying not to bite my nails off, and quelling my nerves with red wine.

I plugged the laptop in to let it refuel itself for our next marathon writing episode and headed for the shower. As I shed my long t-shirt and panties, I thought of what short dress I could wear that would give me the most coverage but the minimum length that Hendrix would be pleased with. I tried to relax. My shoulders were tense from writing, and my ass was still somewhat sore, though the marks had become faint streaks of magenta. I was a little sad that they were no longer glaring red and purple because I was hoping to flaunt them at the club. I felt proud of them, I earned them after all, and it proved that I was a good sub. I knew Hendrix was proud of them too and proud of me, which made me feel warm in a much different way than the water. I took time shaving my legs before I gave the shaving Hendrix demanded a try. I had always trimmed myself, but shaving all the hair off was a totally new experience for me, and I hoped I wouldn't slip and lop off anything important.

Using a little body wash, I began rubbing it in between my hands, and then smoothed it onto the short layer of soft hair. As I was rubbing it in, I brushed over my clit and felt a rush of pleasure. My senses were so heightened. Even though I had tried to keep my mind off tonight, my body had been building with anticipation. I had four hours; that was plenty of time to give myself pleasure.

After removing the hair with the razor, I was surprised to see how smooth and soft the skin underneath felt. Running my hand over the new found skin, I was shocked at how the touch of my own fingers was intensified by the nakedness. I thought of how the night air would feel creeping up my dress, laying its chilled fingers on my hot, bare flesh. I ran my finger over my clit again; it was stiff with need. Didn't men typically jack off before a date so that their entire evening wasn't spent thinking of fucking? I wondered if that actually worked. Probably not, but I was going to try it anyway. Of course, sex was the point of this date, but maybe this way I wouldn't be on high alert throughout dinner. I could imagine my embarrassment if I stood up from the table, and the wetness from my arousal ran down my thigh. Hendrix would love it, I'm sure, but I couldn't bear it, especially not after yesterday. I still couldn't believe he had made me do that. What was it about him that made me do things I would never dream of? Running my fingers over my clit again, I thought of the shame he invoked in me, the horrifying feeling I had when he made me lose control of my body, right there on his floor, but mixed in with all of that, somehow, was a feeling of pure abandonment and pleasure. I couldn't deny that the pressure I felt building behind my G-spot was not enjoyable. He knew what he was doing; I would give him that. He really knew the female body, and that was attractive. I continued passing my hand back and forth, letting my finger slip slightly into the inner lips, barely touching my opening and teasing myself. There were no walls in the shower, only the curtain that wrapped around the claw foot tub, so I propped my foot up on the side of it, exposing my clit to the cascading water. My inner lips blossomed open at the touch, and I took advantage of the position, slipping my fingers inside. I began moving them in and out, letting the water take over my clit, and in no time, I brought myself to orgasm, though it was nothing like what Hendrix had given me, and that was a first. No man had ever given me such pleasure, and

I couldn't wait for him to do it again.

I felt more relaxed, for sure, but pleasuring myself did nothing to make my desire for Hendrix diminish, if anything, it made it worse. Stepping out of the shower, I caught a glimpse of my freshly shaven pussy. It did look enticing, and I couldn't wait for Hendrix to see it. I dried off, wrapped the towel around my head, and walked to the bedroom.

Super short dresses were one thing when you had panties to cover you, but this was another fashion challenge altogether. Once we got to the club, I wouldn't care much if I exposed myself by accident, but in a restaurant, I was pretty sure it would matter to someone. After careful deliberation, however, I stumbled upon something I thought Hendrix and I could both be pleased with: a tight fuchsia mini dress that came to mid-thigh. I wiggled into it, leaving off panties and a bra. Wouldn't Hendrix be proud? Bending over in front the mirror, I checked for visibility. It was good. I had to practically touch my toes before the first glimpse of my outer lips peaked out.

The towel on my head had long since detached itself during all the acrobatics I was performing to see if my dress was plausible. My slightly damp hair was a choppy mess. I shook my head, putting it into place and using product to keep it there. My makeup tonight would be dark and sensual, smoky eye shadow and a deep rose lip color. I assumed the club would be rather dimly lit, and I wanted my eyes to stand out to Hendrix. The look he gave me right before he came made me more aware of how gorgeous his eyes really were, and I wanted to persuade him to look into mine, so I could study them further. I needed the courage, however, to hold his eye contact, and hopefully that would come the more accustomed to being around him I became.

My shower had taken longer than planned, thanks to the curiosity over my new look. My dress choices proving to be more than I had originally thought took up quite a bit of extra time as well. So much so, that I now had only an hour to wait. I slipped on a pair of black high heels with peep toes to showcase the black nail polish, which also matched my fingertips. Taking one long, last look in the mirror, I inspected myself from head to toe. Happy with what I saw, I vowed not to come back into the bedroom to second guess my choices. I flipped the light off and went back to the kitchen for the wine.

My phone rang, startling me in my already hyper state. "Hello?"

"I know I'm early, but I'm out front. Can I come up?"

"Sure." I poured a small glass of the wine and downed it. Damn, he had good timing.

The intercom didn't buzz, and I wondered if he was still in his car, but there was a knock at my door. I looked though the peephole. They let him up without calling me, so now they definitely thought we were dating. When I opened the door, Hendrix stepped right in, grabbing me by the back of my neck, shutting the door with a kick of his foot, and pulling my face into his. He kissed me with so much intensity that I felt like I could die in that kiss, never coming up again for air or food, just that kiss. His tongue licked along the inside of my lips as his fingers gripped tighter to my neck, pressing me harder into his lips. I had never been kissed this way. Placing my hands on his shoulders, I let one slide to the back of his head and ran my fingers up his neck and into his hair. He kissed me deeper, devouring my mouth with his, slipping his tongue over mine, and almost bruising my lips with the pressure of his. Time stood still. I breathed him in; I tasted him. My body was trembling with desire for him to reach under my dress and feel the newly smooth skin, what I had done for him, what I wanted to do to him, everything for him.

He let my head go and looked at me. Most likely, I looked like a drunk teenager with a smirk and half-opened eyes. I was lost in my thoughts and the remnants of the moment.

He spoke to me in that low sexy growl his voice became when he was aroused. "You taste like wine, such a turn on."

"Then I'm glad I drank it before you walked in."

"Mmmmm. You're a fantastic kisser Ashton."

"I was going to say the same thing about you, but you took the words right out of my mouth, along with all of my air and composure."

"You're welcome." The devious smile had returned. Although, now it was exaggerated by the look he had in his eyes, taking in my attire for the first time. I knew he hadn't stopped long enough to get a look at me when I opened the door. "I see you obeyed me, such a good girl."

He took my hand. "Turn for me."

I made a quick turn for him to see me from all angles.

"Bend over."

I turned to face the window and bent forward but not far enough to touch the floor.

"I want to see it. Lift your dress."

I began to stand, so that I could turn and face him.

"No, right where you are. Lift your dress, just enough to give me a glimpse."

Returning to a bent position, I lifted the dress to the middle of my ass. I could feel the air touch my newly shaven skin and I wondered if he could see that my outer lips were swollen with desire.

"You have no idea how hard it is for me not to fuck you right now, but I want to make you wait. I want to see that beautiful pussy swell all night until I finally give you what you want, but don't worry. It will be difficult for me to keep my cock down, knowing that you have that bare, wet, and swollen pussy waiting under there for me."

"Do you want to see it from the front?" That was a risky question. I knew it was a bit out of line, but I didn't think he would mind.

"Are you tempting me Ma'am? Do you think that you'll be able to persuade me before I'm ready?"

"Actually, I don't. You've proven that you have a will of steel. I only wanted you to see that I behaved."

"I appreciate the offer, but I know that you behaved. You

wouldn't disobey me."

"How can you be so sure?"

"Because you want to obey me, and you do what you want."

"You're right about that."

"I know I am."

"Yes, Sir."

"You're probably wondering why I'm early."

"Yes, that and how you got up without my approval."

"Oh, your doorman recognized me and opened the door for me."

"Great, I'm glad I pay extra for my security. I'll make sure to let him know not to let in any questionable characters."

"Oh, I'm questionable now?"

I laughed. "When have you not been?"

"You are walking quite a fine line tonight."

I gave him my best sideways glance with questioning eyes. "Am I?"

"You know you are, and you want punishment."

I was just being cocky now and placed my hand on my hip. "Maybe I am."

"Then your punishment is that I will not punish you."

My hand dropped and my smirk faded. Damn, he turned it back on me again! "I'm sorry, Sir. I won't question you anymore."

"Tell me you're my slave."

"I'm your slave."

"Tell me you'll do whatever I ask of you tonight, without question or hesitation."

I wasn't sure that I could promise that because I had no idea what I was getting into. "I'll try, Sir."

"No, you'll do it."

"Yes, Sir."

"Now, as I was saying, I'm early because I want to get to the club shortly after they open so I can go over some things with you and because I wanted to see if you were already pacing the floor waiting for me."

Dick. I flashed him a sly smile.

"I know you were Ashton because believe it or not, I was doing the same."

Not a dick. I gave him a genuine smile.

"Believe me. I'm very excited to get you into this club. I have wanted to bring you since we met, remember?"

"Yes, Sir, of course."

"Do you feel ready for it now?"

"As much as I'll ever be."

"Tracy will be meeting us there at eight."

"Okay. I'll be glad to see her."

He put his arms around my waist loosely and looked down into my eyes. "Will you? You want to play with her again, don't you?" His smile grew as he said it.

"Yes, Sir." I turned my eyes to the floor.

"Don't be ashamed of it. It turns me on. I want to see you please her again."

"I would love that, Sir."

"I know you will. You're my dirty girl. Tell me, who do you belong to?"

"You, Sir."

"Say my name when you answer. I want to hear you say it. Who do you belong to?"

"Hendrix."

"Say it again."

"Hendrix."

"Tell me you belong to me. Say my name."

"I belong to you Hendrix." My heart jumped at the sound of the phrase.

"And you belong to me, Ashton. I'm your Master."

"Yes, Sir."

He looked into my eyes, but I don't think it was the makeup that drew him in. He looked beyond that, beyond everything I kept on the surface.

Placing his hand underneath my chin, he tilted my head upward so that I couldn't avoid his eyes. "You belong to me Ashton Rhodes, for as long as I say you do."

I liked the sound of that. "Yes, Sir." Maybe I didn't after all. It all depended on how long that was. He removed his hand from my chin.

Smiling, he dropped the domination for the moment. "Are you ready to go to dinner?"

"Yes, Sir."

"Get your things."

I gathered my small purse that surprisingly held everything I would need, including my phone. He offered his arm to me, a perfect act of chivalry. Instead of feeling like an accessory when I wrapped my arm through his, I felt that I belonged there and that I could never belong anywhere else. For me this meant trouble, but I swallowed the knot in my throat and walked out the door.

Thirteen

"The real man wants two different things: danger and play. Therefore he wants woman, as the most dangerous plaything."

—*Friedrich Nietzsche*

The bright green pea coat I wore came down to just below the dress, but the combination of cold air and no panties still left me shivering.

"I'll turn the heat up as soon as we get in the car."

"Thank you. I'm freezing."

"Have you never shaved there before?"

"Not completely. None of the boyfriends I've had asked me to. They liked a little bit of hair. I think it was a reminder of the '70s porn mags they probably found in their parent's bedrooms."

He laughed. "You're most likely right. Just so we're clear, me wanting you shaved has nothing to do with some kind of prepubescent fascination."

"Good to know, but why did you want me to shave?"

"Because I can see your arousal more clearly. I can see the wetness and the swelling of your lips, your clit getting harder, and all without touching you."

"Okay. I can understand that." I did understand it, and as always, the reasoning behind his requests, or rather commands, made me respect him all the more. In fact, I felt that I not only respected him, but that I was learning to trust him and that was a huge step for me.

"Ultimately, it doesn't matter if you understand or not because you would have done it either way, correct?"

"Yes, Sir."

When he placed me in the car, I felt the lingering warmth of his drive over. I watched him walk in front of the hood, thinking of the conversation we had at my door. In the split second it took for him to reach the driver's side, I told myself to relax. It didn't mean anything, and I was blowing it out of proportion. I couldn't help the fluttering feeling in my sternum that threatened to creep up my throat and come out as words. The worst flaw in my character was an insatiable desire to fall in love, but I vowed then and there, as his scent once again filled the car trying its best to penetrate my will, that I would never confuse what Hendrix and I had with love. No matter how much he made me feel like a woman he was dating, he was my Master and not my boyfriend.

"Pull your dress up, so that your pussy is on the seat. I want to see your ass pressed into it too."

I lifted my dress. The seat was cold but not freezing. Instant chills came over my thighs as soon as my warm, wet outer lips touched the leather. He turned to me then, looking me over and grasped my chin in his hand, not forcefully, just holding me there like a possession to be looked over.

"You are the most obedient woman. Thank you for this."

I had no idea what he wanted me to say in return, so I stayed silent and instead gave him a shy smile. He let go, obviously pleased with my lack of response, and started the car.

"I decided that I shouldn't give you a choice in where we were eating. We're going to L'Art de la Seduction."

I liked the sound of him speaking in French, even if it was just the name of a five star restaurant. I had never been there and was impressed and happy to be going with Hendrix. It was across town, so we had a longer ride together than we ever had before. He turned the music up, a college station on his presets. I was possibly more thrilled by the fact that he had an Indie station programmed on his stereo than I was about him taking me to a five star restaurant. That's a requirement of mine though, good listening skills, and that didn't just apply to conversation.

"Put your hands on your knees for me again, like you did yesterday."

When my hands found their positions, Hendrix moved his

right hand to my thigh and began trailing his fingers upwards. His touch was so light that it almost tickled but with enough pressure to stifle the urge to laugh. He moved all the way up, running his fingers over my outer lips.

"You did a wonderful job of shaving, very smooth."

"Thank you, Sir."

He parted my lips, inserting one of his strong fingers into me, moving it in circles and gathering my wetness, and then removed it. Putting it to his lips, he smeared it across them and left it there for a moment. I could see it catching glints off the street lights, and I found myself aching for him to lick it off and to taste me. We came to a red light. He wasted none of the few seconds we had before it changed, and leaned over to me.

"Lick it off my lips."

I leaned into him, remembering the kiss we shared in my doorway. Extending my tongue just enough to graze his bottom lip and turning my head to the side, I licked it and pulled his lip into my mouth with a small amount of suction. His breath was suspended for a moment, but he regained it and kissed me again, not as long as before, because a car began honking its horn behind us. The green light forced us to separate.

"Good girl. I like for you to taste yourself. You're very good at pleasing me, and I'm sure you're going to satisfy other people tonight as well."

Nervousness was setting in. I had been focusing so much on what Hendrix had been doing since he walked in my door that I had almost forgotten about the sharing. It still excited me, but the reality of it was sinking in, and I got a feeling like you might have before going bungee jumping. You plan for it for weeks, but when the day comes, your body turns to nerves and nausea.

"I hope so, Sir."

"If I tell you to please them, you will. By the way, you can pull your dress down now. We're almost there. "

"Yes, Sir."

We arrived at the restaurant and were greeted by valet parking attendants, one of them opened my door, but I sat there frozen. If I turned my legs to exit the car, he would be able to see up my dress. Hendrix was quick to come to my aid and held his hand out for me while also doubling as vision impairment. I was relieved that he didn't make me climb out without him.

As we walked through the elaborate double doors, I was so awestruck that it left me speechless. It had the style of The International Café but scaled up about twenty notches. A tall man in a tuxedo greeted us at a podium, and Hendrix gave his name, "Larson."

"Yes, Sir. We have a table ready for you."

We waked by a baby grand piano, black and shining under the dim chandelier light. The bar was ornate with a faded mirror backdrop and three bartenders, all wearing starched white shirts and black vests. I was thankful for my choice of dresses when I saw how elegant everything was. That was the joy of a mini dress: it could be incredibly classy or provocative. For tonight, I needed it to fulfill both purposes.

Our table was along a dark purple damasked wall with a high back semi-circle booth which enclosed the patrons in a sort of shell, complete with a sheer black curtain that could be drawn closed across the front of the table. There were six tables like this all touching the other, but all creating their own private space. Instantly, I knew that Hendrix had requested this booth specifically.

The host extended his arm, holding the menus, and gestured at the booth. "Is this suitable for you, Sir?"

"It's perfect. Thank you."

I smirked, perfect indeed. He let me sit first. I carefully slid to the left of the center, and he followed, sliding in right beside me so that our thighs were touching.

He spoke low enough that the host couldn't hear him. "Don't think you're going to get too far from me tonight."

"No, Sir." The host handed us our menus and told us our waiter would be over shortly.

"Is there anything you will absolutely not eat?"

I had to think, but I wasn't sure if this question was a double entendre. "I don't like veal."

"Good to know. You may hand me your menu."

I was confused, but handed it over. "Yes, Sir."

"I will tell you what you can eat, what you can drink, and as you already know, what you can wear. I own you tonight Ashton. Do you oppose?"

"No, Sir." It was exciting. All of my choices had been taken from me and I was free to enjoy, instead of decide. A waiter, wearing all black, appeared before us.

"Good evening, and welcome. May I bring you a bottle of wine or a cocktail from the bar?"

I didn't speak but smiled at him politely. Hendrix answered for both of us. "We'll have a bottle of your best Cabernet, and we would like to start with a cheese plate. Thank you."

"Very good, Sir. I'll have that out to you momentarily."

When the waiter walked away, Hendrix reached over and drew our curtain closed. I could still see everything going on, but the scene had been obscured, as well as the view in our own space, the only light coming from the candle in the center of the table and a small amount that leaked through the fabric from the rest of the restaurant. I watched the light dance around him, moving across his face and hands and guiding me to the parts of his flesh I wanted to touch. He reached for my hand then and brought it to his lips. I thought he was going to kiss the back of it, but instead, he licked the tips of my first two fingers, pulling them only slightly into his mouth, and removed them but didn't let go of my hand.

"Play with yourself, but don't let me see any sign of it on your face."

I knew it. "Yes, Sir."

Reluctantly, I took the fingers Hendrix had moistened and reached under the table and under my dress. I ran them over my clit and felt my outer lips. I was wet and wanting, but I kept my face complaisant.

"What do you feel? Describe it to me."

"What if someone hears me?"

"Ashton, don't question me. If you're so worried, just whisper it to me."

"Yes, Sir." I said it aloud, but what I said next was whispered into his ear. "It feels wet, hot, swollen, and smooth."

He didn't bother whispering. "Good girl. Now, tell me what you're thinking."

I could play this game. Words were my specialty. I put my lips to his ear and could smell his dark cologne on the skin of his neck. I suddenly wanted to bite him there and move my lips down his collar bone and onto his chest, but I refrained. "I'm thinking, Sir, that I want to feel your cock inside me. I want you to make me come, and I want you to fuck me right here at this table." He gripped my thigh hard. Victory was mine.

"Do you really want to be fucked right here?"

I took my chances that he wouldn't actually do such a thing because we would most likely be arrested. "Yes, Sir."

"Finger yourself, but don't you dare make a sound or a face that could give you away."

"Yes, Sir." I slid my fingers inside myself and hoped that the wetness wouldn't leave a mark on the booth. It was more difficult than I had anticipated to keep my composure. The waiter made his way to the table, and I started to remove my fingers.

Hendrix's voice growled, "Don't you dare."

Great, the waiter would have to slide the curtain aside somewhat to put the bottle and plates on the table. I took a napkin and draped it across my lap.

"Here you are, Sir." He uncorked the wine and poured a small amount into Hendrix's glass. This was agony and excitement at its best. I thought of getting caught and was turned on by the fear it gave me. I wondered if Hendrix was conditioning me to associate fear with pleasure, like Pavlov's dog salivating at a bell, but I was salivating in a different region and my bell was whatever fucked up situation Hendrix dropped me into. He drank the wine and approved. The waiter filled my glass. Luckily he wouldn't be able to see my lap because even though I had the napkin hiding my hands, he would have been able to see the movement underneath. He took the cheese plate from his tray and sat it near me. "Have you made a decision from the menu, Sir?"

"Yes, the lady will have the vegetable lasagna, and I will have the lavender rubbed chicken."

"Excellent choice Sir, would you or the lady care for a salad?"

"No, thank you."

"I'll have it out to you shortly. In the meantime, enjoy the wine and cheese."

"We will. Thank you."

The lady? I felt like I should call Hendrix the tramp, but it also made me realize that a man treating a woman like his possession was not anything close to a new concept. Maybe the reason a large group of society looked down on the idea of sadomasochism or domination/submission wasn't because it was strange but because it brought back an era of female repression. Maybe that's why there were those of us that craved being dominated and to place a man back into the role his carnal instinct desired. It allowed us both to play our genders to the extreme or, for those men that preferred being dominated by women, to contort their roles for the same effect.

He said it low but very commanding, "Take that napkin off your lap immediately."

"Yes, Sir. I'm sorry."

"You're not yet."

Yes, that tone in his voice was becoming a bell for me. The nerves between my legs twitched at the thought of him raining belt licks down on my ass and to see him in that position again, wielding pain and pleasure in the same hand.

174

"Drink your wine."

"Yes, Sir."

"You may have three pieces of the smoked Gorgonzola, two of the Swiss, and two of the sage cheeses."

He wasn't kidding about delegating. "Thank you, Sir."

"Do you still have your fingers inside yourself?"

"Yes, Sir."

"Pull them out and show them to me."

I removed my two fingers and presented them to him. "Pick up a piece of the Swiss cheese, making sure that those fingers touch it entirely, and then place it in my mouth."

"Yes, Sir." Picking up the cheese, I pressed my fingers to it. He opened his mouth only when I was right next to his lips. I had never fed a man before, and the act of putting food on his tongue was intensely erotic. It was like feeding a wolf, knowing that he could bite at any moment, but giving him a peace offering in the hopes that he would lick my hand instead. I placed the cheese on his tongue and removed my fingers. He closed his mouth around it and chewed slowly.

He smiled. "You make it taste even better."

I looked up into his eyes. He may not have bitten me, but he was looking at me like I was all the better to be eaten. "Thank you, Sir."

I ate the cheese he had allowed me to put on my plate and almost finished the wine. Hendrix sat drinking from his wine glass and I found myself watching the liquid touch his lips, and longing for the feeling of my tongue touching them. To anyone that could see us, we were just another couple enjoying a perfectly normal dinner together.

Thankfully, he didn't ask me to touch myself again because the waiter was back at our table with the food. He refreshed both of our glasses of wine before setting our plates in front of us.

"Is there anything that I can bring you?"

"No, thank you. We have everything we need."

"Enjoy."

Everything we need? That was a loaded statement.

"Cut your lasagna in eight equal parts, then you may eat five of them."

"Yes, Sir."

"Tell me if you like it or not. I want you to be happy."

I took a bite. "It's great. Thank you."

"I just want you to know that I've never been able to take it this far with anyone else. In case you were wondering."

I honestly hadn't thought about it. I was doing a great job of pushing my jealousy instinct aside. Hopefully it would withstand the club. I didn't know what to say to Hendrix, and I didn't think he was searching for an answer, so the moment passed. However, I still wanted to let him know that I was appreciative of what he was doing. I stopped eating and looked over at him. "Hendrix, can I say something?"

He put his fork down and acknowledged me. "You may, and that's very good of you to ask."

"I wanted to tell you thank you, for everything. I enjoy playing with you."

"You're very welcome, but I'm not playing."

"Okay, not playing with you then. Experimenting, whatever you want to call it, I enjoy it."

"I'm glad. Now stop talking and eat."

I didn't answer, but instead focused on the food that I doubted I could finish. However, because I hadn't eaten anything since the morning, I did my best. As I was taking a drink of wine, I felt his hand on my knee. The sudden touch startled me, and I almost choked as I was swallowing.

"Did I frighten you?"

"A little."

"You should be ready for me to touch you at any time."

"Yes, Sir." He slid his hand farther up my thigh and gave it a squeeze, which made me think of his fingertips grabbing my hips as he fucked me. I was ready to leave, I wanted to get to the club, I had to have him again. I noticed he wasn't eating anymore. "Sir, I can't eat anymore. May I stop?"

"Yes, you may."

He wasn't looking at me when he said it. He was focused on his hand on my thigh.

"Reach over and feel how hard I am."

I looped my arm under his and gently touched the visible bulge in his lap. He was solid and ready, but his face gave nothing away. The waiter had terrible timing and appeared at our table.

"Would you care for the dessert menu or an after dinner drink?"

"No thank you. I'll take the check."

"Yes, Sir. I'll be right back with it." He gathered our empty plates and offered to box our uneaten meals. Hendrix declined, knowing that we would never have access to a refrigerator in time to save them. I didn't remove my hand from Hendrix's lap, and he never moved his from my thigh. It was like a dare, who would move first or would the waiter notice? I'm sure he didn't, but it was a fun idea.

After he walked away, Hendrix took his hand from me and put his arm around my shoulders. "Keep rubbing it."

"Yes, Sir." He leaned over and put his lips on my neck, right below my jaw and nibbled on the bottom tip of my earlobe. He found one of my most erogenous zones and chills filled my arms and chest. His cock grew harder when he saw how he had excited me. His breathing was picking up and with his hand that was resting on my shoulder, he began to lightly stroke his fingers up and down the back of my arm and pull me into his chest.

He whispered in my ear, "Will you fuck me at the table, like you wanted?"

Damn it! I shouldn't have baited him. "I would love to, but you know I can't."

"Then you shouldn't say things like that to me because I'll do it."

"How?"

"I can set you on my lap. We don't have to move."

"No, I'm sorry. I can't do it."

"You're lucky I won't make you, but be warned. Don't ever tease me about what you're willing to do, or you'll get what you ask for, whether you like it or not."

"Yes, Sir."

"Take your hand away."

I moved my hand from his lap, and he sat up straight, took the last drink of his wine, and told me to finish mine as well. In a few more minutes, the waiter presented him with the check. I didn't even want to know what it cost him. I could imagine by the décor that it was far more than what I was accustomed to paying at my café.

The waiter nodded at Hendrix. "Thank you, Sir. Have a wonderful evening."

"Thank you. We most certainly will."

I turned to Hendrix. "Thank you."

"My pleasure. Now make yourself presentable to get out of here."

I straightened my dress and tried to focus on anything but how turned on I was. Hendrix got out first and stood at the edge of the table, holding his hand out for me. I reached the end of the booth, and he helped me up. Thankfully, I didn't feel any liquid run down my thigh, but when I began to walk with him, I could feel my outer lips rubbing together. They were more swollen, and I felt the wetness between them. I looked at Hendrix, checking for a sign of his own arousal, but he masked it well. Since I was looking, I took the time to take him in. He was handsome as usual, but even more so tonight. He was wearing a charcoal gray three piece suit, a dark blue shirt, and light blue tie. His shoes were a cognac brown to match his belt. It was amazing to me how stylish he could be in anything he wore, whether it be this or jeans. He looked over at me and smiled, catching me eying him.

"What are you looking at?"

"You, Sir."

"Do you see something you like?"

"I like everything I see." He smiled and held his arm out for me to take once again. I gladly clung to it as he led me outside. The valet had already pulled the GTO to the curb. Hendrix shielded me while I tried my best to sit into the low bucket seat without exposing myself. The car was warm from the valet having it running. Hendrix paid and got in.

"Now, are you ready for the club?"

"Yes, Sir. Very ready."

"So glad to hear it. Remember I wanted to tell you a few things?"

"Yes, Sir."

He drove away from the restaurant. "Some things you need to know are that anyone wearing a blue wristband has been recently tested for all STDs, so we're only going to be playing with them. When was the last time you were tested?"

"Only about three months ago, and you're the first person I've been with since my last boyfriend."

"Good, and I just had my test last month, so we both know we're free to explore."

"Yes, Sir." That made me happy. I was concerned about how those questions would be addressed.

After a few turns, I recognized the scenery. I saw the club as we got closer. There were valets here as well, but Hendrix chose to park his car himself and he pulled into the parking lot where I experienced my first real punishment. I didn't expect the club to have valet or seem so formal. It made me think differently about what the inside would be like. My heart was pounding, and my legs were feeling very unsteady. At the restaurant, I drank just enough wine to keep from hyperventilating, but maybe a bit too much for steady footing. I took Hendrix's arm and we made it to the entrance. A well-dressed man opened the door for us, I inhaled sharply making the breath catch in my throat.

$\mathcal{F}ourteen$

We walked into Club Inhibitions to find Tracy standing with two beautiful women. He would instruct me on what to do with them and how to please them. As his submissive, I would do whatever he wanted of me.

When we approached them, he put his arms around Tracy. I should have been jealous but not here, not with our arrangement. We weren't lovers. We were players in a game he devised, and emotions were not part of the agreement. He wasn't going to ease me into this; he was going to throw me in and hope I learned to swim. Holding his hand out for me, he directed Tracy and me, along with one of her friends, to a large couch at the center of the room. As a voyeur and an exhibitionist, the center was the only place he would want to be. Here, it was certain that no one could miss us. We would be everyone's entertainment and no one's second glance.

Even though it had only opened an hour ago, there was already a crowd of people writhing all around us, drenched in glistening sweat and some crying out in passion. A man next to me feverishly drove his cock into the woman splayed out before him. Two women were fondling each other's breasts with one of them sliding her hand in between the other's thighs, while a man watched them and stroked himself.

The club was dimly lit. The music was loud, but not as loud as a typical dance club. In fact the dance floor, to our right, was quite empty except for a couple of women pole dancing for men that were sitting at tables in front of them. There was a long bar near the entrance, and it seemed that there were several rooms yet unseen because I watched couples disappear through double doors to our left. We stood on a round, elevated floor, with two steps leading up to it, positioned to rise just slightly above the rest of the club. Plush black couches were placed around the circumference of the platform, but we stood in front of one half of the large couch that encompassed a column in the very center, so that the seats faced outward from it. It was more than I had expected, and I was much more turned on than I imagined I would be.

Hendrix invited Tracy and her friend to sit down. I was facing them and he stood behind me, holding me against his body. He ran his hands from the tops of my shoulders, down both arms, then moved to my stomach, smoothed over my hips, and landed at the bottom of my dress. He lifted it just enough to show them only the very bottom of my newly shaven area.

"Isn't she beautiful?"

Tracy answered, "Very. She looks even better shaved. Don't you think she's beautiful, Lindsey?"

The thin woman with dark brown hair I had never met, apparently named Lindsey, answered her, "Yes, Mistress, you weren't kidding. She's hot."

Hendrix pulled me tighter into his body, letting me feel how hard his cock was underneath his pants. He lifted my dress up further, revealing my hips and ass, and turned me around to face him. When I looked at his face, I could tell that he was more than proud that he had brought me, that I was a prize, and that didn't make me the least bit uneasy. He wrapped one arm around me and grabbed the back of my hair with his free hand. Pulling my head slightly sideways, so that my cheek was turned to his lips, instead of kissing me he whispered in my ear. "If at any time you want to leave or you don't like what I'm doing, all you have to do is say the word."

He let go of my hair, and I raised my head to face him, whispering back, "Yes, Sir."

"Bend over for them and wrap your arms around my waist."

I looked past him and saw other people turning to see what we were doing. Bending forward, I wrapped my arms around him.

Hendrix began his commands. "Inspect her Tracy."

I felt Tracy's fingers on me, parting my lips just enough to get a look at how wet I was.

"She's so excited, Hendrix."

"I'm sure she is. I've been toying with her all night. Haven't I, Ashton?"

"Yes, Sir."

"Look at me."

I lifted my head and saw that he was gazing at me with that same questioning look he had the first night with Tracy, silently asking me if I was okay. Knowing after the reminder he had already given me, that this would be the only time he would hesitate before doing whatever he pleased. I gave him a slight smile of approval.

He took the cue and began his instructions, "Tracy, I want you to finger Ashton. Get her even more excited and get her ready."

I wasn't sure exactly who I was being readied for. For Hendrix, for Lindsey, another man? The fear of the unknown could become an addiction for me, like an adrenaline junkie. I found myself craving the anticipation and the flutter it caused in my heart.

Tracy inserted a finger inside me, softly running it in circles and opening me further. "Lindsey, would you like to touch her?"

Wait? Tracy was asking Lindsey if she wanted to touch me? I was confused. Lindsey didn't answer to Hendrix? Did that mean that Tracy could make her do whatever she wanted to me and that wasn't under Hendrix's control?

"If that's what you wish, Mistress."

So that was how it was going to be, a triangle of ownership with me as the toy? I knew I agreed when Hendrix told me he would make me do things to other women and let them have their way with me, but I thought he would be commanding everything that went on. I wasn't sure I liked the idea of Tracy being in charge.

"Now, let's not forget ladies that Ashton is mine. I'm allowing you to play with her, but ultimately what I say goes. Lindsey, you may obey Tracy, but if she crosses any lines, you will stop, understood?"

"Yes, Sir."

Lindsey answered Hendrix the way I had to. I guess that meant she was a submissive, not only to Tracy, but to anyone. Tracy must be dominant because she didn't answer Hendrix in that way. I was beginning to understand the dynamics and assumed that I should answer Tracy the same way Hendrix had ordered me to before.

I was still grasping Hendrix around the waist, feeling Tracy dip her finger in and out of me, lightly flicking the lips at the opening, teasing them to open further.

"Lindsey, lie down beneath Ashton, and watch what I'm doing to her."

"Yes, Mistress."

I looked down as Lindsey crawled beneath me. She turned on her back so that her head was under my hips. Hendrix did nothing but stand as my anchor, though I could see the definition of his cock through his pants as it become larger. I suddenly had the urge to take it into my mouth and hoped this was what he had in mind.

"Lindsey, lick her."

"Yes, Mistress."

Lindsey sat up but remained facing away from Tracy. Leaning back on her hands and tilting her head back, she made a long stroke with her tongue from my clit up to Tracy's finger.

"You may please her, Lindsey, but only with your mouth."

"Yes, Mistress."

Tracy continued to probe me, sliding her finger in and out very slowly, moving it from side to side, and opening me to receive more. I couldn't believe how open I felt, having only one finger inside me. I was glad that Hendrix was permitting me to watch what Lindsey was doing because seeing her lap at my pussy made the intensity of the moment even greater. She traced the same trail as before with her tongue, several times, before resting at my clit. She sucked at it and flicked her tongue in quick strokes, stiffening it. I was becoming lost in the feeling, no longer focusing on who was doing what or caring that there were people all around us. I was learning to focus on the feeling. However, I was very aware of Hendrix's cock at the height of my face. I looked up at him and was surprised to see that his full attention was on me. He was watching my body respond to them and enjoying his own body's response.

He looked into my eyes, knowing exactly what I wanted and unfastened his belt. "Suck it."

"Gladly, Sir."

I unzipped his pants. He looked even larger than I had remembered. I was worried at first that he may choke me with it and push it too deeply into my throat, but I opened my mouth and let him in. He entered slowly, teasing my lips, while I let my tongue run underneath his head, coaxing his cock further into my mouth. He continued to tease me, popping the head of it in and out, wetting it, and making saliva drip from my bottom lip. I had never felt more aroused with Tracy now pushing more fingers inside me and with greater force, Lindsey eagerly sucking and licking at my clit, and Hendrix fucking my mouth. It was euphoric.

"You may come, Ashton. You're going to come many times tonight. I don't want you to hold back."

As soon as he gave me the permission, I let go. I moaned as loudly as I could, though it was muffled by his cock. Lindsey sucked hard at my clit, and Tracy rammed her fingers all the way to my cervix, bringing them in and out quickly and forcefully. I sucked him harder, wanting to feel his come in my mouth and wanting to know that I pleased him, but I knew he would never let himself go this early, not when he had so much more in store.

I opened my eyes, and for the first time realized just how many people were paying attention to us. There were at least ten, male and female, standing around us, unashamedly staring, and some even touched themselves or were touching each other. In this moment, I felt no shame or exposure. To see how turned on our display was making everyone else drove all concern from my mind.

Tracy was easing up with her fingers, now only toying with

me, and Lindsey was gently licking Tracy's fingers at the point that they were entering me. Hendrix withdrew his cock somewhat to go back to the teasing he had done at first, and then it left my mouth entirely. I rested my neck and looked down to Lindsey again.

Tracy's knees came to the floor as she removed her fingers from inside me. Lindsey turned around to face her as Tracy spread my legs wide and ducked under my hips to take Lindsey by the back of her head and press Lindsey's face to hers, kissing her and licking my juices from her lips. Through all the movement, we had managed to move further away from the couch where Tracy had been sitting. This allowed spectators to get closer to us. I could only see their shoes and Tracy pushing Lindsey down to lie back on the floor. Tracy lifted Lindsey's dress, exposing her unshaven pussy, which allowed the collection of moisture to easily show itself off as it clung to her hair. She spread Lindsey's legs apart, lowered her face between her legs, and began to please her with her mouth. Tracy left her ass, which was directly below my hips, turned up in the air, and I watched as she lifted her skirt over her hips, exposing herself to the crowd. I could now clearly see Lindsey's face beneath mine and watch the look of pleasure come across it while Tracy was licking her. All the while, Hendrix kept his hands on the sides of my arms, securing them to his waist. It was like being shackled, especially so now that my legs were so widely spread. I could only imagine the scene people were witnessing from behind me.

Hendrix took one of his hands from my arm and raised it. Though I was unsure of what he was doing, I didn't look up to find out. Still watching Tracy pleasing Lindsey, I noticed several pairs of men shoes get closer. This was it. He had called men over to us with what I assumed was that same confident beckon of his hand, plucking the ones he approved of out of the crowd. Although it gave me comfort to know that Hendrix was making the decision, I was still nervous as to what was going to happen.

I saw one pair of shoes become knees, as the man dropped to the floor behind Tracy. I couldn't see above his thighs, but I quickly saw Tracy's body jerk forward and continue a rocking motion as the man on his knees, I assumed, fucked her. Lindsey began to come when she felt the response of Tracy's body being

186

rammed forward. She moaned and grabbed Tracy's arms, practically sitting up as her body convulsed with the waves of pleasure. I heard the man behind Tracy groan and could tell that he was coming. As soon as he slowed down, he got up. Before I could process what was going on, another pair of men's shoes came forward, but this time he remained standing. I felt no hint of penetration, only the sudden and hard slamming of a cock into me. Whoever this man was, he wasn't fucking me for long because he was going at me hard and fast, trying to come as soon as possible. I was sure he had already been close while he was watching us. I continued looking at Tracy and Lindsey, who were now switching places. Tracy laid on the floor, and Lindsey perched over her, burying her face between Tracy's thighs to begin lapping at her clit. Lindsey arched her back, leaving herself exposed as Tracy had done. The man who was fucking me pulled out and dropped to his knees. I saw Lindsey's body jolt forward as he began pounding her with the same force.

A man's voice I didn't recognize spoke. "Can I eat her, Hendrix?"

"You may."

The man fucking Lindsey began licking eagerly at my inner lips, then driving his tongue into my opening, licking all around, and sucking at my clit. He moaned loudly, pulling his face away from me, gave a few shuddering jerks into Lindsey, and stood up. Hendrix's cock was still out and so rock hard that I wondered how it kept from bursting the skin open, but he never touched it, and he didn't allow me to either, which only made me want it more.

Lindsey still had her ass in the air, softly licking up and down Tracy's pussy when I saw another man walk up. I felt myself being impaled again, hard and fast like the last, and it took him only seconds before I felt his shudder and pull from me. Tracy began to climax under Lindsey's mouth, and I was surprised at how much watching them turned me on. It was intensely arousing to see women please one another. They were so skilled and gentle.

Hendrix was addressing people I couldn't see. "You may please her, but no anal play."

Thank goodness. I wasn't sure if I could handle that yet.

A woman's shoes approached next. She came down on her knees and lowered herself to Lindsey. I assumed she was pleasing her with her mouth, but I wasn't sure. Lindsey began to breathe heavy, her face still pressed between Tracy's thighs, but she soon lifted her face and drove three fingers into Tracy while she began to come under the mystery woman's mouth. All the while, she moved her fingers in and out of Tracy with force. Tracy began to moan, and her body shuddered with yet another orgasm. I felt awkward now because I wasn't being touched at all, though I was immensely enjoying watching the trio of womanly pleasure beneath me.

Hendrix put his finger on my chin, lifting my face to look up at him. "Do you enjoy being used?"

"Yes, Sir." It was the truth. I did like the idea of being an object of pure sexual gratification. I liked not knowing who was behind me, only feeling them relieve their sexual tension with me or one of the women below me.

"Suck on my cock."

"Yes, Sir." I took my hand from his waist and grabbed his cock, positioning it in my mouth. Making deep long strokes, I took all of him in to the back of my throat. The nerves of my clit began flinching at the thought of having his hard shaft between my legs, instead of in my mouth. The anticipation of being fucked at any moment was making my heart pound with excitement. I felt like a common whore, not caring who would fuck me, just wanting the sensation. I didn't dislike the feeling either, which confused me because I had never considered myself a slut or anything of the sort.

I heard heels walking away, and I assumed it was the woman who had been pleasuring Lindsey. It was frustrating not being able to see what was happening beneath me, but I wouldn't have traded the vision for what I was doing to Hendrix. He was gripping my arms now, and I knew he was moving closer and closer to the point of no return. He had incredible willpower, but the mind could only control so much. His body would bend eventually.

Fingers slipped inside me and I couldn't tell if they were male or female, only that I felt more satisfied. They began to flick against my inner walls and then move in and out. A tongue began lapping at my clit. I assumed it was Lindsey because she had been at the right height to do so, if she had been able to lift her mouth from Tracy. I was practically choking on Hendrix's cock now. As I devoured it, I imagined it inside me instead of the fingers, but he pulled from me suddenly and grabbed it with his right hand. He squeezed it hard and put his thumb on the tip. I could see it twitch with the desire to release, but he stilled it and actually managed to hold his composure. Maybe I was wrong. Maybe he was the one man who could control even his orgasms. He was miraculous in every way. I looked up at him and saw the pain in his face at having to stifle the pleasure he obviously desired. He tucked it back into his boxer briefs.

"That's enough for now. I have more to do with it than come in your mouth."

"Yes, Sir."

"You may rest your neck and continue watching."

"Thank you Sir."

I looked to the floor and saw that Tracy and Lindsey had left. The fingers inside me belonged to a man. He was seated on the floor and turned sideways while a woman sucked his cock. He withdrew his fingers from me, and the woman stopped what she was doing to suck my juices from his fingers. They stood up then and walked to the couch where she moved to her knees in front of him and continued to suck him.

As soon as they were out of the way, a man began to fuck me, just as hard and fast as the last. Once again, he was not looking to satisfy me in anyway, only to get himself off. He grabbed at my hips, pulling me into his cock. I held tighter to Hendrix, who didn't seemed concerned about the man's grip. He was driving his cock so hard into me that I thought I would break. His hands tightened on my flesh as he pounded deeply into me. I felt him shutter and heard him moan as he came, and then he quickly pulled out. Not even thirty seconds passed before I was fucked again. How many men were lined up behind me? Hendrix knew, and he would tell me later, but for now I just enjoyed it. I enjoyed the feeling of different cocks pleasing me, though they weren't trying to do so. These men were using me to come, nothing more. The man finished and walked away.

Hendrix's voice rang above the dull roar in the club. "Stand up."

It was hard to move. I felt locked in my current position. Hendrix helped me by holding my arms. My legs felt numb, and my lower back was aching. When I finally stood, Hendrix kissed me as passionately as he had at my door, he slid my dress down for me. It amazed me that a man could be so attracted to a woman that he had just watched be fucked by a line of men. Did he not think of me as disgusting? Was he trying to degrade me to make sure he would never want to date me?

He was smiling brightly. "Good girl."

I was surprised to see that no one stood beside him. Though beyond him I could see that there were many more people in the club than there had been when we arrived.

"Where did Tracy and Lindsey go?"

"I don't know. They play alone and with a variety of others here. I don't keep tabs on them. Would you like a drink?"

"Yes, Sir." He offered his arm to me, and I threaded mine underneath to display his dominance once again. We walked to the bar, and he ordered a glass of red wine for both of us.

"Let's sit down for a moment."

I laughed. "I'm not sure that I can."

His devilish smile again. "What's the matter? Sore? I can't imagine why."

"Funny."

"I can be. Did you enjoy it?"

I was a little reluctant. If I fully admitted to how much I

actually did enjoy it, would that be more than he wanted? Did he want me to keep a hint of disdain for the things he had ordered done to me? I was over thinking as usual. Of course he wanted me to be honest, and I had no reason not to be.

"Yes, Sir. I did."

"I'm very glad. I was a little worried how you would react to not knowing what was going on, but I hope you know that I would never let anyone hurt you, and I wouldn't let anyone I didn't know fuck you."

"Thank you, Sir. I assumed you had chosen the people you approved."

"I did, and just so you know, they were all wearing protection. I wouldn't allow them to fuck you without it."

"Thank you, Sir." It made me oddly happy to know how much he watched over me and protected me, even when he was letting me be violated by other men.

"I noticed that you didn't come with any of them."

"I couldn't."

"You couldn't, or you wouldn't?"

"I guess I wouldn't Sir."

"Why is that?"

"Well, one, you didn't tell me I could, and two, I didn't feel comfortable coming with them."

"I like that Ashton, but you are allowed to get pleasure from others. I want you to. I did say that you would come many times tonight, didn't I?"

"Yes, Sir. I'm sorry."

"It's forgiven. I know this is all new to you. I'm not upset. I just wanted to make sure that you were being pleasured."

"Oh, I did have pleasure. I enjoyed it really. I don't have to come to get pleasure."

"Then I'm happy you had fun."

"Can I ask you a question?"

"Yes, but I can't promise I'll answer."

"I understand. Why do you like watching other men fuck me or other people, in general, pleasure me?"

"I love to see how you enjoy it. I love being the spectator, knowing that you are doing it for me. You're allowing me to protect you, even though you're in a situation that could be very violating or even violent. You have to have complete trust in me to allow that, right?"

"Yes, Sir."

"Would you come here alone and bend over, offering yourself to anyone who wanted a quick fuck?"

"No, Sir." I answered a little too quickly and resentfully, but the thought of it disgusted me, which was odd.

"Why not?"

"I wouldn't want to do it alone. It's not really appealing."

"Don't you find that interesting?"

"Yes, Sir. I think I'm understanding this all a little more."

"I think you are too. I'm proud of you."

"Thank you, Sir. Are most of those men who fucked me here with other women?"

"All of them. They're all married and their wives were watching."

"Are you serious?"

"Of course."

"How are their wives not jealous?"

"They were getting plenty of pleasure themselves. A couple of them were with other men at the time, but they were still watching. The others were focusing only on what their husbands were doing to you, and do you know what else?"

"What?"

"Their husbands never took their eyes off their wives when they were fucking you."

I didn't know what to say. I couldn't fathom how that would make me feel. I wasn't sure I could stand watching Hendrix with another woman, and we were the furthest thing from being married you could be.

"Surprised?"

"Very."

"I told you Ashton. You're in another world here. In my opinion, these people have it figured out. They don't own each other. They love each other. They enjoy watching each other receive pleasure and give it. It changes nothing between them. Their love is just as strong or stronger because of it. It's kind of a test, if you want to look at it that way. Relationships can be broken by this just as easily too. My ex and I are case in point. It depends on the couple and what they want out of their partnership. I want to know that I can watch the person I love receive pleasure from other people because that way I know that they're with me for much more than the idea of ownership. I want to feel that our love goes far beyond the pleasures of the flesh."

I wasn't sure how to respond. I felt that I could fall in love with him then, just for the magnitude of what went on in his mind. How much he thought about love and what it meant to him. I hadn't seen this side of him before, and I liked it.

"Want to get out of here?"

"Really, you mean you're not going to do anything?"

"I've done all I came here to do tonight."

"Then, yes, Sir. I'm ready if you are."

We finished the wine, and he stood to pull my chair out for me. Placing his hand at the small of my back, he led me to the front of the club where the doorman told us to have a good night and released us back to the normal world.

It was freezing. I had left my coat in the car, and the temperature had dropped considerably since entering. We must have been inside longer than I thought because the streets were not as thick with traffic as they had been when we parked. Hendrix put his arm around my shoulders and pulled me into him, trying to give me some warmth. He wasn't wearing his suit jacket either, or I'm sure he would have given it to me in some old movie gesture kind of way. We made it to the car quickly, and as soon as he opened the door, he grabbed my coat from the backseat and held it open for me to slide my arms into. I sat down and Hendrix hurried to his side.

He started the car right away and got the heat going, though I knew it would take some time to warm up. I wrapped the coat tighter around my chest, tucking myself tightly into my body, like a bird trying to fluff my feathers. Hendrix took his jacket from the back and draped it across my legs.

"You can wear your jacket. I'm sure you're cold too."

"Hardly as cold as you are. You're barely wearing a thing."

"And whose fault is that?" I chattered when I said it, but I had meant it to come out in a laugh.

"I'm sorry. I didn't realize it would get so cold tonight. I should have picked you up at the door."

"Oh, no, I'm fine Hendrix. I'm just teasing, really."

"Sure, your chattering bottom lip and fetal position really convince me. Come here."

He put his arm around my right shoulder and moved me into him, which was a bit uncomfortable over the stick shift, but I barely noticed once he had both arms around me, smashing me to his chest.

"The car will warm up in a few minutes, and the heat will kick on full force."

I didn't care if the heat ever came on, not now. In fact, I hoped that it wouldn't. I could let him hold me like this all night. For someone who usually despises being held down, that was saying a lot. With my head on his chest, I peeked around his arm to look out the windshield. I saw the lights of the parking lot and remembered that night, the punishment he had given me, and the excitement I had felt. Tonight was just as enthralling, but in another way. Both instances shared the familiar quality of public display. I had never thought of myself as someone who would be into exhibitionism, but being made to display myself by Hendrix, it felt okay. More than okay, it made me a bad girl, a whore, but being that I was forced to do these things, I could retain my dignity, even though I relished the bad he created in me. In the parking lot, I felt belittled at first, then defiant, and finally at peace. In the club, I felt no defiance, no belittlement, but only trust that Hendrix would never hurt me nor allow anyone else to. I was discovering more and more, that the depth of character I had so admired in the beginning was only the tip of the iceberg. He was intelligent, sure, but so much more than that. It seemed that he could read me and that he knew what I needed more than I did. The thought scared me because I liked to think that I knew myself pretty well. Maybe I was wrong. Maybe all the failed relationships had led me to him, to someone who could pull the me out that was hidden somewhere deep inside, behind walls and protection that I couldn't shake on my own. What would I do when he was done with me? Could I still be this new person, this woman who wanted a Master and could I ever find someone to love and that would love me back in this way? I felt tears coming to my eyes, so I turned my head into Hendrix's chest and breathed in his scent.

"The heat's on now. It won't be long before you're nice and warm again. Then we're leaving here and going back to your place."

I whispered into his chest, "Yes, Sir."

"You're not falling asleep, are you?"

"No, Sir."

He loosened his grasp and lifted me from his chest. Looking into my eyes, he could see that I had lost my excitement and that it had been replaced with something, though he would never figure out exactly what was going on in my mind. I would never let him.

"We're going back to your place because it's my turn to have my way with you, wouldn't you say?"

I perked up at that. "Yes, Sir!"

"Go back to your side and buckle up."

I sat up and moved back to my seat, thinking of how he was going to have his way with me.

"You have no idea the things that were running through my mind when I watched you being used like a whore. Tell me, could you tell the difference between the men? Did their cocks feel different, or did you even notice after a while?"

"I could tell slight differences, but you know it's true. It's not so much about the size. It's all in technique."

"And did any of them have skills you enjoyed?"

"Honestly, I don't think they were using any skills on me. They were just using me."

"You're right. So you don't think they cared whether you liked it or not?"

"No, Sir."

"And do you think that their wives would care as much about them fucking you, if they didn't even care if you were pleased or not? You know, they didn't even see your face, and they barely touched you."

"Probably not as much as if they were making love to me."

"Exactly. So you do agree there is a difference between making love and sex for the sake of pleasure?"

"Yes, Sir."

"And you enjoyed the experience whether you loved them or not, or even knew them for that matter?"

"Yes, Sir."

"Do you think that makes you a bad person?"

"No, Sir."

"Unfortunately, society has made a lot of women feel that way. I'm glad that you don't. I personally think it's very unfair that a man is congratulated for his sexual conquests, but a woman is chastised for them."

"I agree."

"You will never feel chastised at that club, you can be free to explore your sexuality, the things you've never done, and anything you fantasize about, but you have to do it under my command. However, I would like to know what you fantasize about, so I can take it into consideration and possibly make it happen."

"Thank you, Sir."

"You're such a good girl."

He looked over at me and touched my chin, turning my head gently toward him when he said it. I had grown quite fond of him calling me a good girl, though at first I had found it demeaning. Most of the things I would find demeaning were now becoming an erotic catalyst for me. At other times, it was a feeling of accomplishment, as if something so simple as responding to him gave me the pride of completing a tremendous task. I felt that he was breaking me, taking me down to a base level where the most mundane things were becoming exciting. In a way, it was like being stripped bare of my former experiences and having him form me anew. I realized that by doing so, he would own me more completely. He would be the only one I could look to for explanation and guidance within this new perspective. On one hand, I cherished this realization, but on the other, I was fearful of my existence without him. I had never felt tied to a man or in need of one. I was firm in my reliance on myself and committed to a life of my own making, but with Hendrix, I felt exposed in a way that allowed me to feel more, like my thick skin had been removed to reveal the nerves, and I was feeling everything as if it were the first time.

I thought of what Stephanie said about me experiencing all of these things under his control and not being able to keep myself from developing feelings for him. She was right, but so was I. I would never let myself beg for him to be mine. I would not allow myself to be hurt or to cry over him. After all, I knew what I was getting into from the very first day. He may take a great deal of control away from me, but I still controlled the part of me that loved.

We arrived at my building, and on the trip from lobby to ninth floor, I felt my body trembling with anticipation. I knew that when we walked through my door, he would ravage me. Even though I had been fucked more in one night than I ever had in my sexual life, I wanted him with all my being. When he took me, it would be something different. It wouldn't be love of course, but it wasn't just sex either. It was him waiting all night to fuck me instead of touching any other woman at the club, him wanting me to be his end goal, and my confirmation of obedience, my reward and his.

Fifteen

There was no light on in my living room. The only source of visibility was the city from a distance. I took a step towards the floor lamp, but Hendrix grabbed my arm, pulling me into him. His lips were full of want. When he pressed them to mine, I could feel the toll that his earlier restraint had taken on him. While still kissing him, I managed to shimmy out of my coat and let it fall to the floor.

He finally let me breathe. "Don't you want me to get a shower?"

"No, I want you just the way you are, dirty, used, and sore."

Ecstasy, the way he talked to me, the way he looked at me and touched me, the way he wanted me. It was something beyond desire; it was staking his claim. He released me but took the bottom of my dress in both hands and slowly peeled it from mid-thigh to my hips.

"Open your legs."

"Yes, Sir."

I parted my legs only slightly because my muscles were already so sore that I thought I might collapse if I took a wider stance. Hendrix reached a hand between my thighs and slid his fingers inside me, moving them around for only a moment before he brought them to his face and inhaled deeply.

"I love the smell of other men on your pussy. It's still your scent, but a man knows when his woman has betrayed him. A faint smell of something that doesn't belong, cologne? Soap? The unmistakable smell of a condom? Whatever it is, it's a scent of a bad girl who's let someone else fuck her. How many times I wonder, or better yet, how many men? Would you like me to tell you? Would you like to know how much of a whore you are?"

He was being so cruel with his words, but I was dripping

with desire. How could I ever play coy when my body gave me away? "Yes, Sir."

"Four. Your beautiful, tight pussy had four different cocks in it tonight, and it's going to have one more."

He lifted the dress above my breasts and lowered his mouth to my nipple, taking it into his mouth gently, trailing his hands down my sides to rest at my hips and then down over my ass to the backs of my legs. In one fluid motion, he wrapped his arms around my legs and stood up, throwing me like a rag doll over his shoulder. Hanging like I was, my dress fell over my head, and I let it slip past my shoulders onto the floor. He didn't head for the bedroom, but across my living room to the wall which was all window. I knew what was coming, just as he had described. With the lights off throughout the room, I knew people wouldn't be able to see, at least not any detail. If someone looked from the street and concentrated, they may be able to see flesh reflecting light, perhaps steam collecting on the glass, but nothing more.

Hendrix slid me down the front of his body, my breasts and head finally upright, the blood draining back to the proper places, but he didn't let me get my bearings. As soon as my heeled shoes hit the floor, he pressed his chest onto me, moving me back into the window. The cold glass bit at my back, making me inhale sharply. While unfastening his belt, he said nothing but looked into my eyes, that contact which seemed all the more intimate after what had happened to me tonight. Although I liked the feeling of being used, it made me more aware of how I needed acknowledgment. I realized I was coming to crave the after-effect of our little games. Whatever he did or had others do, Hendrix would be there to soothe me when it was over. He was my tormenter, yet he became my comfort. It was like Stockholm Syndrome of a sexual nature.

With his belt open and waving from his hips, he unzipped his pants and removed his cock. I assumed that he was so pent up from holding back that he would use me as the others had, for relief. His fingers dug into the flesh just below my ass as he lifted my legs from the floor and wrapped them around his waist. His body pressed me hard against the glass, I felt him enter me, but instead of beginning to furiously pump away, he simply let himself absorb the sensation. His lips were at my neck, which he began to lick, moving his tongue from my shoulder to my jawline and into my mouth. He kissed me hungrily. I could feel the drive of his body to conquer me, culminating in his mouth on mine. His hands released me, but his body held me aloft, impaled as I was on his shaft and pinned to the window. He flattened his palms to the glass, inches from my head, so that I was wholly encased by him. I heard his hand slide on the fogging glass, as he drove his cock so deep I thought he might come through the other side of me. With his mouth still covering mine, he began to move his hips, slowly pulling back and then entering me at the same pace. I draped my arms around his neck and no longer felt the cold glass, only the warmth of him, the amazing sensation of being weightless, held up by his body and the constant motion of his cock with its measured strokes.

He released my lips but found my eyes, giving me a lingering glance before pressing his forehead to mine. The window had a cloudy halo surrounding us for inches outward in all directions. The heat emanated from us like a small fire that had been touched by a sweeping breeze. Condensation formed on my lower back, and I could feel rivulets of moisture trail their way to the curve of my spine. Hendrix's breath was staggered and hot at my chin, floating onto my chest. His hips began to move faster, so I locked my legs, securing myself around his waist.

"Come for me, Ashton. I know you wouldn't do it for the others but do it for me."

"I will, Sir."

"Good girl."

He leaned back enough to lift me off the glass, quickly catching me in his arms. Now I was held only by him, no solid surface to rely on, only his powerful body. I trusted him entirely. He grabbed my sides, just underneath my arms, and began to move me up and down on his hard shaft. I was poised above him so that he had to turn his eyes upward to see my face. I looked down to find his. The soft bit of light coming in from outside, highlighted the look in his eyes, and his face relayed only desire, but it was desire to please, not desperation for his own satisfaction. I couldn't fathom the strength he had by just looking at him, but moving me the way he was proved that he had unwavering stamina in more ways than one. I had never been taken this way. He drove deeper as I imagined what we looked like or if anyone on the streets happened to see into my window. I didn't care. I let my head tilt back as he brought me down then lifted me up to the tip of his shaft before he drove me down again. The orgasm hit me, tripping the fuse that ran from between my legs, up to my head, striking a match in my body and setting my nerves on fire. I couldn't scream, my voice was caught in my throat, and I could only let my body go, knowing Hendrix was holding me. I felt suspended above him with no surface to ground me. There was only the motion he continued, lifting me effortlessly and the waves of pleasure so strong that it made me feel helpless. He pulled me down, moving his hands up to my shoulders, pinning me in position, which triggered another orgasm almost as strong as the first. I looked down at him. He was staring into my face, smiling, knowing that he was giving me something new. I couldn't understand how a man could please me better than myself. How did he know exactly what to do and when?

He dragged his hands from my shoulders and down until he was cupping my shoulder blades and using his forearms to support my weight, so that I reclined into them. My legs were numb, but I ignored them. I was sure he was ignoring a much more painful strain.

When he could tell my pleasure had subsided, he turned away from the window to head towards the couch, but before sitting down, he popped my shoes off and let them fall to the floor. After unlocking my legs, he unbuttoned his pants to give me better access to all that he had to offer, but never let his cock leave me. He sunk into the couch with me astride him.

His low growl returned. "Fuck me."

"Yes, Sir."

Now, I could show him what I could do. I put my hands on the back of the couch and dug my knees into the cushion. I began to rock forwards and back, grinding my hips to work his shaft as deep as it could go.

He didn't take his eyes from me. "Yes, just like that."

"Yes, Sir."

I moved faster, harder, and it hurt me, but I didn't care. I wanted it to hurt. I wanted to feel the soreness this night had caused me. I grasped his shoulders, using them to pull myself into him. His arms were around my waist, hands holding the shelf of my hips. He began to move me then, taking control, changing the motion, lifting me up slightly, and pushing me back down.

"Move like that."

"Yes, Sir."

Pushing down on his shoulders, I lifted up from my knees and slid up his shaft slowly, then teasingly I slid back down. Moving up again, this time I lingered at the tip, coming down only an inch and lifting up again, before slamming all the way down.

"Mmmmm,yes, yes, that's it."

That breathless low growl of a voice was as much of a turn on as his body. His demeanor dripped with sex, and the best part was that he could follow through with that outward appeal and prove it. While I enjoyed the fullness of sitting on his cock, letting it swell, I felt his need for me to move, so I stayed longer, seeing if I could outlast him. I wanted to move back and forth, to grind him again, but I waited.

"Don't stop! I want you to ride me."

I smiled. That's what I was waiting for, a command. "Yes, Sir."

I began to move up and down, faster now with no teasing. His hands squeezed my waist tighter, his face straining and head tilting back. He brought me down onto his cock and then back up, taking control now. He surprised me by sliding to the front of the couch and dropping his knees to the floor, lying me on my back. He loosened his tie and unbuttoned his shirt quickly, slid the tie over his head and tossed it aside, then tugged the sleeves down and over his wrists with force, revealing his tattooed chest and arms. His body kept my legs spread as he placed his hands by my head and began fucking me hard and fast. He was slamming into me, no composure left, the animal I had seen before. The cool calm he exuded was lost, and I was the only one who got to see him this way, at least for now. His eyes were closed tight, teeth clenched, and the muscles of his chest straining to balance his body above me.

He growled and shouted, "Fuck yes!"

Pulling his cock from me, he began jerking it with his hand, and rose up on his knees so that I could see him more fully. His body was wet with sweat and abs flexed. He moved forward on his arm, still balancing himself, and dropped his head in defeat as his come shot out fast and hot all over my chest and stomach.

He didn't move yet. "Damn, Ashton. I come so hard with you."

I looked up at his face so close to mine. "I'm glad."

He kissed me softly. "You are one of a kind."

"How so?"

"Everything about you."

He sat back on his heels and held his hand out for me. I lifted my head from the floor, but he did the rest, bringing me to a sitting position.

"Let me get you a towel. Where can I find them?"

"I'll get it, don't worry. Stay here."

"Are you asking me or telling me?"

"I'm sorry. Would you please stay here right now, Sir?"

"Yes, since you asked so nicely, I'll stay. I like seeing my come all over you anyway."

"Me too."

He sat down, leaning his back onto the couch, while I stayed immobile. The soreness was setting in. I knew I would be in for it tomorrow, but it would be worth it. We sat there for a moment not speaking, just catching our breath.

He let out a slow breath and ran his fingers through his hair, slicking it back with the sweat that had accumulated. "Ashton, what am I going to do with you?

"Isn't that for you to decide, Sir?"

He laughed. "Such a good girl. In fact you're so good, I think you might fear me punishing you."

"No Sir, I don't. I just want to make you happy."

"You make me more than happy, Ashton."

Why did that statement make me think he was leading us down a road we couldn't go? I sincerely hoped he wasn't going to start teasing me with emotion. That was not a game I would play. My face must have conveyed my thought.

"Did I say something wrong?"

I tried to play it off. "No, why?"

"You look a little lost. Though I certainly wouldn't blame you after all I've put you through tonight."

"All you've put me through?" I laughed. "Do you think I'm regretful? Because, believe me, I'm not. If anything, I'm lost in reenactment scenes."

"Fair enough. I'm so happy that you enjoyed this. You don't know what that means to me."

"Care to enlighten me?"

"Yes, Ma'am. I can tell you that I've had more fun tonight than I ever had at the club, so thank you for that. And thank you for trusting me that means most of all."

"You're welcome." I could have done better than that, but all the words going through my mind sounded far too meaningful.

"What are you doing Friday?"

"I don't know, Sir. What am I doing?"

Hendrix smiled. "You'll be coming to my place."

"Yes, Sir." He was right. I was being much too complaisant. I needed to spice things up. This wasn't my normal demeanor, even though I loved pleasing him. He did admire the stubborn side of me, and I wouldn't want to deprive him of it.

"Now let me clean you off. I need to get going."

My heart sank. I wasn't ready for him to go, but it was late, and I wouldn't dare ask him to stay the night. "I'll grab a towel."

He reached for my shoulder and pushed down to keep me from standing, and instead stood up himself. "No, you stay there. I'll carry you to bed."

As much as I loved the idea, I had to shower before I could sleep. "That won't be necessary Hendrix. I have things to do before going to bed."

"I said, I'm carrying you to bed. Everything else can wait."

"I need to shower."

He stooped quickly and snatched me up from the floor, holding me in his arms honeymoon style. With my head draped over his left arm and my legs hanging off his right, I wrapped my arms around his neck and looked into his still glistening face.

He met my gaze. "Don't even think about challenging me right now."

I answered him in my best sarcastic voice, "Why not?"

"You know, if I wouldn't have just mentioned you not wanting to be punished a few minutes ago, I might think you were sincere, but now I know what you're wanting, and guess what? You're not going to get it. That is your punishment. You should have learned by now that your schemes will always backfire on you."

I was too defeated to argue. He was right of course, which is what I liked about him more than anything. I couldn't fool him, and he loved to call my bluff. "I'm sorry, Sir."

"That's better. Now I'm taking you to bed, no more protests."

I had never been carried like a damsel in distress. Even though no one would mistake me for a damsel and the distress was sought after, it felt comforting. I was a small animal in the arms of a predator, but I welcomed the attack, and as defeated as my body felt, my mind reeled with the possibilities of what he could do to me next.

Walking to my bedroom, still holding me in his arms, he gently laid me on the bed, naked, still covered in his come, which was now dry. He sat on the edge of the mattress with his right arm still tucked under my back. I couldn't say a word because the only one I knew at the moment was 'stay'.

"You can't imagine the pleasure you give me, allowing me to own you. I'm sure any other woman would call me a sadistic prick or tell me I was majorly fucked up, but not you. I can tell you that I enjoyed letting other men use you to get off, then fucking the Hell out of you myself, and that I'm equally aroused by carrying you to bed because you've been fucked so much tonight you can barely stand. And that's what I want from this, the freedom to explore without judgment. I hope I give you that as well."

"Stay." I couldn't stop myself.

He leaned down and kissed me sweetly on the forehead. "I can't."

"Why?"

"I think you know the answer to that."

I was sure our answers wouldn't match, so at the risk of total embarrassment I decided not to push the issue further.

"Yes, Sir." It was for the best. I might wake up with my head on his chest and my heart broken.

"Goodnight, my good girl. I'll lock your door on my way out."

"Thank you, Sir."

"I'll call you, and we'll make plans for Friday."

"Okay, goodnight Hendrix."

He slid his hand from my back and stood quickly, as if he had to leave before changing his mind. I wanted him to turn around, but I knew I would regret it in the morning. When he left my room,

I heard him gather his things and dress, then without a word, walk out the door. I was left with that obnoxious quiet you feel when you've been surrounded by noise for hours and then all of a sudden, silence.

Sixteen

What was that expression? Rode hard and put up wet. I had no doubt what that meant now. All I wanted was a shower, a quick one though because I was starving, and I was anxious to hear from Hendrix. I thought maybe I should text him and apologize for asking him to stay, instead of waiting on him to call. What was I thinking anyway? Thankfully, I didn't beg, and he didn't explain. Maybe I shouldn't mention it, and he would chalk it up to oversexed delirium.

I mulled it over while I sat at my window, which now had a much better view than before. The city didn't even exist because all I saw was Hendrix's body pressing mine into the glass. I felt like my association fee should be raised because of the upgrade.

I stopped deliberating and picked up my phone to send a text. "I just wanted to apologize for asking you to stay last night."

He responded quickly. "Ashton, it's perfectly okay. I asked you to stay at my place, didn't I?"

He did, and I stayed. Why was it such a big deal I had asked him? I was making this into something it wasn't. "Yes, Sir. But can I ask then, why couldn't you stay? You told me you thought I knew the answer, but I have to be honest, I don't."

"Because I had to work this morning."

There had to be more to it than that. He could have easily said that he had to work early and needed to be at home to get ready. "Why didn't you just say that?"

Far too many minutes went by without an answer. Maybe I went too far. I shouldn't have questioned him. I should have just left it alone. Why do I always push? I stood up and walked to the kitchen. I no longer wanted to reminisce at the window. I wanted to get out of the condo. I needed to run, maybe not just a few blocks, but away for a few days. I pissed him off, and now he was going to call it off. We were done. I started to get angry or sad, I couldn't tell, but then I heard the chime of my phone.

"Because I didn't know what to say. It wasn't just work. I needed time to think. I still want to see you tomorrow. Are you okay with that?"

It's never a good sign when a man tells you they need time to think. Even though Hendrix was   different than any man I had ever known, when it came down to it, he was still a man. I shouldn't automatically assume that what he had to think about was negative. After all, I had been doing quite a lot of thinking myself. "Yes, Sir."

"Good Girl. I would like you to come over to my place tomorrow to talk about our arrangement."

"Ok."

"That is not the correct way to respond to me and you know it."

I didn't want to respond the way he would like. I was crushed.

"Ashton?"

"Yes, I'm here."

"Why aren't you answering me?"

I decided that I would give in, but only a small amount, just enough to get to see him on Friday.

"I'm sorry, I'm just tired."

"Get some rest today. I'm sure you're feeling pretty run down."

"I'm doing okay....a little sore."

"I hold you in high esteem Ashton. You don't break easily."

"Haha, very funny."

"Call you later?"

"Yes, Sir."

"Now that's my good girl."

Had to think about what? That thought was going to nag at

me all day until he called and explained, if he ever would. He might not explain at all until tomorrow and I couldn't handle that. I had to stop this. It didn't matter what he had to think about because whatever it was I could deal with it. We weren't lovers, he couldn't hurt me by cheating on me or leaving me, but maybe he could hurt me by falling in love with someone. It was inevitable if he and I continued our game that one of us would eventually meet someone and want to stop. If we didn't, we could never have any real commitment to another person. I plopped down on the couch, put my head in my hands, and began to cry. I couldn't help it. I didn't want to... In fact, I detested crying and feeling like a fragile girl who couldn't deal with rejection or whatever the fuck this feeling was. Sobbing into my hands, the tears pooled in my palms. I could never be this person with Hendrix. I never wanted him to see me this way. To him, I was a fun loving woman who was up for just about anything, who would give herself freely and openly to her Master. I was not a sniveling mess on the couch who didn't even know why she was crying.

"Get yourself together, Ashton!" I wasn't usually a self-talker, but something had to break my concentration. The sound of my own voice cutting through my sobs brought me back. I wiped my eyes with the bottom of my t-shirt and lied back on the couch. The thought of Hendrix and I eventually committing ourselves to other people really stabbed me somewhere I wasn't aware. I couldn't allow myself to be a part of his life when that happened. I had to be vigilant and watch for the signs he would start to display: avoidance, lack of conversation, and his kisses would surely become less passionate. This was not going to be easy. Since sex didn't have to be part of his idea of love, we could easily still go on with that before he told me he wanted out. I could see the scene in my mind, him fucking me the way he did last night, so much intensity, and then when it was done he would tell me nonchalantly that it had been great to find someone he could be like that with, but he was in love now and wanted to have a real relationship. He would leave, and I would feel helpless. Who was I when compared with love? I was a toy and nothing more.

Sitting up, I reaffirmed in my mind that I would not allow myself to be hurt. I would not allow myself to run after him and beg him to be with me. I barely even knew him. How could I tell if I loved him? God, I hated being a typical girl! Fuck this stupid insecurity and genetically programmed need to be in love! I really felt like I had gone off the deep end because I started laughing. Laughing at the drama I had somehow just managed to conjure in my mind and at the idea of being in love with Hendrix when I barely knew him. This was a new experience. It was exciting and scary, and Hendrix was my only still point. Of course I felt attached and he had already told me that was okay. Why was I getting so bent out of shape?

I stood up feeling like I was once again as normal as I ever dared to be and that my life was just as it should be, with or without Hendrix. I was fine before he came into my life, and if he left, that was his decision to make, nothing I could do about it anyway, so let him go. This was only a game and I was having fun, great sex with an attractive man, meeting new friends with benefits, and so many things I would probably never had experienced if it wasn't for Hendrix. He was my toy too, I told myself. I was using him for the same satisfaction, and if some kind of situation like I had imagined ever truly arose, well I could just as easily be the one falling in love and telling him I was done being his good girl. Get over yourself, Ashton and, get back to your life.

Seventeen

"Disobedience is the true foundation of liberty. The obedient must be slaves."
—*Henry David Thoreau*

When Hendrix called hours later, I had almost forgotten that I was waiting on the phone to ring. I was sitting in my favorite, long Fleetwood Mac t-shirt, typing on my laptop and was so sure of my place in all of this that I no longer needed confirmation from him, and I was ready to let him know it. He wouldn't be able to hurt me, because I was going to be the one that made the decision.

"Hello?"

"I'm on my way home. Can you talk for a bit?"

I wasn't going to play his game today. "Sure."

"I'm sorry, what?"

"I said sure."

"Is that how it's going to be? Trying to get into more trouble?"

"No, just answering your question."

"Inappropriately, and acting coy about it is not going to sway me."

"Look Hendrix, I've done some thinking too, and I think I'm letting you get away with treating me with less respect than I deserve."

His voice lost its dominance, instead he sounded truly concerned. "Why would you think that?"

"Because being submissive to you is a huge break in character for me, and I don't think you appreciate that."

"Well, you're wrong. I absolutely realize that and that's what I appreciate about you."

"Sure."

"I think you're just wanting punished and you're bating me. You're doing a good job and I almost fell for it, but no more. You're mine, remember?"

"No, I'm not bating you. I want to make sure that you understand what part I play in this."

"Oh, I'm well aware of what part you play."

"We're in this together, but I feel like I'm being...." My sentence was cut short by a knock at the door.

"Hold on Hendrix, there's someone at my door." I put the phone down to my thigh and looked through the peephole. Fuck! He was here, and I was in trouble. I could see it in his face. He had his arms folded and was looking directly at the door, knowing that I could see him. I wasn't sure what to do, so I raised the phone back up to my ear.

"Why are you here and why didn't you tell me you were coming over?"

"Open the door."

"No, this is what I'm talking about Hendrix. It's not fair that you think you can do whatever you please all the time. It's one thing when we're playing, but right now it's not okay."

"Open the door."

"You can't just boss me around when I don't want you to."

He still didn't raise his voice, only kept it low, but in a commanding tone, "Open the door, Ashton."

"No."

"Ashton, if you really don't want this, then say the word."

I wanted to. I really wanted to hurt him. I didn't know why exactly, but I just wanted to put my foot down and take a stand against him. I was tired of being pushed. We stood there for a few seconds, neither of us saying a word. He was waiting for an answer, but I couldn't bring myself to go through with it. I wanted to see him, but I wanted to make him understand.

"If I let you in, what then?"

"Open the door."

"God damn it, Hendrix! Can't you just act like a normal person and tell me what the fuck you want?"

"That's it!"

He burst through the door. I jumped back so I didn't get knocked out. I stared at him in disbelief. He was not the debonair gentlemen anymore; he was dressed in jeans and a t-shirt, speckled with tarnish, smelling of sawdust, and wearing a ball cap. This was a side of him I don't think he ever intended on showing me. I tried to act strong as I had been on the phone. "What the fuck do you think you're doing? You broke my lock!"

"I'll fix it, but I have to fix you first."

He pushed the door back into place and latched the chain lock so it would stay shut. I moved to the kitchen, trying to get closer to sharp objects. "You're scaring me, Hendrix. I don't appreciate it."

"You should be scared. You've disobeyed me, questioned me, and in not so many words, called me an asshole. If you think that you're not going to be punished for this, you don't know who you're dealing with. I know you mean everything you're saying, and I'm pissed off. You don't talk to me that way. You are not to disrespect me. Is that understood?"

I was trembling, but I couldn't stop looking at him. I had never found him more attractive than at this moment. He was sweaty, dirty, and standing up to me. He was intimidating, but I was determined to get my point across. "You need to understand that I don't want to be ordered around all the time."

He moved closer, which made me back up, right into a corner. Grabbing my hair, he forced me to turn around and pushed my upper body down to the counter top. Since I was only wearing my t-shirt, I knew he would take advantage of that. He raised the shirt angrily and began to administer hard, sharp slaps to my ass. He yanked my panties down, uncovering the tender skin and spanked it harder. My ass was burning and I was crying. I sobbed his name. "Hendrix, please stop."

He leaned down to me and whispered in my ear, "All you have to do is say the word and I will." He gripped my hair tighter, twisting his wrist, pulling my head back to his shoulder. He let go and wrapped his hand around my throat. I couldn't breathe, and when he continued to hold, I started to panic. My vision was becoming fuzzy at the edges and my hearing was dulled. I was going to pass out. This wasn't funny.

He released his hand at the last moment before everything went black. I got my voice back. "What the fuck do you think you're doing?"

He grabbed my arms and pulled them behind my back, holding them solidly with one of his hands and using his forearm to keep me pressed to the counter top. With his other hand, he covered my mouth tightly. "Shut up!"

I tried to protest, but all I could do was mumble and thrash my body against him, pressing my ass to his hips, trying desperately to move him back. He bent down to my head again and whispered in that low growl I loved. "All you have to do is say the word and this will all stop." He uncovered my mouth only long enough for me to say the safe word, but I didn't.

"That's what I thought, you little bitch. As much as you want to make me out to be an asshole, you fucking love it. So what the fuck do I think I'm doing? Is that what you want to know? Well, I'll tell you. I'm putting you back in your place and teaching you a lesson you won't forget."

He was still holding my mouth closed. I was crying, fighting him with my body, but he was too strong. He released my mouth and moved his hand down to my throat again, but this time pinched the sides of my neck, cutting off the blood to my head, depriving me of oxygen in another way. I didn't feel as panicked as before, but the sensation of passing out was still coming to me. He was pushing down on my arms and back so hard I knew I would be bruised. My ribs were painfully mashing into the hard counter top. All of my senses began to dull, all but smell and touch, which made those two heighten. I could smell the sawdust on him, and I could feel his hard body pressing into me and the heat of his arms. The fear he instilled in me was humbling, to know that I could become so powerless.

As before, he released my neck just before I blacked out. I was left shaking and weak. My legs were ready to give out, but I couldn't fall with Hendrix's body holding me up. He lifted my shirt higher and rained down several more hard and proficient smacks to my ass. My mind and body were pliable now. He could do anything he wanted, and I couldn't fight back even if I tried. I heard him unbuckling his belt and pop his jeans button open. Then came the zipper.

"You're mine, Ashton. You gave yourself to me, remember? Whatever I want to do to you or make you do, you will. I won't tolerate this behavior, is that clear?"

Why did I have to provoke? Why couldn't I just say what he wanted to hear? I wanted to hurt him. I wanted him to think I no longer wanted to please him. "Fuck you!"

He pushed my face down to the counter, and the surface was cold against my flushed skin. He held me down. I couldn't lift or turn my head and he still held both of my arms to my back. I felt his hard cock against my ass. "Fuck me, is that right? From my perspective Ashton, it looks like you're the one who's fucked."

My mouth was uncovered, but I couldn't say it, whether it was out of fear that I would never see him again, or because in some demented corner of my mind, I wanted this. I wanted to be held against my will and fucked angrily. No matter what he did, I still trusted Hendrix.

He rammed his cock into me, and to my surprise, I was soaking wet. He slid in without a hint of resistance.

"See, little whore, you were so wet for me. You wanted this didn't you?"

I didn't say a word. He picked my face up off the counter top by my hair and bent me upwards. I was eye level with the cabinets, my back was arched, and Hendrix was pumping hard into me, slamming my hips and stomach into the counter. "Answer me!"

The way he yelled the command at me, I instinctively

answered, "Yes, Sir."

"Ah, that's better you bitch. You want to be my good girl again?"

"Yes, Sir."

"Tough! You're not my good girl, not today. You're a little whore who wanted this cock forced on her. All that taunting and misbehavior was all for this, wasn't it? You wanted to make sure I wouldn't let you get away with anything. You were testing me."

"Yes, Sir."

"When are you going to learn that I will always call your bluff? You can't intimidate me Ashton. I own you."

"Yes Sir." I was crying and tears were running down my face, into my mouth. He pulled me by my hair away from the counter, letting his cock slip from me, and pushed me to the kitchen floor. I got a quick glance at him, his cock wet and shining from being inside me, his ball cap turned around backwards, and the look of utter dominance in his eyes.

"Don't look at me! Get on your fucking knees!"

"Yes, Sir." I sat up on my knees, but he pushed my back down so that I had to put my hands on the floor. He didn't start fucking me again but began slapping my pussy with his hand. The sting radiated through my clit and excited me.

"Who does this pussy belong to?"

"You, Sir."

"I didn't hear you." With every word, he slapped my pussy. "Who does this pussy belong to?"

I practically yelled it at him, but I was sobbing so hard I could barely get the words formed. "You, Sir!"

"That's right. This is mine." He drove his fingers into me, deep and hard, before he pulled them back out and slapped my clit again. "In fact, it's mine and anyone else's I say it is. Isn't that right?"

I said it loudly again so that I wouldn't have to repeat it.

"Yes, Sir!"

"That's right, but you're still not a good girl. You're a little bitch, aren't you?"

"Yes Sir!" I was so turned on, I wanted to come. His sharp slaps to my clit were making me shutter with pleasure and the way he was treating me. Every part of it was making me more and more aroused and drawn to him. What was wrong with me? How could I be so self-deprecating?

"And does this little bitch want some more of my cock?"

"Yes, Sir!"

He dropped his knees to the floor, grabbed the bottom of my shirt, gathering it in his hand until it was tight against my body, and pulled it back, using it like reins. He drove into me and slammed his hips into my ass, again and again, fast and hard. Putting his hands around my neck, again he only pinched the sides, not cutting off my air supply. I didn't panic this time because I knew he would let go before I passed out. He knew what he was doing and I trusted him. The blackness came and my head began to drop, my legs going limp; only then did he let go. I hung my head in defeat, ready to fall. He slid his arm under my shoulders and pulled me upwards so that my hands left the floor, but didn't keep me up on my knees. Instead, he pressed my chest to the floor and pinned my arms behind my back, my ass still in the air, while he drove his hard shaft into me. He made those guttural grunting sounds I had heard the first time he fucked me. Every time he slammed into me, I heard the deep growl of pleasure…or triumph.

Pulling from me, he flattened me to the floor, releasing my arms. My body now prone, he laid his own down on top of me, all of his weight bearing down, smashing me. I could feel his hand spreading my lips apart for him to slip back into me. I could only lift my head slightly, straining my neck. He placed a hand on both sides of my head and moved them so close together that he trapped my neck in his forearms, not choking me but holding my head like a vice. He slid his cock in and out of me, his boots gripping the floor, using them to propel his body forward, and pushed his forearms against my neck and shoulders to move himself back.

Never had I felt so mistreated sexually. He didn't care what he did to me. All he wanted was to fuck me.

"Who is your Master?"

"You are, Sir."

"Say my name!"

"Hendrix!"

"Tell me I'm your Master!"

"Hendrix, you're my Master!"

He pulled out of me again and released my head from his forearms.

"Get up on your knees."

I was so weak. My arms barely supported my efforts to raise my body from the floor.

"I don't have all day to wait on you. I'm ready to come. Now get up here so I can finish fucking you."

"Yes, Sir." I was crying again, but my inner lips were pulsing and swollen. I wanted him to fuck me this hard for hours. I didn't want him to come yet. Raising myself, I sat up on my knees. He stood, I couldn't see him, but I heard him. He wrapped his arm around my chest and shoulders and picked me up to stand on my feet. I was weak and wobbling. He kept his arm locked around my arms and chest, keeping them pinned at my sides, and dragged me to the living room. My feet tried to keep up with his pulling but did a terrible job. He threw me to the couch.

"Get your knees on the floor and bend over the couch."

"Yes, Sir."

He tugged his belt off. I heard the sound as it passed the belt loops of his pants. Then I felt the sting, the leather lashing my ass harder than he had whipped me in the parking lot.

"Count them!"

"Yes, Sir. One!" He sent another, lighter but stinging. "Two!"

"I own you, you do what I say. You don't tell me I don't treat you with respect, understood?"

"Yes, Sir. Three, four!" He whipped me unexpectedly in the midst of my answer, but I didn't miss my count.

"If I didn't respect you, I would have hung up the phone, driven home, and never spoken to you again. Because I respect you, I came here to teach you what you seem to have forgotten."

"Five!" I was still crying, but even more so now. I could tell he was breaking me again. I could tell that my sharp edge was dulling. It wasn't so much the lashes of his belt that broke it, but his words. "Six!"

"If you ever disrespect me again, I will make this punishment look like a warning, understood?"

"Yes, Sir. Seven, Eight!"

"You like being punished, don't you? You like me forcing myself on you, don't you?"

"Yes, Sir. Nine!"

"I knew you wouldn't say your safe word because you're a dirty little whore who wants to be roughed up, you want to be taught a lesson, don't you?"

I was sobbing now, barely able to breathe, let alone speak, but I choked out my answer, "Yes, Sir. Yes, Sir."

"Tell me you're a dirty whore."

"I'm, I'm....."

"Say it!"

I hung my head, still crying. "I'm a dirty whore." I said it quietly because it made me feel defeated. Of all the things he had done to me, making me say that phrase jerked the rest of my pride from me. "Ten, Eleven." My mind searching for anything to cling to, to hold to myself. I began writing my experience in my head. It was my escape, and I was losing myself. I had to keep my mind occupied so I didn't succumb to him.

"I could taste the salt of freedom as my identity slid down

my face in the shape of tears. Punishment caused an irreparable break in my psyche, leaving me a hardened adversary to weakness. I no longer feared it, and I felt closer than ever to discovering the ecstasy of life with every infliction.

He told me, "Face the pain and you face yourself." I had learned well that the strength of yielding was the key to release. This time, I allowed him to cut all the way to my soul. It was not merely a wound, but a blood-letting, dripping with my relinquishment.

I knew this time I would not emerge the same person. I would be the property of the one who tamed me. There was no longer any doubt; I belonged to him. My Master, my savior, Hendrix was now the name of God upon my lips."

I only cried harder because what I had dictated to myself was true. I didn't want to be so hard that I couldn't feel, and I didn't want to get to the point that I blocked out everyone who attempted to get close to me. Hendrix was freeing me by treating me this way. I loved him for it, but I hated him too.

I heard the belt hit the floor. He sat down on the couch and lifted my face with his hand. I couldn't look him in the eyes, so I stared ahead at his chest.

"Look at me, Ashton."

I looked up and met his eyes and immediately began to cry, my bottom lip trembling. I had never felt the need to be held like I did now. I wanted to be comforted, especially by the person who caused me pain. Hendrix had zipped and buttoned his pants back, seemingly done fucking me, though I knew he hadn't come.

He helped me up from the floor, sat down on the couch, then brought me down to sit across his lap, wrapping his arms around me, all the while looking into my eyes. Tucking my head into his chest, I sobbed unashamedly. He only held me tighter and ran his fingers through my hair. I was starting to calm down but was becoming more concerned as I did. What was I supposed to do when he let go? What should I say? Thanks for the great beating, see you tomorrow? I may have lost the anger I had tried to build against him, but now I was pushing away from something more.

This comfort in his arms, similar to last night in his car, wasn't something I anticipated or wanted for that matter. It only complicated things. Why was he doing this to me?

"Ashton, can I talk to you? Are you okay?"

I could only whisper, "Yes, Sir."

"Please look at me."

I looked up from his chest, knowing that my face would be red, eyes swollen, such a pretty sight I was sure. He looked changed, almost sad. "As defeated as you feel right now, know that I feel the same. Breaking you down like this takes a lot out of me, and I'm not talking physically. I think I feel the same way you do, but I can't be sure because you haven't told me how you're feeling. Will you?"

"I would if I knew what to say, but I'm sorry, I don't."

"Are you angry?"

"No, Sir."

"Are you hurt?"

"I'll have bruises, but I'm not really hurt."

"You know I would never truly hurt you and that you could make it stop anytime."

"Yes, Sir, I know."

"Then why didn't you?"

"Because I wanted it."

"So did I."

"Does that mean there's something wrong with us?"

"I don't think so. I think it means we both need things that no one else has been able to give us. I feel like I've needed someone to break down. I know that sounds bad, but I mean, I want to get to the core of someone who will truly let me. Does that make sense?"

"Yes, Sir."

"And you giving me that power, freely giving it, you have no idea what that does to me. Why do you like the punishment?"

"Like you said, getting to the core of someone, which pretty much sums it up, I think. Sometimes, I think you know me better than myself and you help me."

"How?"

"You help me break down this shell that I didn't even know I created until you came along. I guess I owe you a thank you for that. You've helped me know myself better. I had no idea that was possible."

"You've done the same for me. I know you probably see my role in this as superior and sadistic, but honestly, I feel honored. I know that sounds crazy, but I'm grateful that you trust me so completely that I can do what I've just done to you. I know you're giving yourself to me in ways you've never given to anyone else and that makes me happy."

"I do trust you, Hendrix."

"Thank you."

We looked at each other in that moment for what felt like several minutes, but I'm sure it wasn't that long. It was somewhat uncomfortable, but I couldn't look away. He leaned down and closed his eyes, lifting my head to his, and kissed me, the same deep, passionate kiss he had given me yesterday, which now felt like weeks ago. When his head rose back up, he opened his eyes slowly and that moment of tranquility on his face just before he did, was the most peaceful expression he had ever worn for me.

"Hendrix, what did you have to think about last night? Can you please tell me?"

"I can."

"Will you?"

"Sometimes I feel closer to you than I want to be. I know that sounds terrible."

"It doesn't actually. I understand."

"Look at me, my good girl."

I started to cry again when he said it. I didn't realize how much I needed that affirmation. He held it like a ransom from me, and I wanted to earn it so badly.

"You are my good girl, Ashton. You are a very good girl."

He was petting my hair, holding me tighter in his arms, like a father-figure comforting the child he had to spank. "Thank you Sir, thank you." I tucked my head to his chest again. I knew he could feel the sobs racking my body, but he held me tight until they passed.

"I'm sorry Hendrix. I don't know what's wrong with me. I know this isn't part of our experiment, our game. I'm ruining it."

"Hardly Ashton, if anything you're confirming it."

"What?"

"Remember I wanted to see if you could be my submissive and we could have sex for pleasure only, and we did, didn't we?"

I was looking at him quizzically. "Yes, I suppose so."

"Have you not experienced pleasure and had a great time with me?"

"Yes, Sir."

"But, of course, you've confirmed something else for me too."

Oh no, he was going to stop it. He was ending it because it didn't work the way he anticipated. This wasn't the way I wanted it to be. He would pat my head and call me his good girl, then tell me I confirmed that I was just like every other girl, getting all emotionally attached and not wanting to let him go. "What?" I knew he heard the disdain in my voice.

"That I can't...."

"No, stop, don't do it, don't say it, not right now, just hold me and stay for a minute. Then you can go."

"Ashton, I don't understand. Why don't you want me to tell

you?"

"Because you're going to hurt me."

"I'm not trying to."

"Just please, don't."

"Okay, okay, I won't say anything more about it."

"Thank you. You can go if you want." I sat up from his lap but stayed on the couch with him.

"I wasn't planning on leaving yet, but I will if you want me to."

"Why stay?"

"What is going on with you? One minute you're crying into my chest and now you're telling me to leave?"

I moved away from him towards the opposite arm of the couch. "I can't handle this Hendrix. You break me down, you build me up, you share me with your friends, and then you practically make love to me last night and carry me to bed. I'm lost."

"Why are you lost? Lost from what? We don't have a rule book and you know what we wanted to do."

"What *you* wanted to do and I went along with it."

"Do you not enjoy it?"

"I do, but I can't take this part of it. You tearing me down and then leaving. I try to be strong, but all you manage to do is make me weak."

"You're asking me to leave remember?"

"So that you don't hurt me."

"I told you, I wasn't planning on it."

"But you will."

"Ashton, I can't promise you that I will never hurt you, that's impossible, and you can't promise me that either. I'm not asking you to."

"But I'm not ready for this to be over and I'm not ready to

keep going either."

"Who said it was over?"

"Well, no one, but I feel that's where you're going with your confirmation of the experiment talk."

"Are you always so sure of yourself?"

"Not since I met you."

"Then that makes two of us."

"What do you mean you're not sure of me either? I wouldn't blame you."

I sat cross legged, pressed as far as I could into the arm of the couch in a protective position. I was ready to run, to yell at him to get out, to just make this stop. I wanted to go back to me in his arms and the comfort I felt.

Hendrix wasn't swayed by my display. "I'm not sure of myself. I'm sure of you."

I didn't have a response, so I looked at my hands.

"Ashton, I'm sure that you are unlike any woman I have ever met. I have so much fun with you. I feel free when I'm with you. You give to me what no woman has ever given me, your complete trust and if you must know, you're hurting me right now. I know I may be strong and dominant, but don't mistake that for a lack of emotions. I have them and I thought that I have always shown you that by respecting you, treating you kindly. I only dominate you when you want it, and yes I know that you want it because I can see it. It's strange for me too. I didn't expect this to work as well as it has. At the most, I thought I would get you to be with another woman, and we could have a threesome, maybe get you to the club, but honestly I thought you would bow out before that. Then after the night in the parking lot, I knew that you were more complex than I thought. Don't get me wrong. I've never looked at you as naive or shallow, but I had no idea of your depth. We haven't known each other very long, but we've crossed a lot of bridges that some couples never do. I feel like I know you in a way I've never known anyone. I may not know when your birthday is, but I know what you're afraid of and I know how to make you brave again. You say I make you weak, but you want that, you want to feel weak, I know you do. I take your control away so that you can feel free and you give me a sense of possession I've never had. And before you get upset about that, let me explain. I don't possess you in the way that I make you respond to me. I don't own you, and we both know that, but you give yourself to me and that is true possession."

"September 8th. That's my birthday."

He turned to sit as I was and moved closer to take my hand. He brought it to his lips as he had done before and kissed the back of it before flipping it back over and kissing my wrist gently. He continued to hold my hand in his. We had never touched this way before.

"Ashton, I want to know those things now. I didn't at first, but now I do. I want to know about your life."

"I'm not sure I can do that, Hendrix."

"Talk to me, why not?"

"Because I have been hurt too many times in ways you can't imagine. You want to know me now, but you've already broken me down. What does knowing my life do for you?"

"It lets me see who you are, what you've been through."

"Maybe I don't want you to see those things." I withdrew my hand from his and returned it to my lap. He didn't try to take it again.

"That's fine. You don't have to tell me, but please don't push me away."

"I'm sorry, Hendrix. I don't mean to, but it's the way I am. I know you've tried to break me of it and I'm thankful for what you've made me realize about myself, but I don't know that I could ever bring you into that part of my life. What am I going to do when I bring you to meet my Mom or my friends, introduce you as my Master?"

"Of course not. Why can't we have our own way of being together and then another way in public, like we have been already?"

"But we're also like this, today, in public, remember?"

"Only around certain people, not your family of course."

"Hendrix, please stop. I can't let you into that part of my life. I don't want to bring the perfect man to meet my Mom and then tell her it didn't work out two weeks later. Every man I've ever been serious with has let me down and I leave them."

"So you're afraid of running from me? Like you're doing right now."

"Yes."

"How can you ever be sure if you already have the end planned out? You assume you'll have to run. Why would I make you run? I know what you need better than you do, you said that yourself."

"I know I did and that scares me."

"What are you so afraid of?"

I was getting angry. I wanted this to be done and to watch him leave so I could be alone with my thoughts. I couldn't handle the pressure he was putting on me. I would rather have the worst lashing he could give me than to sit in front of him feeling so exposed. "What happens when you start fucking other women in front of me?"

"Nothing happens. It will be the same as me watching you be with other men."

"But I'm not with other men. I'm with you, and you just let other men fuck me. It's not the same. If you fuck another woman, you're fucking her, you're choosing her, don't you see?"

"I'll let you choose her then. The point is, I want you there. I wouldn't do it just to do it. I want to look at you. I want you to get the same pleasure out of seeing me please another woman as I do from seeing other men enjoy you."

"I don't know that I can feel that way."

"I know you don't because it hasn't happened, has it?"

"No, you know the answer to that."

"I know I do. It's rhetorical. In case you haven't noticed, I have never even touched another woman since you and I have been playing."

He was right. Not once had he laid so much as a finger on any woman besides me. I didn't realize it was a deliberate act until now. "I didn't look at it that way."

"I see that. I'm not telling you that to shame you. I'm telling you so you will understand that my focus has been thoroughly on you and I haven't wanted it to be anywhere else. Why do you automatically assume you will be jealous and hurt if you watch me with another woman?"

"Because it's just human nature."

"But if you know without a doubt that I don't want to be with her, that I'm doing it for fun, why should you be upset? You would be there. I wouldn't be trying to hide it from you."

I put my hands in front of my face and ran them up into my hair, in a look of total exasperation. "I know, I know, it doesn't make sense. I know it doesn't. I know I'm being hypocritical, but I don't want to feel like I'm competing for your attention or that you like the way another woman pleases you more than I do." I let my hands fall back into my lap.

"I understand. You're still not getting it and that's okay. It's too soon for you to realize it all right now. I think in time you will see that it's not a competition. I'm more concerned about you being present for that kind of play than what that woman does or doesn't do for me."

"Why? Why do you care?"

"Because I feel close to you. I am sharing this with you. I'm not sharing anything besides skin with this hypothetical other woman."

"But you could be close to her just like you are with me."

"I don't think I can. I didn't plan on feeling close to you. I planned on us having frivolous sex with a group of people and only talking when we were planning our encounters, but in case you've missed this too, I've spoken with you every day since we've met."

He was right about that too. It had only been a little over a week, but it felt like months, and the days were running together. I had overlooked the fact that he had kept in constant contact with me when he certainly didn't have to. "Yes, you have."

"Ashton, I don't know what else to say to show you that you don't have to run from me. If you want me to tell you that I'll never sleep with another woman, I don't think I can do that. It's part of who I am. I enjoy expressing myself sexually, and I think it's wrong to limit a human being of their most basic nature to conform to some ideal societal norm. I've told you and shown you that married couples can love each other just as much, if not more, even when they allow their spouse to have sex with another person. Sex doesn't have to mean love. Haven't I shown you that?"

"I've seen the sex part, yes, but how can I see the way these other couples' relationships work? I don't know them. I don't even know how marriage works for that matter. I see my friends get married and settle down, whatever that means, and some of them seem miserable."

"Maybe they seem miserable to you because it's not the life you want for yourself."

"You're right, it's not."

"Well, then we're agreed on that point. I don't agree with the typical idea of marriage either, but I think it can be what you make it. I want to love someone, but also be free to be myself and explore what life has to offer. But you know what? If my wife wanted me to stop, I would because the person I love enough to actually walk down that road with will know what it means to me and know how much I love them to give it up. It's not having sex with other people that I would be losing. It's losing the fun I have in the pursuit. If my wife knew all of that about me and I agreed to give it up, she would know that her love was more important than sacrificing that part of myself. I assume that's what normal married people feel, but to me, it's not a necessity, the pledge of monogamy. There's a difference between monogamy and fidelity you know? Monogamy is having sex with the same person for the rest of your married life. Fidelity is staying true to that person. You can have fidelity in a marriage and still share each other sexually. The one true mark of love in this lifestyle is that the spouse knows what's going on. It's not behind the others back or with intent to hurt or hide. It's out in the open and it's approved of. Just think of the extent of trust they have for one another. They're probably more open and honest with each other than any 'normal' married couple because those couples have to keep feelings of sexual desire for another person hidden, and then it becomes something much more than it would have been, and before you know it, one of them is leaving the other for this other person, who later down the road they realize they don't love at all. Is that better because it's normal?"

"No, it's not. I'm not saying that I want normal. I'm saying that I don't know how to see you with another woman. All this time you've been talking, you're telling me about couples, about marriages and love, but we don't have that. We're just people having sex, so it's hard for me to see things from your perspective. And, honestly, I don't understand why you have this perspective. Why do you presume to know what these lovers feel?"

"I had a long term girlfriend, remember? Yes, things ended badly, but that was because her idea of love was ownership. I don't think you feel that way. I think you're just afraid of something you've never experienced. Are you jealous of Tracy? You know that I've been with her, yet I haven't had sex with her since you and I started hanging out. Do you think she's jealous of you?"

"How do I know? And yes, I was jealous of her at first."

"But you're not now. Why is that?"

"Because I've been around her. I know she's not secretly trying to make you fall in love with her or something."

"Exactly. So could you have watched me fuck her yesterday at the club?"

I thought about what he asked because I wanted to know the real answer, not just my knee jerk reaction, and he was right. "Yes, I could have."

"Why?"

"Because I know you don't want to be with her or you would be already."

"That's right, and to answer my other question, no she's not jealous of you at all. Because she doesn't want to be with me either. We may have fun together, but we would never work as a couple."

"Why not? Have you tried it?"

"When my ex left me, I took her out a few times. We don't have a lot in common. We may share the same ideals on sex and marriage, but everything else in between is just not compatible. Just another example of how sex can be something altogether separate."

"Okay."

"So what are you running from? I can see it in you right now that you want to get me out of here as fast as you can, possibly to never see me again. Why?"

"I'm confused. I don't know how to keep doing this."

"Why are you confused? About what?"

"As much as I try to just drift along and wait for the next encounter you setup, I do feel a need to know the end result."

"You can't know the end result. No one can, not ever. Whether it's a marriage, a date, a quick fuck, you can't know without a shadow of a doubt the end result. Trying to nail that down is a waste of effort. Live your life. Don't try to write the ending."

"But that's just it Hendrix. I am a writer. I have to know the story. I have to know where it's going."

"Don't waste your life worrying about how it ends. Enjoy reading it. Let someone else write the ending because you'll be gone. The only ending you can be sure of is death, and you don't want to only focus on that."

"Aren't you metaphorical?"

"You know what I mean."

"I do and I admire it, but that doesn't mean I can change."

"You're right. It doesn't, but you're too smart, funny, creative, and passionate, you name it. You're too much to fit in to a norm or to try and plan your whole life. If I told you today how I felt, would it make you happy or would it make it worse? I don't know the answer to that, but I would be willing to risk whatever came of it, if I thought it was worth it."

"Is it?"

"Yes, you are worth it."

"Worth what exactly?"

"Worth the risk."

I didn't say anything else. I wasn't sure where he was going or what he was risking, but I wasn't going to make him tell me. I wasn't sure if I wanted to know. It was a good question, would it make it better or worse, and that showed me that he did know me more than I thought possible in this short time.

"Ashton." He took my hand again and used his other to direct my chin so that I could see his face. "Look at me." I was shaking. It would be worse. I already knew the answer the minute he looked at me, that it would make me run and it would make it worse for us both. I needed to stop him, but why? What was the point whether he said what he felt or not? If he felt it, it would still be there, and I would always know it. We could never go back to the way it was before today. It was already happening.

"Please look at me and just quiet your mind for a second because I can see it's going a million miles an hour. Breathe and look at me."

Might as well say it one last time. "Yes, Sir."

"No, no Sir right now, no submissiveness, just you. I love you and I mean that. I know it seems crazy because I've know you for such a short time, but I love you. You have a soul that I want to know for a very long time. I can't promise you forever, no one can, and if they do, it's a lie because no one can be sure of everything. I can promise you that I have never felt like this with anyone else. I knew the moment I saw you that you were unique, that you and I

234

were cut from the same cloth, but I didn't know I would fall in love with you. I told you that day that I wasn't looking for love, but I wasn't afraid of it either. It's a good thing because I fell in love with you when you spent the night at my house. I walked into the bedroom after you had fallen asleep and looked at you, so at peace, so beautiful, lying there in my bed, and I knew that I never wanted to see another woman lying there asleep. You belonged there. I'm sorry that I left last night, but what I was thinking about, was whether or not to tell you that I loved you, but after today, after breaking you down the way I did and the love I felt for you when I was holding you, I knew I couldn't hide it any longer."

I couldn't move. I was furious, amazed, ashamed, and so many other things. I couldn't process them. He just sat there looking at me for some kind of reciprocation, but I couldn't. I just couldn't. I just wanted him to leave. "I'm sorry Hendrix, but I don't feel the same." Anger won out and I used my trusty shield of indifference to push him back.

"Okay."

He looked utterly defeated, and I thought I saw a hint of a tear in his eye, but he didn't let it fall. He stood up and offered me his hand to help me stand. I didn't take it. How could I after what I had just done to him? I didn't look at him. "Goodbye Hendrix."

"I'll leave Ashton, but please know that I understand why you're doing this and I know that you love me too. If it takes a week or a month, or even a year, you'll see that I won't love anyone else the way I do you. I found what I have been looking for my entire life without even trying, and no matter how much you're hurting me right now, I don't regret coming up to talk to you that day in the vintage shop."

He leaned in, kissed me on the cheek, and turned to walk out the door. "I'll have someone fix your lock."

When it shut, I fell to the floor and cried harder than I ever had. I felt like someone had died, but I knew it was only me. Whatever part of me was left that could let a man get close to me or that could potentially love in return was gone. There was music from the record player I had left on, playing low, Chopin's

Nocturnes. I finally knew what music belonged to him and our short time together.

Interlude

I threw myself into my writing, mostly staying in my condo, staring out of the window that seemed ruined now somehow. It wasn't flawed just because of the passion that had occurred there, but also because somewhere in the streets of Atlanta Hendrix was living his life, walking down the street, maybe with a woman on his arm or looking lonely and depressed. This giant piece of glass would surely find him. I was afraid of what I might do if I caught a glimpse of him walking through my neighborhood, so close but so out of reach. I wouldn't be the girl to run to him and throw myself at his feet begging forgiveness; although it felt like the right course of action. I stayed away, locked inside myself and my embarrassment and began a new project, something that would keep me busy for a long time, a work that would exorcise some demons and maybe help me in the long run.

I remembered reading Nietzsche, and one statement that stood out was, "Be careful, lest in casting out your demon, you exorcise the best thing in you." I was willing to risk it though. What I had done to Hendrix to "save" myself couldn't possibly be the best part in me. I wanted to be an open wound again, to let the pain in, and to feel the rawness that love creates, so that the joy is that much more apparent. I let Hendrix break me down so many times, and I enjoyed it. He made me open up and feel life, not just the physical pain of being whipped or spanked, that wasn't really it, but the pain of realization. Life hurts, love hurts, and there will always be pain and suffering, but without it, without allowing yourself to feel it, you can never know the other side. This was me suffering. This was pain like I had never experienced. Losing him was an awakening, and I was going to make it count.

To Feel That We Exist, Even in Pain

"The very essence of romance is uncertainty."

-Oscar Wilde

I was writing at my laptop, sitting in the International Café which, after several months, I was finally able to enter again. I saw him crossing the street, and I thought of running out the back door, but I stayed put. In a few moments a shadow moved beside my chair. I looked up to see Hendrix, whose face was framed by the bright sun, making it seem like an afterimage I couldn't blink away, one that dredged up painful yet blissful memories.

"It's nice to see you, Ashton. I thought you might be here. Can I sit down?"

I was so shocked I could barely think, but I wasn't going to come off as desperate. I wanted to make sure he knew I hadn't spent the better half of a year missing him. "That depends. Are we going to talk about the weather, or do you need answers I can't give you?"

"You know I don't start conversations off with some cliché excuse to talk. I just wanted to see you. Look, what we had is obviously over, but after eight months of not speaking, I'm tired of hiding. We had something different. I can't ignore that."

"Different, Hendrix? No, what we had was an experiment that went wrong."

"Maybe you're right. Let's not talk about that. I just want to know how you've been, Ashton. I haven't seen you anywhere. I've been worried about you."

His voice was trying to pull me back into the past, but I couldn't go there. "You don't have to worry about me. I'm fine."

"Good to hear. What have you been doing?"

"Mainly writing."

"What are you working on?"

"A novel actually."

"Really? That's great! Do you mind if I ask what it's about?"

"I was working on a piece back when, well, you know, and I began thinking about this story, so I started writing things down and eventually it came together. It's about life, I suppose."

"Well, if it's about life, then I guess that means you're out there living yours and that makes me happy."

He couldn't have been more wrong. "How about you? What have you been doing?"

"My business is picking up. I had to hire a couple of people to help out."

"That's great."

We both nodded, and Hendrix beckoned the waitress. I got chills watching him do it, the simple hand motion reminding me of so much.

"Do you mind if I have a drink with you?"

"Not at all." I smiled, but I was starting to tremble inside, I didn't know how far this conversation could go.

The waitress came to the table and Hendrix ordered an absinthe. "Would you like one? My treat."

What was I doing? My mind was telling me what to say, but I was ignoring it completely and going with casual conversation. "Sure, why not, maybe it will help with my creative process. I've had some writer's block lately."

"You, writer's block? Why?"

"I'm just stuck at a part of the story because I don't know where I want to take it."

"What's it about? Maybe I could help unstick you?" He smiled and looked into my eyes, the same smile he had given me the first time we went out. All I could do was smile back. I couldn't tell him what it was about. I couldn't tell him that it was about us, about me and my idiocy when it came to love. About the time I let the man of my dreams walk out my door and never talked to him again because I was ashamed. Now here he was and I was still too afraid to say what I really felt.

"I don't think you can, sorry."

"Being secretive, that's okay. I can respect that."

The waitress came over with two glasses of absinthe and sat them in front of Hendrix because the space in front of me was taken up by my laptop. He prepared it as he had done before at the Blue Rhapsody and slid my glass to me. "Don't let me interrupt you. If you need to write, go ahead."

"No, no, I'm glad you're here. The writing can wait."

"I'm glad I'm here too. I've missed you."

I took a drink and remembered the flavor in my mouth after I had returned home from our first date, if you could call it that. Hendrix was still as handsome as he had ever been, his dusky blue eyes trying to stare their way into my soul, and he was here talking to me, even after what I had done to him. I was used to breaking guy's hearts, and as terrible as it sounds, it wasn't that hard to do, but Hendrix was bullet to the chest. I had cried for months and picked up the phone so many times to text him, but I didn't want to talk to him, only to hurt him again. He deserved better than I could give.

"So, are you seeing anyone?" I know it was ballsy to ask, but he was the one that came to see me, and I thought if he was with someone, then I could stop thinking about what could never be.

"No, I'm not and I haven't. I've been to the club occasionally, but I haven't dated anyone. Tracy asked about you."

"Oh, what did you tell her?"

"I told her that you weren't ready and that I rushed things, and that if I saw you on the street the first thing I would to say to you, would be that I'm sorry. And I *am* sorry Ashton."

"You have no reason to be sorry. It's me who is sorry."

"The way I see it, you don't have a reason to be sorry either.

I rushed things. I pushed my feelings on you when I knew you weren't ready. I should have known that it would scare you, but I was cocky and I thought it would be different because it was me."

"It was different."

The devilish smile I had come to miss so much, returned. "Oh, it was? I thought we were just an experiment that went wrong."

I laughed sarcastically. "It wasn't that the experiment went wrong. I guess it was that the experiment itself was wrong."

"I'll agree with you there. I'm sorry that I started us out that way."

"I'm just glad that you started it, really. It may not have been the outcome you were expecting, but it was a great experience."

"Yes, it was."

The absinthe was working its magic, and I was feeling more relaxed. I had even pushed my laptop aside to leave more room for my hands to inch closer to where Hendrix held his glass. I felt like telling him I was wrong and that I wished I could take it back and do it over, but that was impossible.

"Tell me about your book, please. I want to know what kind of writer you are. I never got to read any of your work."

I guess it wouldn't hurt. I could leave it vague. "It's about two people who meet and enter into an agreement, but one of them is a chicken shit who can't get beyond her need to control and the other is a stunningly handsome man who fell in love with her and she broke his heart." That wasn't vague at all. My mind's dialogue was starting to overpower my sense of protection.

"You're writing about us?" He smiled at me with a genuine look of pure happiness. How could he not hate me? If I were him, I wouldn't even talk to me.

There was no use trying to play coy. "Yes, I am."

"Why?"

"Because I wanted to see if I could figure it out by going over it all again and writing it out so I could see where I went wrong. I know you're going to laugh, but it started that last evening you were with me. I have a terrible habit of writing in my head when I get upset or nervous. It calms me and helps me focus. I remembered what had come to me, and I wrote it down a few days after you left."

"I wouldn't laugh at that. What was it?"

I slid the laptop over to him and brought up the page. He read and I watched his eyes dance back and forth. His smile got bigger and brighter. "Silly, isn't it?"

"No, not at all, I love it. You write beautifully. Of course I never imagined it any other way."

"You don't think it sounds stupid?"

"Are you kidding me? What man would ever tell a woman it sounded stupid to call him a God?"

We both laughed and took a drink. I could tell there was tension building between us, but instead of trying to break it with a witty remark, I let the moment be what it was. One thing I had learned while I was writing our story was that Hendrix was right about me in so many ways. For one thing in particular, I did have an annoying need to know how everything would end. I finally had a chance to sit with Hendrix and he came to find me. I was going to enjoy this and for once not think about what was coming next.

"So, where are you stuck?"

"What came after you left."

"I'm so sorry, Ashton."

"Hendrix please, stop telling me you're sorry. I'm a terrible bitch, and I owe you the biggest apology ever."

"You are certainly not a bitch and I promise I won't apologize about it again, if you won't."

"Deal."

"Can I read the chapter you're on?"

"Sure." What could it hurt now really, why hide anything from him?

He read for a while. I saw his face rise and fall as the time passed. It must be hard for him to read about himself from my perspective. I could only imagine if the tables were turned. He finished and slid the laptop back to me.

"Well, what do you think?"

"I think I could help you."

"Really? I know it's probably hard to read."

"No, it's great. It tells me more than I could have ever hoped for."

"How so?"

"It tells me you love me."

I blushed and looked at my drink, which was almost empty. "Yes, I did."

"You did? Did you stop?"

I looked up at him. I was tired of hiding. "No. Well honestly, I wasn't sure until I saw you standing next to me today."

Hendrix smiled so brightly then, like I had never seen him do before. He took my hand. "I love you, Ashton, and I would do anything to have another chance with you. No games, no experiments, just us and whatever that entails."

"I would like that, Hendrix." I closed the laptop and pushed it aside.

He moved over and put his arm around me, pulling me to him. Then he kissed me, lightly at first, but it soon became the deep kiss I longed for. I had missed him so much, but I hadn't let myself dwell on it. I had put all of my sadness into my writing in hopes that I could avoid dealing with it in real life and work on it in a way that I could control. All I really wanted was the freedom of having my control taken from me again.

When the kiss ended, he looked up to find the waitress and gestured for another round.

I broke the silence. "So, you think you can help me?"

"If you'll let me."

"You can try."

The absinthes arrived and Hendrix began to prepare them.

"Can you get your laptop back out so I can look over the last few paragraphs again?"

"Sure." I turned away from him to get it and brought the chapter he had just finished back up.

My drink was sitting in front of me, but Hendrix was on the floor. I thought something was wrong. "What are you doing?"

"Helping you with your book." He smiled and looked at my drink. I followed his eyes, and there on top of the spoon was a diamond ring, vintage, of course. I looked back at him in disbelief.

As always the chivalrous contradiction, he was perched on his left knee and took my hand in his. "Ashton, you know that I can't promise you forever and I can't promise you that everything will be perfect, because both would be a lie. But what I can promise you, is that I've never felt so much like the man I always knew I was, than when I was with you. Just like you said I knew you better than you knew yourself, well, you did the same for me and I don't want to go through another empty day without you. Though I'll never truly own you, would you do me the honor of becoming my wife?

The tears were forming. I couldn't see anything. He was a blur, and my heart was racing. This was it, my chance to be who I wanted to be, someone who wasn't afraid, who didn't want to run, and I realized that I didn't. The only place I wanted to run was to him.

"Yes, yes." I was nodding my head stupidly.

I sunk down to the floor with him and wrapped my arms around his shoulders. He held me in his arms for a few seconds, then reached up to the table and took the ring from the spoon. When I held my hand out for him to slip it on my finger, it fit perfectly.

All my thoughts were jumbled, so I said the first thing that came to mind, "When did you get this?"

"I saw it months ago, but I picked it up yesterday. I knew I was going to find you, wherever you were and one way or another ask you to marry me. Even if you didn't want to speak to me, I had to ask. It was the only way I could know that I did everything I could to show you that you were safe with me. If you want us to be monogamous, then we can be."

"No, there's no need for that. I love you the way you are. I don't think I'll be jealous now. Maybe, this is what I was missing before."

"A ring?"

"No, being able to love you."

"You are my good girl, aren't you?"

"Yes, Sir."

He stood and held his hand out for me, helping me up. After sitting back down, we noticed that everyone in the restaurant was looking our way. Hendrix smiled and gave a simple wave which was met with an embarrassing round of applause.

"So I guess this is how you're helping me with my book?"

"Does it help?"

"No."

He looked perplexed, and I didn't blame him. "Why not?"

"Because I don't need to write anymore."

"Ashton, you should still finish it. I would love to see our story in print."

"If I finish it, that means I have to write an ending, and our story doesn't have one."

Hendrix smiled and took my hand, bringing it to his lips to kiss. I looked at the ring, shining in the sunlight and imagined what marriage with him would be like. It wouldn't be normal, that was for sure, but it would be what we made it, our kind of crazy.

www.ingramcontent.com/pod-product-compliance
Lightning Source LLC
Chambersburg PA
CBHW030915120626
46554CB00001B/162